GLENN ROLFE

UNTIL SUMMER COMES AROUND

This is a **FLAME TREE PRESS** book

Text copyright © 2020 Glenn Rolfe

FLAME TREE PRESS
6 Melbray Mews, London, SW6 3NS, UK
flametreepress.com

Distribution and warehouse:
Baker & Taylor Publisher Services (BTPS)
30 Amberwood Parkway, Ashland, OH 44805
btpubservices.com

Thanks to the Flame Tree Press team, including:
Taylor Bentley, Frances Bodiam, Federica Ciaravella, Don D'Auria,
Chris Herbert, Josie Karani, Molly Rosevear, Mike Spender,
Cat Taylor, Maria Tissot, Nick Wells, Gillian Whitaker.

The cover is created by Flame Tree Studio with
thanks to Nik Keevil and Shutterstock.com.
The font families used are Avenir and Bembo.

Flame Tree Press is an imprint of Flame Tree Publishing Ltd
flametreepublishing.com

A copy of the CIP data for this book is available from the British Library
and the Library of Congress.

HB ISBN: 978-1-78758-394-8
PB ISBN: 978-1-78758-392-4
ebook ISBN: 978-1-78758-395-5

Printed and bound in Great Britain by Clays Ltd, Elcograf S.p.A.

GLENN ROLFE

UNTIL SUMMER COMES AROUND

FLAME TREE PRESS
London & New York

For all the Lost Boys out there.
Thou shalt not fall.

PROLOGUE

I didn't know what her arrival meant, not really, not then. I was just a lovestruck kid who became a shaky bundle of nerves when November Riley came to Old Orchard Beach. How was I to know she was a monster?

It started the summer of 1986. I was fifteen. Unlike the vast majority of people in our small beach town, we, me and about six thousand other people, were year-round residents. That number easily doubled in the summer. We weren't too far from Portland. In fact, the Amtrak Downeaster ran constantly to and from both Portland and Boston, delivering all sorts of summer people.

We had plenty of things that drew the tourists to us like flies to shit. For the kids, there was Palace Playland, an old-school seaside amusement park, complete with roller coaster and Ferris wheel that stood seventy feet tall. Or they could travel fifteen minutes over to Saco to Funtown, the bigger, newer (if 1960 qualified as new) amusement park on Route 1. Funtown, however, lacked the carnival-like charm of our place. Plus, our dual arcades beat their one lame one every day of the week.

If rides and games weren't your speed, Old Orchard Beach was also home to the Cleveland Indians Triple-A team, the Maine Guides. The Ball Park, yes, that was and still is the actual name of the field, also opened up for rock concerts on the nights between games. My older sister, Julie, brought me to see Foreigner there at the end of summer in '85. That first concert experience also supplied me with my first contact buzz from what Julie called Mary Jane. I had a smile for miles and wound up kissing a tall brown-haired girl up from Virginia. I can't remember if I ever got her name, but I'll never forget her kiss.

For the grownups not wishing to headbang, go on thrill rides, or watch a ballgame, the pier offered a plethora of bars. Places like Duke's, The Gin Rail, and Barbara Ann's were packed full of rowdy drinkers from afternoon through well after midnight. I can't count the number of times I was woken up by motorcycles and trucks cruising by my bedroom window out on East Grand Avenue. The loud blats of Harleys and big-wheeled Chevys stole me from dreams of flying, chasing ghosts, and kissing Heather Thomas or Madonna one too many times. I always envied Julie for choosing the room on the other side of the hall. She was up and ready for the day, while I met my cereal and cartoons bleary-eyed, and in a daze, as if *I'd* been the one partying on the pier all night.

It was a morning after one of these long nights of listening to my Walkman in my room that I met the girl who would change my little seaside world. That's the day I first ran into the girl of my dreams…or at least my girl of that summer.

CHAPTER ONE

Screams, cheers, and laughter rang out before eventually fading as the hours barreled toward midnight. By one in the morning, the bars near and around the square were the only sound. Rock music, motorcycles, and jeeps revving. Mustangs growling and bellowing through the beachside community as tires squealed on the still-hot blacktop.

The roller coaster and Ferris wheel of the amusement park had both gone dark for the night as their shadowy silhouettes loomed over the beach and pier like sleeping giants. The smells of fried dough, burgers, and fries lingered in the air, scents that he knew had a way of sticking around until after all the tourists and kiddies packed up for the season and went back to their normal lives.

Craig Sheehan had been drinking since work let out at the shipyard. He couldn't believe Darlene had dumped him. Darlene, his fiancée of the last two years, told him last night that she was done. They were finished. After five damn years of devotion, she'd had enough waiting around.

Drown your sorrows. That's what Craig's old man had always said. And hell, the man practiced what he preached. Drank himself into the grave, gone three years now.

"Like father, like son," Craig said aloud.

"What's that?" Duke asked.

Duke was a good guy. He was the reason Craig drove down here rather than going to one of the old haunts up in Bath. Duke was a stocky, tan, barrel of a man with a long black ponytail and a huge smile. The guy was straight out of Hawaii and drinking at his new place here in Old Orchard, surrounded by the tiki torches, the tables skirted in straw, the ukulele music; it made Craig feel like he was in an episode of *Magnum P.I.* Plus, Duke really was a great dude.

"Nothin', Duke," Craig slurred. "Just nothin'."

Duke walked over, wiping down the bar as he did.

"Let me call you a cab, huh, Craig?" he said.

"I ain't got enough money for a cab back to my house."

He didn't want to go back home. There was too much of *her* there. Everywhere. Her Snoopy coffee mug, her uncomfortable wicker sofa, her flannel sheets.

He was crying before he knew it.

"Shit, Craig," Duke said. "I'll take care of the fare."

Craig shook his head and then downed the rest of his beer. "I don't...I don't want to go home tonight."

"Why, bud? What happened?" Duke asked.

"Dar...Darlene...." He sobbed like a child. "She left me, Duke."

Duke leaned down and gave Craig's forearm a pat. "Hey," he said. "Let me finish closing up, huh? I'll put you up at my place for tonight. Sound good?"

Craig clamped his lips tightly to keep himself from bawling and nodded.

After a few minutes watching as Duke put the chairs and stools up for the night, he felt tired. So damn tired. He just needed to put his head down for a minute.

"Okay, bud," Duke said, startling him awake as he patted him on the back. "Let me go take a leak and then we'll head out, okay?"

Craig nodded.

As soon as Duke disappeared into the bathroom, Craig climbed off his stool and stumbled for the door. It wasn't Duke's job to take care of him.

No, it's – it was – Darlene's.

Craig hurried down the pier, passing a few drunk couples necking. He managed to make it to the ramp before his stomach rejected the last three beers. He heaved over the railing. Knowing Duke would be looking for him, he forced himself onward. He shuffled down to the beach and found a cool place in the dark beneath the pier. Duke might come looking for him, but he didn't think the guy would come all the way down here. Nice guy or not, he'd probably figure Craig had drifted off in the dispersing crowd and stumbled down the road.

As if on cue, he heard Duke calling his name. The voice never came close and only faded, until he stopped calling completely.

Craig dropped down onto the cold sand, briefly wondering if the tide came in this far. He couldn't recall. He doubted it but wouldn't that be something, to pass out now and wake up dead in the sea?

★　★　★

His eyes shot open. The water hadn't come for him yet. He listened as the waves lapped the shore. He must have passed out. Luckily, his stomach hadn't revolted again. He climbed to his feet and realized he was still hammered drunk. He braced himself with one of the pier posts and rested his forehead against the back of his hand.

Outside of the waves, there was nothing but silence. The pier, the beach, the whole damn town had retired for the night. For all he knew it could be nearing morning. Wondering what the hell he was going to do now, he regretted not taking Duke up on his offer.

When he lifted his head and turned around, he nearly screamed.

A tall man with long black hair stood there, gazing at him behind dark eyes.

"Hi," Craig managed. He couldn't think of anything else to say. A chill raged down his spine. He felt his skin break out in goose flesh. There was so much about this person standing here that wasn't right. Where the hell had he come from? Had he been there the whole time? Had he been watching him? Was he homeless? A beach bum? No. The fancy long coat and boots said he was probably well off.

"If this is your spot, I'm sorry. I'll juss be on my w—" Craig started.

The man came at him fast. So quick that Craig hadn't even seen him move his legs. As if he had glided like an evil Peter Pan across the sand.

Evil?

The man's hand was on his throat. Craig tried to fend him off, batting at his arm. It was as useful as a toddler trying to break free from a parent. The man had yet to make a sound. Not a breath, not a sigh. Even now, lifting Craig from the ground with one hand, he did so in silence.

"Puh-puh, pleeease," Craig managed.

"Yes," the man said, his voice smooth as silk. "Beg."

And with that, Craig was pulled to the man. Pain exploded in his neck as the man bit into his throat. He felt the guy sucking on him.

Drawing from him. Craig's limbs grew weak, his breathing slowed. A strange sense of peace washed over him. His heart seemed to fall in line, beating with each pull from this man's mouth, and swooshing with the waves.

Craig had just enough time to think of Darlene when she'd still loved him. And then, he would have laughed if he'd had the time or ability as the word *vampire* crossed his dying mind.

CHAPTER TWO

Rocky wiped the drool from his cheek and covered his head with his pillow. Those friggin' bikers, man, when the hell did they sleep? Try as he might to fall back into the dream of the random blonde taking him someplace only she knew about, it wasn't happening. He lifted the corner of the pillow and reached for his watch on the nightstand.

"Argh," he growled. Eight in the morning. And on the second week of summer vacation, that was just wrong in so many ways. He put the watch back on top of his new Superman comic and slipped his feet out from under the covers.

His back brace stared at him from in front of his bureau across the room and he glared back. He should put it on, but he didn't want to. Not yet.

It can wait until after breakfast.

He'd been diagnosed with severe scoliosis in fifth grade and that uncomfortable, hard plastic torture device was his grand prize. His mother and father liked to remind him of the alternative – surgery. Two steel rods fused to his spine.

On second thought.

He picked the lightweight brace up and squeezed it around his ribs and hips. The pinched nerve in his hip that never seemed to go away made him wince and curse as he reached back, pulled the straps tight and Velcroed them in place.

Breathing a sigh that was equal parts depression and submission, he pulled on a Journey *Raised on Radio* t-shirt and crossed the hall.

Julie was singing some lame Madonna song. Madonna was hot, but her music sucked. He pushed his sister's door open.

She spun around, placing her arms over her chest.

"Jesus, Rocky," she said. "Don't you know how to knock?"

Julie turned her back to him, snagged a t-shirt from the top of her bureau and pulled it on.

"Sure, but I figured you must have your headphones on. You sound like a dying cat."

"Screw you," she said.

Julie actually had a good singing voice, but he loved messing with her.

"Are you working today?" he asked.

"Yeah, I'm leaving in, like, half an hour. Why?"

"Can you bring me with you?"

She had a job at the Maine Mall. He normally only went to Portland once a month. He preferred the square, but he'd been out there every day since vacation started.

"I can't. For one, Mom and Dad would kill me for leaving you on your own all day, and besides, I have a date right after work, so you'd need to find a way home."

"What? You mean you're seeing Brick again?"

She reached for a bunch of jelly bracelets and chucked them at him.

He dodged them and they landed in the hallway.

"You know I'm just kidding. I don't care if you guys are trying to be the real-life Nick and Mallory."

She reached for her canister of Aqua Net and held it back over her shoulder like she was going to chuck it.

"Kidding," he said, holding his hands up in surrender. "Honestly, I just need to get out of here."

"It's not happening," she said. She lowered the Aqua Net and looked at him with sympathy. "Maybe I'll bring you in tomorrow. I have the day off and need to do some shopping anyway."

He smiled.

"Now get out of here," she said. "Let me finish getting ready."

"All right, all right, don't have a conniption fit," he said. Rocky smiled as he made his way down the hall.

After relieving himself, Rocky checked his face in the mirror. His nose was a little on the big size and had a slight bump on the right from when his sister broke it by slamming the front door in his face two summers back. His teeth were crooked, especially the bottom ones. Paul Bilodeau once called them Freddy Krueger teeth. His earlobes were long, not circus-freak long, but he could tuck them in his ear if he tried. Axel thought it was a neat trick, but it wasn't the sort of thing to impress a girl. He wet his face with a handful of cold water from the sink and slicked his floppy hair back from his forehead. He wasn't a total monster or anything, but he certainly didn't have the charisma it took to get a girlfriend. His back brace only added to his ever-growing list of anxieties.

He sighed and headed to the kitchen.

He grabbed a bowl of Cocoa Pebbles and a Pepsi from the fridge and plopped down in front of MTV to wait for a Twisted Sister or Ratt video. He'd just have to suffer through Wham! and Duran Duran first.

Julie came out singing along with Cyndi Lauper's 'Time After Time'. She was messing with her hair, trying to make it taller – her bangs were at least half a foot high – as she stepped next to the couch.

"Have you talked to Mom about setting up your driver's test yet?" she asked.

He swallowed and said, "Yeah, she's still worried that I'm too young, but she said if I do good when we go on the highway this weekend, she'd consider it."

"Well, that's cool. You're gonna do fine," she said. "You do have the best teacher."

"Thanks, sis."

"No problem. I'll see ya."

He couldn't complain about his sister. She'd been taking him out driving behind their parents' backs since he got his permit. She'd always been super cool to him, minus the slamming door incident, but she'd become even nicer when they'd found out his scoliosis was bad enough to warrant the back brace.

Rocky decided that if he was going to be up this early, so was Axel. He took his bowl and empty bottle of soda to the kitchen and called his cousin.

His aunt answered, said Axel was still asleep, but that she'd wake him. His cousin's groggy voice came on the line. "Hello."

"Hey, cuz," Rocky said. "Meet me out front in, like, fifteen minutes."

They lived three roads apart.

"Why? Why are you up already?" Axel asked.

"This damn street, man. I can never sleep in except on Sundays. All the bikers must go to church. You gonna be ready?"

"Yeah, sure," he said. "Want me to grab some quarters?"

They would need to start the morning off at the arcade.

"Yeah," Rocky said. "I'll see if I can scrounge some cash for snacks."

★   ★   ★

Axel came down the street in his neon green shorts and Motley Crue t-shirt. His long dirty-blond hair was mussed like he'd just gotten out of bed and didn't know what the hell a brush was or how to use one.

"Got the quarters?" Rocky asked.

Axel raised the near-full mason jar and shook it, wiggling his eyebrows.

"Whoa, that's awesome," Rocky said. "Where the hell'd you find all that?"

"It's supposed to be my money for England," he said.

"Man, summer is gonna suck without you here," Rocky said.

"I told my mom I didn't want to go," Axel said. "Told her that I could stay with you guys, but she said no. We're going as a family. My dad's parents and family are all there and they can't wait to see us."

Knowing his cousin would be gone most of the summer also made the need for Rocky to get his driver's license a matter of life and death. At least then he could cruise to the mall or shop the record stores in the Old Port.

"Well, let's get to it, man," Rocky said.

★   ★   ★

Rocky used the ten dollars he'd made helping his Uncle Arthur rip down an old porch last week on Reese's Peanut Butter Cups, M&Ms, Andy's Hot Fries, and a six-pack of Orange Crush.

They picked the arcade closest to the beach to start. This one had *Ms. Pacman* and the brand-new racing game, *Out Run*. An hour later, they were forced to take a break from *Out Run* after two Frenchies

the size of Andre the Giant and Big John Stud, and greasy as the oil
bins at Lisa's Pier Fries, hovered over them, muttering a bunch of
foreign threats.

★   ★   ★

"Well, shit," Axel said. "Should we head to the beach and watch
for babes?"

"You read my mind, cuz."

They found a spot near the crabgrass, sat down and popped open
a couple of their orange sodas. This spot gave them full view of the
beach and any bouncing beauties that might be strolling around and
showing off their assets.

"I'm gonna miss this," Axel said.

"Yeah, do they even have beaches in England?"

Axel sipped his soda, wiped his mouth with the back of his
hand, and said, "Dude, it's gonna blow. They don't have girls like
we do. They watch *Benny Hill* and *Doctor Who*. I won't have anything
to talk about even *if* I can find a babe to talk to."

"You can talk to them about Iron Maiden and Led Zeppelin,"
Rocky said.

"Won't be the same, man. It won't be the same."

They watched the beach fill in. By the time the sun was directly
overhead, the place was jam-packed with bodies of all shapes and sizes.
Young and old, big and bold. Slick and ready to make two perverts
such as them drool to dehydration.

"Dude," Axel said. "Why do the old Canadian men think that it's
cool to wear Speedos?"

"Who cares? Their ladies are just as shameless. I'll take that trade."

"Not me, man. It's gross." Axel stood. "I'm hungry, dude."

"I have another packet of M&Ms."

"No way," Axel said. "Those are definitely melted."

Rocky picked them up and could feel that they were indeed ruined.

"You've got to at least be thirsty," Axel said. "We finished the last
soda, like, an hour ago."

Rocky's mouth felt like it was coated with flour. It'd been a while
since they got forced from the arcade's canvas cover. Now the white-

hot sand was cooking them like two eggs. He thought of the anti-dope commercial, 'This is your brain on drugs,' and laughed.

"What's so funny?" Axle asked.

"Nothing, man. Let's go."

★   ★   ★

Crossing from the beach to the square, Rocky nearly tripped, and that's when *she* came into view.

"Oh my god," he said.

"What?"

Rocky's mind went blank. All his summer plans, his cousin leaving for England, his driver's test, his back brace, all of it, gone. She had ice cream smeared across her upper lip and wiped it away with the back of her right hand. She was wearing one green high-top Chuck Taylor and one yellow. The guy working the Dairy Queen window was staring at her with his mouth open like a dumb kid trying to catch snowflakes from a winter sky. Two older men, older than his dad, were checking her out from the metal fence that separated the DQ from the train tracks. Rocky's gaze moved from the multicolored shoes to the ripped blue jeans, paused at the Twisted Sister logo and the two mounds beneath it, and then froze on her face. She was absolutely gorgeous. Not a crooked angle to be found and eyes that, god knows why, found his. Her lips spread in a smile as she slid the sunglasses from the top of her head down into place. And then she turned and walked away.

Rocky had never wanted to risk it all before, but at that moment he threw caution, good sense, and reality to the wind and ran after her.

"Rocky, man, what the hell?"

Axel's voice slid away in the background, somewhere from a galaxy far, far away.

Keeping his eyes on her long, shiny black hair, he shouldered his way through the crowd crisscrossing the busy street. Part of him wanted her to look back, to see him again, to stop and wait; the other part thought she'd see his determination as insanity and run.

Axel was still calling out from Tatooine, but Rocky kept going, closing in. Ten feet from her, his heart started pounding through his chest, going so berserk he felt it throbbing in his neck. The world beneath his feet swayed as he stumbled. His stomach flipped. And then, he fell.

She turned around as he hit the ground.

Everything went black behind a series of light spots tap-dancing in his vision.

"Are you okay?" she said.

Her face appeared. He took in her brown eyes, thick, dark eyebrows scrunched in concern, and full red lips parting to speak to him.

"Hey," she said.

"Ah...."

He was on his back. The clear blue sky above suddenly filled with a variety of sunburned faces that were just out of focus in her presence.

"I...I think so," Rocky said.

He tried to get up. Her hand pressed against his chest.

"No. Don't get up yet," she said as she raised her chin. "Anyone got some water? I think maybe he's got heatstroke."

She accepted a water bottle from someone, thanked them, and then lowered it to his lips. Under her spell, he opened up his mouth and accepted the cold wet drink. The bottle could have been filled with battery acid or Pepto Bismol; he would have taken any remedy she had to offer.

"There," she said. "Give me your hand."

She stood and pulled him to a sitting position. He still felt a little fuzzy, but better than before.

"How do you feel?" she said.

Her face reminded him of someone.

"What's your name?" she said.

Someone on TV.

"Hey, you got a name?"

"His name is Rocky," Axel said, as he waded past the old woman behind this dark-haired angel and knelt next to him. "You okay, man?" he asked.

"Rocky?" she said. "Like in the movies?"

"Yeah," Rocky said.

"And who are you? Apollo?"

"Ha! That's a good one," Axel said. "Nah, I'm Axel. I'm his cousin."

Rocky never wanted Axel to disappear from this planet more than he did at that very moment.

Go to England already!

"Well," she said, sliding her shades down over those deep brown eyes, putting her hands in her back pockets, and shrugging her shoulders. "Glad to see you're okay, Rocky. You better keep that water. And maybe you should go back inside the arcade. Stay out of the sun for a bit."

With that, she turned and vanished into the dispersing crowd.

"Hey, hey!" Rocky shouted. He tried to get up, but moved too fast, and dropped back down on his ass. "What's your name?"

He couldn't see her, but out of the static of voices he heard it loud and clear.

"November."

CHAPTER THREE

He wanted to spend the night at Axel's. With his cousin leaving for most of the summer, it was their last chance to hang out, but Axel's dad had said no. He said they were leaving too early in the morning; they had a six a.m. flight. They let him stay over until almost six and then sent him home. He said goodbye to his cousin and aunt and uncle and made the short walk back to his house.

His mother was making dinner. With Dad coming home late during the week, they tended to eat dinner at six thirty most nights. Sometimes, they didn't have supper until nearly eight. Rocky waltzed through the living room without mentioning his episode of heatstroke that afternoon or the gorgeous girl who had saved him. Instead, he told his mom to call to him when the food was ready and slunk into his room. He tried to play Atari to keep his mind off everything. Unfortunately, *Pacman* and *Galaga* were more exciting at the arcade and try as he might, he just couldn't concentrate.

His gaze drifted to the second controller. The thought of Axel not being here all summer seemed like a strange dream. The impending loneliness crept its way into his head, crawling down into his guts just as his stomach rumbled. Who was he supposed to play games with? Who would stay up and watch Dee Snider's *Heavy Metal Mania* with him?

There was November, but he didn't really know if he'd see her again. And what if she spaced out and avoided him, or worse, what if she had just been messing with him?

He hung his head as Blinky caught up with him, taking his last life.

He dropped the controller to the floor.

"Dinner's ready," his mom yelled.

As he shut off the machine, his guts rumbled like an oncoming thunderstorm. He wasn't just hungry, he was starved. He hurried down the hallway to the kitchen and took his place at the table. His mother had made hamburgers, scalloped potatoes, and green beans – a Clarise Zukas Specialty, if a meal that made its appearance every Monday night could be considered special. Her food was always good, and even with a stomach floundering full of spiders, his mouth watered at the sight of those scalloped potatoes.

"You look worn out," she said as he pulled out a chair and dove into the meal.

"Where's Dad? Where's Julie?" he mumbled through the first mouthful of potatoes.

"Oh, your father made a pit stop over at your Uncle Arthur's, helping with some project or another. My brother can always find an excuse to get your father over for a drink."

Uncle Arthur was a beer man. He'd worked for a company in Portland for years until he got hurt on the job. He won some lawsuit and now got to sit at home tinkering on things or tearing them apart so he could put them back together. His uncle was a peculiar guy, for sure, but he told great stories and had a smile that made you feel good to be somewhere with someone *real*.

"Your sister is out with her boyfriend."

"Brick?"

"Rocky," his mother said, cocking her head and giving him her *be nice* face. "You know his name. And besides, I think he might be a good guy for your sister. He has a job, he has a—"

"A motorcycle."

"Well, I don't care much for motorcycles, but he's nothing but nice when he's over, so you should at least give him the decency of using his actual name. Understood?"

He couldn't argue with her. She held the keys to his future and his freedom. Mom would decide when he could set a date for his driver's exam, the one thing that could save his summer, so if that meant being nice to Julie's meathead boyfriend, so be it. He could handle that, at least in front of his mother. If he got that license and cruised down the avenue, maybe the girls would notice him.

The thought brought November back to the front of his brain.

"Mom?"

"Yes," she said, finally taking up the seat next to him. The smell of her flowery perfume was comforting, part of her motherly ozone that always drew him to her. She forked some green beans, looked at him with her blue eyes, holding the steaming veggies before her mouth.

Rocky swallowed his burger and cleared his throat. "Would it be all right if I went out for a little while?"

She chewed up her food and placed her soft hand in front of her lips. "Back to Axel's? I thought they sent you home so they could get ready for the trip?"

"No, I was just going to go out for a walk on the beach, clear my head, get some fresh air. It's cooled off quite a bit." He knew she didn't like him venturing out alone, especially during tourist season. He and his mom had spent too many Friday nights together watching episodes of *20/20* where children were kidnapped and never seen again. Grieving mothers and fathers, sisters and brothers. If anything, the paranoia the show ingrained in him gave him an edge around crowds. He was always looking over his shoulder and ready to run at the first sign of someone creepy.

"I'll be safe. I won't even stay out for long. I just need...." What did he need exactly? Just to get out, to be where *she* might be. "I just need the fresh air."

"I guess I could eat dinner by myself," she said, lowering her chin.

"I can finish supper and then go," he said, reaching across the table and putting his hand on hers.

She looked up and smiled. "Okay, but I want you back shortly after dark, if not before."

"Deal," he said.

He started to shovel green beans into his mouth, and then slowed down. Looking up at her, he grinned.

"It's okay," she said. "You can head out now. I'll be fine. Go."

"You sure?" he said. The green beans made him sound like Mushmouth from *Fat Albert*.

"Yes, and don't talk with your mouth full."

He swallowed, forked the final corner of potatoes down his gullet and grabbed the remainder of his burger. Taking a bottle of Crush from the fridge, he gave her a peck on the cheek. "Thanks, Mom."

"Back by dark," she said.

He walked out the front door and headed toward the thriving seaside attractions.

★   ★   ★

The lights and sounds of a summer beach town played all around, a carnival that stayed on for the season. The melody of voices – the laughter, the hoo-rahs, the French-Canadian back and forths – accompanied the roar of specialized mufflers that blatted out from tough-looking cars and Hell's Angels-ready bikes. Nestled in between these sounds were the cheers, screams, and music from the amusement rides, the live band playing at Barbara Anne's, and if you walked to the edge of it all, you could hear the Atlantic whisper promises of serenity to the shore. Rocky had lived here his entire life and this orchestra, this show, every year, never got old. If anything, it revitalized him. Reminded him how great it was to live here, to get this experience that a lot of these people milling around paid big bucks to feel, year in year out, for nothing. Locals had to put up with loud nights and strange people passing through, but that too was a part of the charm. A young man couldn't ask for more, with all the babes from Massachusetts, New Hampshire, New York, and all points Canada to gawk at and dream about. Some spoke with great accents, some were completely foreign, couldn't speak a lick of English and just smiled instead. That was more than enough. The girl he'd kissed at the Foreigner concert last year spoke terrible English, but that hadn't stopped them from holding hands. He still couldn't believe he'd had the guts to touch her let alone kiss her. Julie told him it was because he had a contact high from the Mary Jane. Whatever it was, it had been wonderful. At the end of the day or night, talk is overrated. It's all about the spaces in between, the whispered promises that you have to go to the edge to hear.

"Hey, Heatstroke," a voice called out.

There she stood, her back against the front of Louie's Sports Shop, yellow Chuck on the building, green Chuck planted firmly on the ground. She'd swapped out the Twisted Sister shirt and jeans for a yellow *Star Wars* ringer t-shirt and a purple skirt that met the knees of her pale legs. Her dark hair, darker lips, and the gleam of the neon light in her eyes spilled his thoughts to the ground. He mumbled something but didn't know what.

"Come on," she said.

And just like that, they were off.

He wanted her to reach back and take his hand. She didn't. She walked, glided was more like it, pacing every other person on the block. He followed, his heart thumping as fast as Pacman on power pellets, as they made their way out past all the shops and entered the gates of Palace Playland.

"Hungry?" she said, calling over her shoulder.

"Yeah, sure," he lied. The Clarise Zukas Special in his belly was being fed to the spiders from Mars that seemed to have been planted there with November's arrival. She might not have been Ziggy Stardust, but she was every bit as intriguing and mysterious.

She stopped at Palace Dough Boys.

"Two fried doughs, please."

He stopped behind her, trying to catch his breath, and wiped his sweaty palms on his knees.

Stay cool.

After a few seconds of crossing then uncrossing his arms, rubbing his hands together and then scratching at his ear, Rocky put his hands in his pockets just to settle the whirlpool of emotions trying to swallow him.

"Where are your parents?" he asked, unable to think of anything else to say.

The greasy-looking, gray-haired guy at the dough stand handed her two paper plates. She thanked him and handed him a five.

If she'd heard his question, she didn't answer. She took the plates to the side counter and applied both powdered sugar and cinnamon.

"I could have gotten mine," Rocky said.

"Nonsense. You have to get the mix just right." She finished up and handed the plate over. "Here. Take a bite and let me know what you think."

Never one to put cinnamon on his fried dough, he hesitated for a split second before trying it. "Wow," he said, chewing the warm bread. "That's really good."

"I know," she said. "It's perfect."

He watched her gaze all around, taking in every sight, sound, every breath like it was the first time she'd ever been someplace like this. It was hard to imagine, she seemed so comfortable here, and navigated through the crowds and buildings like she'd been here since the days of the settlers. She gazed up at the darkening sky, nodded, and added, "Perfect. Just like tonight."

While she got lost in the beauty of his town, he stared at her. Her smooth neck, her chin, and he even managed to be a gentleman only taking a quick glance at the way her boobs pressed against the fabric of her t-shirt. Luke and Han were two of the luckiest guys on Earth right now and they didn't even know it.

He snapped his eyes back up to meet hers as she smiled.

"So," she said. "What else do you do around here for kicks, beside playing arcade games and chasing girls you don't know?"

"Ahh...swim?"

She nodded. "Okay, that sounds like fun. Let's go."

"What? You mean like, right now?"

The thought of her seeing his back brace and yucking out like Becky Colby made his chest tight. He wished he'd taken it off before he came out, but he hadn't thought to. Hell, he didn't really think he'd see her again.

"Sure," she said. "Why not. The water's probably still warm and—" Her eyes dropped to his jeans. "I bet you left your trunks at home, huh?"

My way out.

"Yeah," he said. "I was just coming out for a walk—"

"No problem." She nodded back toward the square and shoved off in that direction.

"What are we doing?" Rocky said, his stomach turning on him again.

"Getting you some swimwear. Unless you wanna chance going in in your tighty-whities."

His face flushed with warmth.

"Here," she said.

He followed her into a tourist trap he'd never been in before. It was one of many little shops with Hawaiian shirts and vibrant-colored shorts and swimsuits in the window.

She snatched green trunks from a rack, placing them against his waist.

He pulled his hips away from her before her hands could make contact and bumped a large woman behind him with his butt.

"Oh, I'm so sorry," he said to the woman. She harrumphed at him and moved along.

"Sorry," November said, her gaze drifting to the floor. She looked slightly wounded.

"No, it's okay," he said. "I didn't know what you were doing is all."

She looked up, her lips making a slight upturn.

"Well, I think these should work. What do you think?"

"I think they should be fine," he said.

"Good. Are you ready then?"

Before he could answer, she took them to the lady behind the counter and paid for them.

"Here you go, Heatstroke," she said, slapping the green shorts to his chest. "Now we can get wet."

He stopped panicking about his brace enough to wonder what she was going to wear. She probably had something on under her clothes.

He had to think of a way out of this without looking like a wimp or a weirdo.

The beach was just a couple minutes ahead of them. All the way his body filled with dread. How the hell could this be happening? She wasn't even supposed to be here. He should still be at home in his bedroom playing video games or listening to music.

As they reached the sand, he remembered the bathrooms.

"I have to go to the bathroom," he said. "I'll be right back."

"Don't go sneaking off on me," she replied. "I'll be waiting right here."

He hurried to the bathroom, fished a quarter from his jeans, placed it in the coin slot on the door, and entered.

What the hell was he thinking? His original thought had been to come in here and take off his brace, but then what? He couldn't just leave it in here. Could he? And if he walked out with it, she'd see him and ask about the ugly thing.

"Fuck it," he said. Nobody ever used the quarter potties. They smelled awful and like this one, were a mess. There was still someone's shit on the lid of the toilet seat and pissy toilet paper on the floor. He looked at the lock. Maybe he could lock it and step out. No one could get in, and he could find someone to open it for him after November left.

It was a terrible plan, but he wasn't about to let her see him in this damn thing.

He undid the Velcro straps and placed the brace down in the cleanest corner.

"I hate you," he said, talking to the brace. "But for the love of god, please be here when I come back."

He stepped out, hit the lock button and shut the door. He plunked another coin in the slot and pulled. It wouldn't open.

Good.

She was people watching as he joined her.

"All set?" she asked.

"Yep."

They were on the sand, heading toward the water – he hadn't warned her that despite her assumption that the water was still warm, they'd be lucky if it was fifty-four degrees. The Atlantic didn't get 'warm' until late July, early August at best. The tide was in, which meant they had some pretty big waves – *big*, like *warm*, being a relative term when it comes to this slice of the ocean. You wouldn't see anyone hanging ten out there tonight or any other night.

The sun was dropping at a steady rate behind them. Twilight had a firm grasp on the sky, a bruising purple, and would sooner than later turn them into a couple of shadows.

There were plenty of people still sitting on blankets and walking where the water met the land, but it was dwindling down for the day.

November pulled her shirt over her head, revealing a black bikini top. His eyes betrayed the noble knight within him and took her in. Without turning to him, she bent over and slipped her skirt down her legs to her feet. She might as well have shot him with a hormone dart. He felt his dick come to life and had to turn away and try to get myself under control before it became blatantly obvious and totally embarrassing.

"You gonna hold those all night or put 'em on?" she asked.

"I, uh...." He remembered the green trunks in his hand.

"No one's gonna look. Just take your pants off and throw 'em on real quick."

Under normal circumstances he would have excused himself and gone to the pay-to-piss restrooms again, but this was no normal circumstance. He didn't want to leave her again. He dropped his jeans, grateful that his chubby had vacated the premises, and pulled on the trunks.

"Hey, look at that, I was right. Perfect fit. You look real cute,

Heatstroke. Last one in has to buy lunch tomorrow." She bolted toward the waves.

Beating her to the water, knowing how cold it would be and still diving head-first into a crashing wave proved to be either the bravest or dumbest thing he'd ever done for anyone.

The icy water attacked his flesh like a bazillion tiny, hate-filled blow darts from an indigenous tribe.

Your kind is not welcome here. Leave now or we will make it much worse for you and your friend.

Rocky exploded out of the salty water, slicked his long bangs out of his face and crossed his arms in a vain attempt to appease his frozen flesh. Goose pimples popped up like white flags to the hateful Tribe of Cold Ocean.

November's laugh made it easier to stand there shivering to death. The fact that she stood there clapping from the shore filled him with another urge: revenge.

"Oh, I see," he said through his already chattering teeth.

"No, no…" she said, raising one palm between them.

Rocky was too fast, and she was too busy laughing. He bolted from the sea and had her over his shoulder in seconds. He didn't send her in alone; he was courteous enough to join her as he tossed her to the waves and dove in for another round of attacks from the Tribe of Cold Ocean.

She was already up when he stood.

Shivering, her dark lips quivering before his own, she gazed into his eyes like someone searching for a soul. They were kissing before his brain could find a chance to ruin the moment. Fireworks exploded behind them, lighting up the sky to applause and *oohs* and *ahhs* from the entire population. You couldn't have scripted this any better. It felt like the world was sharing in the greatest moment of his life.

When their lips parted and their eyes locked, gravity abandoned, he was lost in the dark space of her gaze.

"Wow, Rocky, you're a pretty good kisser."

"Thanks. So are you."

"I'm freezing."

"Yeah, me too."

She stepped forward. He pursed his lips, ready for another kiss, when he felt her leg behind his. She shoved him backward and bolted for the shore as his back hit the water.

He scrambled to his feet, but she was already at her clothes.

"I owe you lunch tomorrow," she yelled back. "Meet me at the pier."

He started for the shore as she sprinted away, pulling her shirt on as she took off.

"Oh man, am I in trouble," he said. "Big trouble."

The fireworks continued going off overhead. The thought occurred to him that Palace Playland waited until nine fifteen or so to set them off on Mondays, Thursdays, and Saturdays. It was dark already. He'd made his mom a promise.

He threw on his t-shirt, tossed his jeans over his shoulder, hopped into his sneakers, and headed for home.

It hit him as he reached the square. After they kissed, she'd called him by his name. The smile dropped when he looked over at the pay-to-piss potty where he'd left his back brace.

"Oh shit."

He hurried over and tried the door. It wouldn't budge, but at least it was still locked. He glanced around. Who the hell did he ask to help get the door open?

Serious anxiety cinched his insides as he scanned the crowd for help. There was a cop over at the DQ.

He was gonna feel like an idiot, but touching his lips and remembering her kiss, it was totally worth it.

"Hi, Officer Nelson," he said.

"Hey, kid, what can I do for you?"

Pete Nelson was kind of a jerk to most of the kids Rocky knew, but he was always super nice to Rocky, because Uncle Arthur had helped Officer Nelson fix an old snowmobile a couple winters back. Rocky had even seen him from time to time drinking beers with his uncle on the stoop.

"I need your help. I kind of locked something important in one of the pay-to-piss porta potties."

"Can't say I've ever heard that one before," he said. "But you're in luck."

★   ★   ★

Officer Nelson knew the guy at the Seaside Motel, Gordon something or other, and fortunately, Gordon oversaw the crapping facilities.

It was ten o'clock by the time he walked in the front door.

Motley Crue had a song called 'Looks That Kill' and the expression on his mother's face held his death sentence.

"I'm sorry," he said.

"I told you to be home by dark. You had me worried sick," she said, arms crossed over her chest. Dad came up behind her.

"You just bought yourself a day's worth of chores," his father said.

"Dad," he whined.

"Never mind," he said, waving Rocky off before he could plead his case. "Give your mother a hug and then go to your room."

When his father busted out *never mind*, it was useless to resist. The Force was strong with this one.

He hugged his mother.

"Don't ever do that to me again," she whispered.

"I won't. Promise."

She let go, crossed her arms again, and nodded toward the hall. "Go."

His father was already planted in front of the TV; Clint Eastwood's *Escape from Alcatraz* was playing from the VCR.

Rocky only hoped that fate was nicer to him than it had been to Frank Morris.

CHAPTER FOUR

Her hair dripped as she hurried down the beach. She didn't feel bad about leaving Rocky behind. There would be time for them, but she couldn't risk being out with him at night for too long. Gabriel could be anywhere. Her brother wasn't exactly what you would consider the approving type.

Her family wasn't like other families.

After spending years hiding away from society, her father and mother moved to Ohio and had her brother, Gabriel. Eight years later, she came along. Their father passed when she was ten. Gabriel was barely eighteen when he eagerly took over as the patriarch of the household, moved them northeast and dropped the demand that they stay in the shadows.

Mother drifted into a depression. She slept most days, and nights were spent in her room. She was slow to warm to Gabriel's more open ideas of living, but eventually she gave in and agreed that blending into the small community was best for all of them.

Gabriel enrolled November at school and made sure that she got a proper education. She wasn't permitted to bring friends home, but between her mother and TV, she really didn't care about people outside the four walls of their new home in Aroostook, Maine.

Once Gabriel started with their summer excursions, that's when she really became intrigued with people. They went to places flooded with tourists, places like Ocean City, New Jersey, Cape Cod, Massachusetts, and Virginia Beach, Virginia.

Each vacation bought her more and more freedom. Gabriel and Mother knew she could more than handle herself should some stranger try and take her or make her do anything she didn't want to, but they also knew she was stealthy when she needed to be.

Last year, they wound up in York, Maine, where she discovered the wonder of boys.

And the true face of what she and her family really were. What Gabriel really was.

Monsters.

She'd hated her brother ever since. He said she'd get over it. You can't change who or what you are. Of course, she knew what they were. She always had, but Mother and Father managed to live alongside humans for years without much trouble. They were humble, careful, and smart enough to know what would happen if anyone found out that they were vampires.

God, thinking it made her want to do another sweep of her surroundings as if someone might have the ability to read her mind. She didn't want some beach city bastard trying to shove a stake through her chest or some religious freak burning her for Jesus.

It wasn't quite like everyone thought. They weren't that hard to kill. Her father suffered a heart attack. His father fell ill with pneumonia. If you shot one of them in the head or hit their vitals, that would do the trick, too. They weren't deathly allergic to the sun, although it did tend to weaken them and make them slightly more lethargic, but November loved its warmth and the beauty it dropped on the earth. She was quite certain she would die if she couldn't be out in the day.

They could fly, possessed above average strength, and moved faster than you could see. Drinking blood enhanced these abilities greatly. They needed to drink, but the amount to maintain health was minimal and did not have to be human. November had spent the majority of her life surviving off the occasional rabbit or fox. Her kind was able to get by for quite a while without a good dose of blood, but along with lessening the potency of their gifts, it made them more susceptible to viruses and disease.

She'd only drunk the blood of humans three times that she could recall. It was the memory of her last that still deeply saddened her.

It was Gabriel, of course, who demanded it of her. Gabriel, who in the last couple of years had taken to dressing in black, sleeping in a coffin, and even talking like some sort of noble jerk straight out of a bad Hollywood horror movie. It was almost like he was getting into character. She didn't understand it, but figured it was maybe a strange phase he was going through. By far the worst change in him was his willingness to kill and the lack of remorse he seemed to have in doing so. He made excuses for taking lives, trying to convince her to do the same. He'd insisted that she would need the extra boost for their move here. He'd taken an elderly gentleman from a bench somewhere near Cleveland. He promised not to kill the man, to return him to where he'd abducted him, so at the time, November didn't feel so bad. She drank until she was full, and not a drop more. Mother did the same. When it came to Gabriel's turn, he gorged himself. When the man began to convulse, Gabriel let him go, only to then grab hold of the man's head and snap his neck.

The awful cracking sound the man's neck made haunted her. Gabriel claimed it had been done out of necessity. Saying they couldn't chance the man seeing one of them again before they left and remembering what they'd done, although that seemed unlikely as they were leaving the next night.

She learned more than she wanted that day. Her brother was not like Mother, Father, or herself. He was going to be trouble. Somewhere, sometime, he would do something that would threaten their safety. She was hopeful it wouldn't happen until he'd gone off on his own, but he'd yet to leave her and mother, claiming she wasn't strong enough to take care of herself or Mother. That they'd be dead in short order. November knew better. Despite all his skills and arrogance, Gabriel was a coward.

★　★　★

Stepping from the beach to the slim path into the woods, she felt a chill sweep by and knew he was there.

She stopped and said, "You can come out."

Gabriel dropped from the tree behind her.

"Ah, little sister, you're getting good."

He always acted so surprised when she knew he was there before he revealed himself. She *always* knew. Even last summer before he tried to ruin her life.

"What do you want?" she asked.

"Now, now, no need to have a poor attitude. You should be happy I'm looking out for you."

He snaked around her, practically whispering the last line into her ear.

She shrugged him off, turned and crossed her arms.

"I don't need your protection."

"Oh, darling," he said.

She hated it when he spoke this way. Calling her *darling*, the word spewing from his mouth like he was some sort of noble gentleman casting it upon a peasant.

He placed his hands on his hips and flipped his long black hair. "I know you think you've got enough defenses to take care of yourself, and you do possess admirable control of your abilities, but don't hate me for being cautious."

"That's not why I hate you."

"Oh, please," he said. "Don't tell me you're still upset about that silly boy from last summer? Really? Is that what this is all about?"

She didn't answer. She couldn't. His conceit and callousness made her seethe all over again.

He stepped forward and reached for her shoulder. November swung her arm, knocking his hand away.

Rubbing the wrist she'd struck, acting like it actually hurt him, more of a pathetic attempt to gain her sympathy, he said, "I see."

He turned, placed his arms behind his back and gazed toward the beach with a sigh.

For the tiniest second, she almost felt bad. It was possible, a slim chance but possible nonetheless, that he was being sincere in his watching over her. Deep down, he may have meant well with all his intrusive behavior, but he was just too self-centered and childish to understand how his actions and reactions affected others, or more precisely, how they affected her.

"I'm going home," she said.

She left him there to brood on his own.

She was sure he'd follow her, but he did not.

She prayed that Rocky had made it home already. For the briefest of moments, she considered turning back and checking to make sure, but thought better of it. She'd never forgive herself if she led her brother right to him.

★   ★   ★

Gabriel hadn't always been a devil.

When she was a child, he was her hero. There weren't much worse things than seeing your idol transform into something less than that before your eyes.

Prior to their father's passing, they were just relatively normal kids.

They ate human food, wore regular clothes, played in the woods, and even watched programs on the black-and-white television that father brought home one day. They got one channel, PBS. They watched *Mr. Rogers' Neighborhood*, *Electric Company*, and *Sesame Street*, which featured a lovable old vampire named The Count. Seeing him there, interacting with kids, it made her childish mind believe they were more normal than they'd been taught. It showed her they could live among people and be fine. She knew better now, of course.

Gabriel used to lead her around to see the things he'd discovered in the woods or take her on long walks just to see what they could find. They built forts; they fished and hunted with spears or with their bare hands. They swam in ponds and lakes deep in forests that looked untouched by humankind. If she fell or got hurt, Gabriel lovingly tended to her wounds. She had no doubts that he cared for her, and there could be no doubt of her adoration for him.

Somewhere near the end of their time in Ohio, she could tell he was struggling with the charade. With Mother and Father's demand for secrecy. He wanted to be in the city. He wanted regular friends. He wanted to show people what he could do. It was around this time that he stopped taking her with him. He stopped smiling. Even now, she couldn't remember the last time he'd laughed.

When Father died, Gabriel only grew worse, mean even.

Mother said it was a phase. That Father's death dropped a lot of responsibility onto Gabriel's shoulders. And that the circumstances would be difficult for anyone, man or monster.

They never shied away from that word – *monster*. They knew their place. Unfortunately, in that regard, knowing their place, she'd begun to fear Gabriel may have passed a point of no return. If not, he was certainly on the edge. He'd grown angry, dark, and after last summer, sinister.

★　　★　　★

Although she could fly, most of the time she chose not to. She enjoyed walking and liked to feel the dirt beneath her feet. It made her feel closer to nature. Father ingrained the importance of keeping up appearances. And one of the fundamentals was keeping their feet on the ground. It taught humility and grace. It also greatly lessened the chances of people discovering them.

Their home came into view. It was a lovely, three-bedroom cottage at the edge of a cemetery on the outskirts of town. Mother was asleep in her darkened room. She'd been sleeping a lot again lately. Not a good sign, but as old as she was, it was to be expected.

November swept through the house to her own bedroom, grabbed her headphones, and put on the new Van Halen record. She still couldn't believe the 'I Can't Drive 55' guy was singing for them, but it was so good. Side B had just the tune she was looking for.

The keyboard intro to 'Love Walks In' warmed her heart and made her smile like a fool.

The lyrics were about aliens pulling strings – love was an out-of-this-world experience, for sure. Not that she was in love, that would be crazy, but there was something about Rocky. It was instant. She saw him and knew she had to hang out with him.

Contact. That's all it takes.

CHAPTER FIVE

Marcy Jackson sat at the window watching the fireworks from the beach. She'd always loved the spectacle of it all. Her late husband, Eddie, hated them. When they first moved up to Old Orchard Beach from Biddeford, the young interracial lovers stuck out like sore thumbs. It was fall, the tourists had all hightailed it home, and the mostly white community left behind could do nothing but talk about the new mixed couple on Gage Street. But a Frenchwoman had fallen for a colored man from the south. Eddie was thirty when they started dating, she was just twenty, but it was love at first sight. He was beautiful, strong, and had the heart of a lion and a laugh that lit up her world. Married three years by the time they came to OOB that fall of 1968, they'd experienced two lifetimes' worth of dirty looks and hardships. When her friends warned her what mixing races could do to her reputation, and lord forbid if they had a child, Marcy set them on their heads and told them god was the only judge she concerned herself with. Eventually the new beach community warmed to them, and as recently as two summers back, Eddie, who'd been a career fireman, was awarded the city's Citizen of the Year Award for his contributions with the fire department as well his years with the town council, and for the volunteer hours he put in at the Boys & Girls Club.

He'd endured racism on a daily basis, and she couldn't have been prouder of his ability to turn the other cheek. She missed him dearly. He'd been a diabetic his entire life and succumbed to a stroke at the young age of forty-nine, just four months after receiving his big award.

Nights like this, the fireworks and the hubbub of the busy season, made things a little bit easier. They'd never had children of their own but knew plenty of the local kids and had watched many of them grow up before their eyes. Even the younger kids in the neighborhood knew them and said hello when they passed by.

Eddie had touched so many lives in town, his legacy endured.

Marcy was getting ready to go into the TV room when she heard a yelp from the front yard. She hurried to the window in time to see something streak across the small lawn. She placed her forehead to the glass, trying to glimpse what was just beyond her sight. Her hand fumbled along the wall and found the switch to the front porchlight. The Chaplins lived next door. Their little white picket fence contained a splotch of dark, dripping paint.

Paint, she told herself. *Definitely paint. Just because it looks a little like blood, doesn't mean it is.*

Marcy went to the door and stepped out into the warm night. She could hear nothing but the summer people carrying on. A chill crept over her flesh. She hugged herself as she started down the steps and edged toward the corner of the house, her gaze flicking back and forth from the dark splatter across the Chaplins' fence to the shadowy space between their houses.

She dug her nails into her arms as she inched closer to the fence. The splatter glistened and was indeed dripping in the soft light from her house.

Fresh.

Someone was out here. She thought of the boy, John. He was maybe thirteen or fourteen. Maybe he and his friends were fooling around.

"John?" she called out. "Is that you, sweetheart?"

A deep moan came out of the dark.

That was not the boy. That was something awful. She knew it in her guts. She swallowed hard, backing away from the small alley, and hurried up the steps and into her house. She was near tears as she fumbled the slide chain lock into place. She cursed herself for calling out and drawing attention to herself. It seemed so stupid, but the thought that she had suddenly invited trouble to her front door nestled inside her chest like a fast-growing cancer, heavy and black.

"Please, god, please, Eddie," she whispered, her head bowed before the door. "Please make it go away. Whatever it is, sweet Jesus. Let it be gone."

After a moment, she dared a peek through the yellow curtain over the door's little window and caught sight of it. A blur, ever so slight, and then it disappeared. She exhaled, her breath coming out in a staccato sigh as she battled between a cry and a nervous laugh.

And then she screamed when he appeared.

A man dressed head to toe in black stared toward her from the lawn. And just as quickly, he vanished.

Marcy stumbled away until her back hit the wall. She slid down to the floor, brought her hands to her face and wept.

★   ★   ★

John Chaplin was out that night, but the blood on the fence was not his. He and his band were jamming up the street at his friend Jonas's house. Jonas was the only kid on the block with a PA system. His dad played in a cover band that performed gigs on the pier twice a month. When John's mom helped him get a guitar from the music shop over in Saco, he made a beeline to his friend's place and demanded they start their own band. And they weren't going to follow crappy bands like Ratt and Dio with their over-the-top sex and wizard lyrics. No, they were going to tear shit up. Like The Misfits or Bad Religion. Jonas didn't know any of the bands, but John made him a mixtape crammed with thirty-something songs from The Ramones, The Clash, Black Flag, and others. And knowing what they were doing with their instruments took a back seat to the attitude and energy, of which John and their drummer, Brandon, had plenty. Jonas owned a bass and knew how to play. He showed John some basic power chords and they were off and running. It wasn't long before Jonas saw the light and came over to the dark side. They called themselves Freddy's Nightmares due to John's love for horror movies, but soon shortened it to The Nightmares after Jonas said it sounded better.

They'd been jamming for two months now and Brandon wanted to invite the neighborhood kids over to watch.

"We're not ready," Jonas said. He pushed his glasses up his nose and pointed at John.

"What? I think we sound awesome," John said, hitting an A chord that was all out of sorts.

"See, John can't even tune that thing right," Jonas said to Brandon. "And we don't even have enough songs yet for a setlist."

"Jonas, it's your job to tune his guitar until further notice." Brandon pointed a stick at John. "And you, you got all the songs, man. Why don't you show Jonas what you showed me last night?"

John had songs. Despite all his bravado, he also happened to be really private about his lyrics. Which pretty much went against the whole punk rock rebel thing. How were you going to stand up to authority or oppression or piss off the Republicans if you couldn't even share those stances with your bandmates?

"Oh yeah," Jonas said. "What songs? Why haven't I heard 'em?"

John hated being teamed up on. At the same time, he asked himself, *What would Joe Strummer do? What about Jello Biafra? Would they act like pussies?*

"Show him 'Rock, Riot, Revolution'. That one is rad as hell," Brandon said.

He could feel their eyes upon him. His face felt way too hot. He needed air.

"Come on, John," Jonas said. "Let's hear it, man. This is all your idea."

John bent over and shut off his amp, set his guitar down, and headed for the garage door.

"What are you doing? Where are you going?" Jonas asked.

"I can't breathe in here," he said, stepping out into the night. As he closed the door, he could hear Jonas whining, and Brandon defending him. Truth of it was, he cared what Jonas thought. Jonas was the most musically gifted of the group. If Jonas thought his songs sucked, it would crush him.

John pulled a pack of Camels that he'd swiped at the corner store from his back pocket, slipped one between his lips and sparked it up, making sure to watch for Jonas's mom. She'd bust him and tell his dad and he really didn't feel like getting his ass whooped again.

Jonas came out and joined him.

"Look, man. I get it. It's hard, right?" Jonas said. "Music is personal. But even though I haven't heard your songs, I know they're going to be awesome."

John was going to wave him off but something across the street stole his attention.

"No, man. Listen," Jonas said, grabbing his arm. "I'm only playing with you because your energy...it's...it's like, contagious, man.

You're like a stick of dynamite set to blow someone's face off. You have something to say. I know you do."

"Yeah," John said. He squinted into the shadows behind the big red garage across the street. "Do you see something over there?"

Jonas let him go and turned. "No, where?"

"Shh, right there, back corner of the garage. I think there's someone watching us."

"Why are you whispering?" Jonas asked. "Hey," he yelled. "If you wanna watch us play it's gonna cost you one dollar to get in."

Just then, something was on top of the roof of the garage across the street.

Both boys stepped back.

"Shit, what was that?" Jonas asked.

John didn't know and he didn't want to find out. Tossing his cigarette to the blacktop, he pushed Jonas back toward the door. "Fuck this, let's go back in."

He followed Jonas inside, glancing back before closing the door; he could swear he saw a man crouched atop the garage, smiling at them.

★　★　★

Gabriel enjoyed this early part of the night. Letting people see him, if only for a split second, just a glimpse to set the hairs on end and spill enough dread to give their dreams a malevolent turn. Watching them was wondrous, but picking one…ah, that was the greatest thrill. He'd gone against his preferences earlier, taking the mongrel he'd found next door to the woman's home. He despised taking pets. Not morally, of course. He couldn't care less about the sentimentality these humans held for their animals; it was the taste he'd grown tired of. They offered nothing. Hardly even a morsel compared with their counterparts.

He'd been coming out earlier and earlier, making the wait for the moment of gratification longer. He could feel the urge prickling beneath his milky flesh, a constant hum that stayed with him until his teeth made penetration. All those years, Father preaching self-control, minimalism, fear. It was not they who should fear. These humans dispensed pheromones like a beacon, and it offered the greatest sensations Gabriel had ever felt. It was worth living or dying for. Father had been weak and timid. And what had he gotten for it? A quick death and a life unlived. With the gifts that they possessed, it was a tremendous waste, one that Gabriel refused to duplicate.

There was beauty in this world. He found himself drawn to these seaside towns not just for the bountiful collection of victims, but also, their life. Everywhere you looked, there were people going for it. Taking chances, living on the edge, pushing boundaries and treating each day and night as if there were no tomorrow. They did not hide in shadows or cower under the covers. Even the elders watched from windows and doorsteps, sucking on the tit of youth, absorbing all they saw and experiencing it vicariously. The youth were out in droves, celebrating with reckless abandon well into the midnight hour, fearless.

Thinking of it now made the blood ache in his veins. He should have waited until later to come out. Should have slept a little longer. The small amount of sunlight he'd been exposed to was enough to sap some of the power he'd garnered from last night's feast. Had it not been for his sister and her need to be around humans, he would have postponed this excursion until later tonight. He preferred the traditional way of resting through the day, but November was far too curious for such things. She was more than curious, she was desperate. Desperate to be like them. To be one of them. Coming here, he was certain last summer's little lesson would at least cause her to be more cautious. To guide her more in line with him. Make her an observer. But her will and her stubbornness were strong. She could welcome trouble. That is why she needed his protection, his guidance, his influence, and maybe in time, his intensity.

It was a harrowing ordeal to get his sister to take nutrition from a human. A feat he hadn't succeeded in getting her to partake in since the week they left the Midwest. Like him, she could be so much more if she'd see these delightful creatures for what they were – sustenance. But alas, in the end, her supplemental approach of sucking off rabbits and deer would only shorten her time with her precious humans.

She would come around to seeing things his way.

One way or another.

CHAPTER SIX

Warren Dubois whispered sweet nothings into the ear of the tan Southern girl named Vanessa, hoping his accent would charm the shorts off her. He came down to Maine's top tourist trap every year. Forty-four years young, he loved the way the pretty young things treated the beach town excursions like Sin City. They were up all night and open to anything. And Warren liked to take full advantage of it all before going home to his government job back in Quebec. All year among the boring, stuffy government types, driving through crappy snowstorms and blustery northern winds, mingling in sweaty dance clubs surrounded by the same women he'd known all his life, he looked forward to these summer getaways.

"So, *ma chérie*, where are your mother and father? Do they know you're out here so late at night?"

"I'm old enough to be out until I'm ready to go home," Vanessa said, her hand resting on his golden thigh. "Don't you worry about me, sugar. Us Southern gals know how to take care of our gentlemen."

The waves lapped the shore beneath stars that couldn't quite breach the carnival-like lights of the town. Warren leaned forward, inhaling her bleached-blond hair and sunblock. She wasn't a knockout like the woman he'd had two nights ago in this very spot, but she had a better body and she was nearly half that one's age.

"I do like the sound of that," he said. He caressed the back of her head and placed his lips against the salty flesh of her neck. He let his hand trail down her spine, resting just above the waistband of her shorts.

She moaned as she slid her hand to his crotch and squeezed his dick through his jeans.

He'd been with plenty of wild women, but he had a feeling about this one. There were three other couples on the beach, an old man and his dog, and a group of long-haired teens blasting obnoxious heavy metal music from their boombox about a hundred meters away. Sweet Vanessa hadn't hesitated or flinched as he continued kissing from her neck to her breasts. Instead, she pressed her chest to his mouth and squeezed his dick harder. This little girl was an exhibitionist.

Cheers went up from the metalheads as she slipped her tit out from beneath the bikini top and let Warren have her nipple.

He came up and looked into her eyes.

"You are amazing," he said.

"I know."

"How about we go back to my place and—"

She pulled her top back into place and touched a finger to his lips.

"I know a quiet spot just off the path over there," she whispered.

He craned his neck and saw tall grass swaying in the light summer breeze.

"In the grass?"

"It's a little farther in, just after the trees over there."

He turned and kissed her cheek before standing and reaching out a hand to her. "Lead the way, my little mademoiselle."

He watched her ass dance beneath the tan fabric of her shorts as she pulled him along.

Aren't you just one eager beaver? he thought.

The longhairs hooted and hollered as they passed.

"Who's your daddy?"

"Someone's getting lucky."

"Get some."

Warren put his hands on her hips as they headed into the woods.

"Hey, what the hell?" he said, stopping behind her.

He'd seen someone. Standing off to their right.

"What are you doing?" she asked.

"I...." He scanned the grass but couldn't see anything. "I thought I saw someone."

She stepped to him, wrapping her arms around his neck and kissing him. "Let them watch."

His arousal conquered the odd sense of dread.

"Eyes on me, sugar," she said, reaching behind her back and undoing the bikini top. The purple fabric slid from her breasts.

She smirked and pulled him along.

She shoved him as they reached a narrow path in the woods. He stumbled back just beyond a large rock. The ground was bare save for a few discarded beer cans and a red bandana that someone had left behind.

She dropped to her knees and undid his jeans.

Within seconds she had him in her hands, in her mouth.

A shadow fluttered.

He jerked back, his eyes straining to find the source of the movement.

Vanessa pulled him to the ground and shoved him onto his back before standing up and slipping out of her shorts, then kicking them to the side.

Stradling him, she grabbed his chin. "I said eyes. On. Me."

He gave the trees one last glance before locking on to her body again.

She rose up and slid down onto him. He closed his eyes, groaning as her warmth enveloped him and she began to writhe up and down.

He clamped his hands on her ass and guided her movements.

She grabbed his wrists and brought his hands above his head, leaning her breasts over him and slipping her tongue into his mouth before sitting up again with her hands upon his chest.

"You're so—" he started.

Before he could finish, she was gone.

He sat bolt upright, searching for her.

What the fuck?

"Vanessa?"

His jeans were still around his ankles. He could still feel her wetness on him as he went limp. The sound of the branches jostling above drew his attention. He had to roll out of the way as the body dropped down next to him.

Vanessa's dead eyes stared up at nothing. Blood ran down over her breasts from the open wound in her throat.

"Jesus!" he cried. "Oh Jesus Christ!" Trying to get to his feet, yanking up his pants, he stumbled forward, nearly falling to the ground.

"I too like the young pretty ones," a voice said from behind him.

Warren cried out.

A man in black wiped a trail of blood – Vanessa's blood – from the corner of his mouth. His dark eyes seemed to draw Warren in like the tide.

"Seems we both got a taste of her tonight," the strange man said. "Come to me."

Warren didn't know why, but he stepped forward. He knew he should run. This was no man. This was...something evil.

"I can see your life is empty. You are so alone."

He was...alone. In his mid-forties and never married. He could never seem to open up.

"I can take it all away," the man in black said.

Warren shuffled to him, a meter between them.

The man reached up and took Warren's chin and tilted his head to the side. Warren felt a sudden warmth crawl over his mind and body. Happiness. His lips curled upward as he closed his eyes.

He continued to grin as the man placed his mouth to his throat.

It wasn't until the man bit him that the warm fuzzy feelings ran for the hills. He tried to pull away from this thing in his neck but couldn't. The creature sucked at him until all the fight in his soul fled.

Warren fell to the ground. He glimpsed Vanessa's face again in the dirt, pale and devoid of life. A piece of magnificent art lost in the woods, lost for eternity.

Au revoir, ma chérie, he thought just before he closed his eyes forever.

★   ★   ★

Gabriel finished the man off and stumbled back as he let him go.

He clenched his fists and felt the strength from the man's blood coursing through him. It was glorious. He flew upward. Up above the trees, gazing down upon the beach, he could see everything as though it were twilight – one of the many enhancements that drinking human blood had to offer. Although Father had never explained the vast difference between draining beast or man, not that it was a subject the old fool would dare traverse, Gabriel was certain it had to do with the soul. Human consciousness held so much more than any other creatures on earth. And it was absolutely divine. His heart pounded heavy, a tribal drum calling to the gods of the night. The rush was intoxicating. He could feel every pore of his flesh. There was a world of flesh and blood upon which to feast.

He breathed the life below him in deep.

The power that awaited him.

Slowly, he made his way back down to the dead couple.

The man was a bloodless husk of dried-out flesh and bone.

He turned his attention to the naked girl. There was some blood left in that one, but he didn't enjoy sucking from the dead. He stepped toward the beach but forced himself to halt.

The entire summer was ahead of him. There would be time to feast again. And again.

For now, he would discard the bodies where he had the others, and head to the pier.

He thought of walking amongst them while the high was so intense; he would feel each and every soul flickering and begging to be taken. A thrill that was nearly as addictive as the kills themselves. Yet, it could prove dangerous. The temptation could be too much, but it was his restraint that promised to make the next one all the more... exhilarating.

First things first. He must clean up his mess.

CHAPTER SEVEN

Rocky waited outside the bigger of the two arcades, the one with *OutRun*. Just like yesterday when he and Axel were here, the two big Frenchies were all over the new machine again, not that he'd step foot inside and chance missing November.

The sun was high above. He stood just under the shade provided by the tented canvas covering the arcade. It was a few minutes before eleven in the morning. He was early, but it was better to be early than late. The arcade always played 102.9 the Blimp, Maine's rock station from Portland. 'Cum On Feel the Noize' from Quiet Riot ended, giving way to 'Black Dog' from Zeppelin. Rocky hadn't really gotten into Led Zeppelin.

Sipping on a bottle of Orange Crush, watching the out of towners going past in every direction, Rocky wondered what Axel was doing. Probably still on the airplane. How long did it take to cross the ocean? Maybe not that long. Maybe he was grabbing fish and chips somewhere right now. He'd promised to call when his parents let him. Rocky couldn't wait to update him on November. Hell, Axel probably wouldn't believe that she'd kissed him. More likely, Axel would make up his own love story from England. His cousin had a thing for trying to either one-up him or act like he had the same stuff going on. Like when Rocky got a keyboard two Christmases ago, Axel claimed he'd gotten a drum set. Problem was the drum set was always at his Uncle Geoff's house in Portsmouth, because his mom didn't want to hear it all day. He kept promising Rocky it was coming, but the drum set never materialized at Axel's house. Rocky had given up asking about it. He wished Axel didn't think he needed to make up things like that. He was the coolest kid Rocky knew.

His stomach growled at the sight of children passing by with their cups of Lisa's pier fries. It'd been three hours since he'd had his cereal and watched *M.A.S.K.* He'd been awake since six a.m. He couldn't even remember the last summer morning he'd woken up that freaking early. It seemed almost against teen law, but he knew it was because of her. He'd thought about her all night before he fell asleep. It was so crazy. He kept getting this swarming feeling stirring in his guts. There was a part of him that kept whispering that he was gonna get hammered by this girl. She was going to be his doom, except that didn't feel right either. She'd seemed so genuine, but you never could tell.

He swiped his bangs out of his face, finished the soda and ducked his head inside the arcade to check the clock over the quarter machine. Half an hour had passed. He sighed.

"Waiting for someone?" she asked.

Spinning around, he said, "Oh, hey."

November was dressed in a blue tank top and cut-off jean shorts. Her hair was in a ponytail. Her face looked pale, her eyes a little heavy, like she hadn't slept well. Maybe she'd been up all night thinking of him, too.

"I hope you're hungry." The smile brought her face back to life. "Starved."

She nodded for him to follow. "Hold my hand," she said.

He reached over and their fingers intertwined.

Another thought tried to ruin this moment for him. What if she hugs me or tries to put an arm around my waist? She'd feel the back brace. He wished he'd left the stupid thing at home. After yesterday, he wasn't about to ditch it somewhere. If he lost the thing, his parents would kill him.

Please, god, don't let her touch my brace. Please, I'm begging you.

It seemed like a dumb thing to ask of god, but he just didn't want her to know about the contraption.

"Are you all right?" she asked.

"Uh, yeah. Sorry, I was just thinking about my cousin. He left for England today.."

"Oh, well, going to another country sounds pretty cool. I'm sorry you didn't get to see him off. How long will he be gone for?"

"He'll be back in August," he said, his head drooping slightly.

She squeezed his hand. "Well, I guess I'll just have to be your best friend while he's away."

His face flushed as he smiled and glanced at her.

Just looking into her eyes, he knew she meant it.

"How long are you going to be in Old Orchard?" He hated the question the second it left his lips. He didn't want to think about her leaving. She'd just gotten here for crying out loud. What if she says next week? What if she says—

"Sometime around then. End of summer, I guess. When Gabriel's ready to head back up north."

"Gabriel?"

"My brother. He's the one who decides where we vacation. Last year, we went to Kittery."

"What about your parents?"

"My mom is with us, but she's not well. She stays at the cottage. My dad passed away a few years ago."

"I'm sorry."

"Thanks. It sucks sometimes, but it's...it's...."

"You don't have to talk about it if you don't want. I didn't mean to—"

"No, it's okay. I just haven't really talked about him with anyone else before."

He wanted to ask about her friends or her home up north, but he decided to just drop it. He didn't want to make her uncomfortable.

A silence fell between them.

He chewed his lip, hoping he hadn't screwed up already.

"Come on," she said.

She led him to a place he'd never eaten at before. A food truck with a cartoon portrait of a dude holding a steaming burrito that read: Greg's Burritos.

"Have you eaten here yet?" she asked.

"Ah, no. I don't think I've ever seen this truck here before."

"Hey, guys," the punk at the window said. "What can I get ya?"

November stepped right up, pulling Rocky along.

"Can we get two full supremos?"

"Sure thing," he replied. "Anything else with that?"

Rocky noticed some sketchy things about Greg – sweaty hair sticking out the side of his backward Red Sox cap, the scabs on his elbows and knuckles, and the Band-Aid on his chin – and wondered if they were destined for food poisoning.

"We'll grab a side of guacamole and two Cokes."

"Guac comes with the supremo. I can add some extra on the side."

"Yes, please," she said. "Thank you, Greg."

"That'll be $3.62."

November paid for him, pulling a five from her back pocket. "Keep the change," she said.

"Wow, really?" he said.

She nodded.

"Of course, yeah. Thanks. I'll have those right out for you guys."

They walked over to the lone picnic table to the right of his truck. The meat and spices smelled good. Rocky had never really been a big fan of Mexican food; it wasn't really on the Clarise Zukas menu. Outside of a night of tacos at his old friend Logan's house a couple years back, he'd never had it. He couldn't even remember if he'd liked the tacos or even if he'd eaten anything other than the ground beef and the cheese.

"How'd you find this place?" Rocky asked.

"Just walked by and thought the sign was fun."

He checked it out again. And recalled the scabs and sweaty hair. Not that he was one to judge about greasy hair. He was not immune to showers despite what his sister often claimed.

"Did you notice the scabs on his arm?" he asked.

"Yeah, and he hurt his chin, too. Skaters always have wounds like that. I tried it once and fell right on my butt. Thought I broke my tailbone."

Skateboarding, of course. Rocky shook his head at not guessing that. He could hear the punk tunes cranking from the kitchen.

"I'm not allowed to try it." He said it before thinking.

"Not allowed?"

Shit.

He couldn't tell her his mom told him she didn't want him doing it. After he got his back brace, she'd seen him staring in awe at some of the local kids skating down his streets. They were flipping their boards beneath their feet and coming off the ground grinding down the sidewalk curbs. *Don't let me catch you doing something that foolish,* his mom had said. *The last thing Dr. Mellick wants is for you to scuff up your brace or hurt your back more falling off one of those.*

"I mean, my mom doesn't want me doing it. She thinks I'd break an arm or something," he said, hoping it sounded good enough.

"It's not that bad," November said. "But I guess it'd be easy enough to break something if you tried a big trick right off."

"Here you guys go," Greg said, bringing the two fat burritos and Cokes to the table.

"Thanks, Greg," November said.

"You're welcome."

"Hey," she said.

He stopped and turned, his hands in the back pockets of his Dickies.

"You skate, right?"

"Sure do. You?"

"Not really, but do you have your board with you?"

"November, can we just eat?" Rocky said.

"I do. You want to try it out?" Greg said.

Why did he have to be so cool? Damn him, Rocky thought.

"Maybe after we eat these," she said, holding up the beastly burrito.

"Cool. Just come up when you're done."

Rocky battled the dumb fears that wouldn't let him go. He wasn't afraid of skateboards. Hell, he thought they were super rad, but if he did fall, and he was pretty sure he would, she'd try to help him up, or what if his shirt flew up and she saw his brace. He wasn't going to do it. He just hoped she didn't think he was lame for not trying.

He brought the burrito up to his face and took a whiff; his mouth watered in response.

"You're gonna love it," she said.

He took a bite and felt his eyes roll back in his head. It was delicious.

"Told you so."

He finished chewing and took a sip from his drink. "Wow, that's really good."

"Can't judge a cook by his scabs," she said.

Rocky's Coke shot from his nose. He couldn't help it; she was too damn funny.

"I'm so sorry," he said.

She laughed, covering her mouth with her hand.

He'd never seen anyone so cute in his life.

They finished their food and drinks. Discussing Van Halen, of all things.

"You can't listen to Sammy Hagar," he said. "That's like...like... rooting for the Emperor and Vader."

"Oh, come on," she said. "That's not fair. The new album is good. You shouldn't have to pick sides. And besides, David Lee Roth is no Luke Skywalker. He's more like Lando Calrissian."

"No way. Roth is...or was Van Halen."

"Well, that's just silly. I love the new album, and I bet you would, too. Just like the burritos."

"You think so?"

"Good thing we've got the whole summer, it looks like you've got a lot to learn." She got up and headed toward the window of Greg's truck.

"Hey, ah, yeah, November...I don't want to skate."

She turned and placed a hand on her hip.

"Please? Maybe we could try it another day."

"What would we do now then?"

He thought for a minute.

"Bikes," he blurted.

"I don't have one here," she said.

"You can use my cousin's."

"Okay, you're on."

★   ★   ★

They said goodbye to Greg and thanked him for the food. Axel's bike was in the shed out back of his house. There was a lock on it but Rocky knew the combination. Fetching Rocky's Huffy from his front yard, they were about to set out when his sister pulled into the driveway.

"Hey," Julie said, killing the engine and getting out of the car. "Who's this?"

Rocky wiped the bangs from his eyes and said, "This is November. November, this is my sister, Julie."

"Hey," November said.

"Hey," Julie said, smirking up a storm.

Please don't embarrass me. Rocky tried with all his might to telepathically send the message to Julie's mind.

"Where are you two off to?"

"Not sure, just gonna go riding, I guess," he said.

"Well, Mom and Dad are going out for dinner tonight. If you want to practice parallel parking, tonight sometime before it gets dark would probably be best."

He definitely needed to practice parallel parking; it was the one thing he really hadn't done yet.

"Yeah, we should do that." He checked his watch.

"Listen," Julie said. "Go out for a while. Be back around six and we'll just go downtown for a bit." She lifted her chin toward November. "If she wants to come or hang out after at the house, that's fine with me."

Rocky turned and found November grinning.

"What do you think?" he asked.

"You mean I'd get to see you drive?"

"I'm not promising that it'll be fun."

"No, this I've got to see."

"So, be back here by five thirty or six," Julie said.

"Okay," he said.

"See you guys later."

Julie disappeared inside.

"So," November said, pulling up beside him. "Lead the way."

Before shoving off, he noticed her looking around, almost like she was searching for someone.

"Everything all right?" he asked.

"Huh? Yeah, no, let's go."

CHAPTER EIGHT

Rocky saw Julie sitting in her car in the driveway. He could hear her singing along with 'Papa Don't Preach' as he and November rolled into the yard. She glanced at him then looked at her watch. "Jesus, Rocky. It's nearly six thirty, come on," she said. "Mom and Dad left like an hour ago."

"Sorry," he said. "We lost track of time."

She got out of the car, went to the passenger side and got in.

Rocky held the driver's-side door open and pulled the lever to lean the seat forward so November could climb in the back.

She ducked and sat back.

Rocky put the seat in its upright position and got behind the wheel. He reached over and turned the radio down.

"Okay," Julie said. "You've done this bit plenty. Just take us to the avenue nice and slow."

He pulled the lever behind the steering wheel, putting the car in gear, and pulled out of the driveway.

"Wow," November chimed in from the back seat. "You really are a good driver."

"Ah, thanks," he said.

Julie turned back. "So, November. Are you new in town or are you here with the summer people?"

"I'm here with the summer people."

Rocky gripped the wheel, his palms suddenly sweaty.

"You here with your parents?" Julie asked.

"My mom and my brother."

"Oh, brother? Older or younger?"

"Older."

"Is he cute?"

"Hey," Rocky chimed in. "I thought you were going out with Brick?"

"His name is *Derek*," she said. "And we're not exclusive."

"My brother's in his twenties. He's not that nice."

"Ooh, so he's a bad boy?"

"Ah...well," November said.

"I thought you had to be a preacher's daughter to be attracted to bad boys?" he said.

"This isn't *Footloose*, Rocky," Julie said. "All kinds of girls like bad boys."

"Yeah, well, Brick seems like a dude destined for jail. You should be all set."

"Hey, don't be a jerk. I'm taking you out when Mom and Dad would kill me. This is risky business."

"All right, I'll shut up," he said.

"I do like Derek. I was just making conversation. Turn here."

Rocky made the turn onto Plane Street. He glanced at November in the rearview mirror. She was once again scanning the sidewalks.

"Okay," Julie said. "Pull up alongside that green Dodge."

She talked him through the steps. He managed to get a good angle, but cut his wheel too late; his back tire hit the curb.

"It's okay," Julie said. "Just pull back up beside it and try again. You can do this."

She really had an amazing ability to calm him down. Going out with Mom or Dad was like riding with someone holding a ruler, ready to snap it across your wrist at the slightest wrong move. Julie managed to keep cool no matter the situation. It was something he'd picked up on when he was pretty little. It was almost like her superpower.

He pulled out, lined up with the green Dodge and tried again. This time he nailed it.

"Whoa, bro, that was smooth. I told you you could do it." She punched his shoulder.

November leaned over the seat and kissed his cheek.

"Good job," she said.

"Okay," Julie said. "Now, let's try it again."

He managed to do it flawlessly four more times, only having to try again once.

When they pulled onto their street, Derek and his on-road/off-road dirt bike sat waiting in the driveway.

"Oh, look," he said. "It's Brick."

Julie nudged him again.

"Be nice," November said from the backseat.

Julie smiled. "I like her."

They pulled in beside Derek and his bike and got out.

"If you two want to hang out and watch a movie, you probably have time," Julie said. "Dad left fifteen bucks so we could order pizza."

November was scanning the houses around them.

"What do you think?" he asked.

"No, I'd love to, really, but I've been gone all day. I really should get home."

His heart dipped.

She took his hand. "Tomorrow?"

"For sure," he said.

"Do you need a lift home?" Julie said.

November gave his hand a squeeze, before letting go and starting for the sidewalk. "No, I like the walk," she said. "But thank you. And, Heatstroke, I'll see you tomorrow, okay?"

"Cool," he said.

He watched her walk down the road.

"Heatstroke?" Julie asked.

"She calls me that sometimes." He kept the story to himself.

"Hmm, well," Julie said. "Whatever. She's cool, Rocky. And she really digs you."

"Hey," Derek said, "maybe you'll even get laid."

Julie elbowed him. "Jesus, Derek. Shut up."

"Sorry, babe."

"The money for the pizza is on the kitchen counter. Order whatever you want, okay?"

"What are you guys doing?" Rocky asked.

"We're gonna go hang out in my room for a bit, then maybe we'll come watch something with you."

He knew full well what went on in her bedroom; he'd heard them doing it the other afternoon before Dad got home.

"Yeah, all right. I have to bring Axel's bike back first."

"Okay, but right back here after, okay?" she said.

He nodded.

Julie and Brick walked into the house, Brick's hand on his sister's ass.

Rocky shoved his hands in his pockets and kicked rocks down the driveway.

He wished November would have stayed and hung out awhile longer. She'd seemed pretty skittish for the last couple hours. He hoped she didn't get in trouble for being out all day with him. It would suck if he didn't get to see her tomorrow.

He also wished there had been a goodbye kiss. Not that he had tried.

He walked his bike to the porch and then got on Axel's and coasted down the lawn and onto the sidewalk.

It only took a couple minutes to get to Axel's. He locked the bike up and started his walk home. He paused as a man sweating through his collared shirt stapled a poster to one of the telephone poles ahead. The guy pulled a handkerchief from his pocket and wiped his forehead before continuing down the road.

Rocky walked over to the pole and checked out the white piece of paper and saw the picture of a cute blonde who looked about his age. Beneath the black and white portrait, read:

Missing
Vanessa Winslow.
Sixteen. Blond hair, she's 5'2, 112 lbs.
Last seen wearing khaki shorts and a bikini top.
If you've seen her please contact her parents, William or Mary Winslow
at the Atlantic Ocean Suites.
207-678-0909

Rocky couldn't recall the last time he'd seen a missing persons poster outside of TV. He and his mom used to stay up watching *20/20*. They had all kinds of kidnapping stories. They used to give him the creeps and make him paranoid when he was younger. As he looked at the poster, that childish fear crept over him.

He thought of how nervous November had seemed tonight. She was so cool and composed the other night on the beach. The man making his way down the sidewalk stopped to hang another poster. Rocky wondered if that was Vanessa's father, William. He wondered if the girl would turn up. He didn't know her, but he hoped so.

He gave the poster another look before starting toward home, a little more urgency in his step than normal. The sun would be setting soon. He didn't feel like being out when it finally did.

CHAPTER NINE

November made it home just as the sun fell behind the trees. Gabriel was still in his room; she could feel him. She breathed a bit easier knowing that he'd been asleep this whole time, rather than out in the daylight watching after her. Good. Maybe he was learning to trust her a bit.

The small television was on in the living room. Her mother lay on the sofa, curled up in a brown blanket despite the heat and humidity.

"Evening, Mother," November said.

"Evening, love," she said.

She'd been ill for the better part of the year. That winter she'd had trouble breathing for nearly two months. Despite all Gabriel's demands for her to drink human blood to help give her the strength to get well, she refused. Instead she made November fetch her small animals from the forest, and eventually worked herself out of it, mostly. She never fully shook whatever was afflicting her, but her breathing had improved. Now she just seemed fatigued all the time. She was pale, of course, but that came with the territory. November was worried. She wished they could take her to the hospital and make sure it wasn't anything serious. Unfortunately, their kind could not go to the doctors' without it leading to more questions and inevitably, more trouble. They'd never been discovered, not that November had ever heard of, but Father had told them of a cousin named Jeffrey who had sought treatment for a wound and when the doctors got a look at his blood, they demanded he come back for more tests. When their cousin went back to the hospital, he saw men in black suits waiting for him. They stood talking with his doctor. Cousin Jeffrey turned around and left. Terrified that these men in black suits would come looking for him, suspicious that they knew what he was, he ended up packing up his belongings and moving south.

November never met the man but knew they could never risk hospitals.

She took a seat next to her mother on the sofa, leaning down and kissing her forehead.

"Should I go get you something to eat?"

"No, dear, you don't have to do that. If I get hungry, I can look for myself."

This was what she said every time.

The air changed, the dust molecules shifting, dispersing, as they sensed his presence seconds before she did.

Gabriel.

He stood with his hands on the back of the sofa.

"Mother, sister," he said.

"My dear Gabriel," Mother said. "Come to me, my son."

As he came around, November stood and went to the kitchen. She wasn't hungry, not for any of its few contents, but she wanted to give her brother space.

She watched Gabriel take up her spot sitting with mother.

"You must let me do for you what I can, Mother," he said, placing a hand to her forehead.

"When was the last time you fed?" Mother said, more than a hint of harshness in her tone.

She smelled it upon him. November knew her brother's thirst for human blood was great, but she was unsure how often he indulged. A single kill could fulfill a vampire for many weeks, months even. He had held the scent since their arrival two weeks ago.

She found herself eager for his reply.

"Now, Mother, you needn't worry about me. It is I who is looking out for us."

"I can see it in your eyes," Mother said. "Your scent is ripe with it. Oh, what would your father say?"

Gabriel's features tightened. He gripped Mother's arm. The ill woman gasped.

"Father is dead."

The words filled the room, hanging in the air with menace.

November came out of the kitchen.

Gabriel released Mother and stood, staring at November.

"See to it she feeds tonight."

And with that, he was at the door and gone into the night.

November hurried to her mother.

"Are you all right?"

There was something she'd never seen in her mother's gaze before. It dressed her face like a shadow in the dark – fear.

Mother placed a hand on hers, which November knew was meant to reassure her but did nothing of the sort. Her hand trembled, slightly, but the tremor was there.

"He's a good boy. Your brother is…he's his own man. He will find his way. He will take care of us."

"But the way he just grabbed you—"

"I'm fine, my love. Besides, he's right, I should feed. An old woman can give in to stubbornness. Will you be my sweet, and bring me something?"

"Yes, Mother."

"And maybe when you come back, we can discuss this boy you're seeing."

November had been staring at her own hands against her mother's. At this, she met the woman's gaze.

"There's nothing you two can hide from me. I may be old, but a vampire's senses are the last to go."

"Would you stop this talk of being old? You act like you're a hundred and riding with the reaper."

A small grin creased her mother's face. "Not yet, I suppose. But there will come a day. And when it does come, you must learn to trust Gabriel, yes?"

She truly wanted to believe in him. She did, but she just didn't have her mother's faith. Perhaps she was judging him too harshly lately.

"Yes, Mother," she finally said.

After a few minutes of sitting with the woman, watching some prime-time soap opera, she got up and went outside.

She could see the graveyard just through the trees. The way the streaks of moonlight shined across the graves. It was a dark beauty that she adored. She'd walked among the headstones when they first arrived. As with every graveyard she visited, ever since she was a little girl, she wondered if any of their kind might be buried within.

They were good at keeping secrets, maybe not from one another, but from others. You learn to be great at something when your livelihood depends upon it.

She paused at the steps, wondering if Gabriel was near, or if he was hunting again.

She decided she didn't want to know, either way.

*   *   *

Rocky unfastened the straps on his back brace. His body beneath the pads and harder contours exhaled in response. The air felt cool hitting the sweaty, white tank top he wore under the contraption. He tossed the brace to the end of his bed, pulled the soaked shirt off, and tossed it to the hamper across the room. Summer was wonderful for a bevy of reasons, but it was hell on his particular predicament. The heat made him sweat like crazy, irritating his skin beneath the brace. And while everyone else in town was roaming the beach and the square shirtless, soaking in the sun, he had the tank top, the brace, and a t-shirt to boot.

He was only supposed to be out of the brace for an hour. He needed to take a shower and he was supposed to do some exercises to strengthen his core, but right now, he didn't want to do either. He grabbed his Walkman and put on his headphones. He opened his little brown suitcase of cassettes and found the newest one. Julie had given the few extra bucks he'd needed to get *The Final Countdown* by Europe. It had a bunch of great songs on it, the title track had made him and everyone else have to have it, but he was a sucker for a good love song. Call him a hopeless romantic. His favorite track from the tape was called 'Carrie'. Their singer, Joey Tempest, was great, and the guitar player, man, the solo in this song sang almost just as good. Rocky lay back, kicked his brace from the bed and cranked the song up.

He rewound and listened to it twice before his door opened.

"Hey sweetie," his mother said. His father appeared beside her.

He took the headphones off.

"Hey," he said.

"Did you do your exercises?" she asked.

"Not yet."

"Make sure you do, buddy," his dad added. "Did you get pizza?"

"Yeah. How was your date?"

"Well, it started out great, then your mother made me watch some chick flick."

"Dale," she said, slapping his arm. "You liked it. I heard you laugh."

"Hey, I've been playing this game long enough. I know what I gotta do if I want to get lucky."

"Dale!"

"Ugh, okay," Rocky said, setting his Walkman aside. He slid his feet to the floor and slipped past his parents. "I think I'll take my shower now."

"A shower? At this time of night?" his mother asked.

"Oh, come on, hon," his dad said. "It's only ten thirty."

"Okay, just make sure you wipe up the floor when you're done."

"I will, Mom."

"And do your exercises before you put your brace back on," she added.

He stepped into the bathroom and shut out her nagging.

★   ★   ★

Clean, half of his exercises completed, Rocky pulled the brace's torture straps tight and peeked his head out his bedroom door. He didn't want to go to bed just yet. His mother had gone into the bathroom after him, to take a shower no less. As he entered the living room, his father finished off a Schlitz and placed the empty brown bottle on the coffee table.

"Staying up for a bit?" his dad asked.

"Yeah, I was gonna see what's on."

His dad stepped beside him and kissed him on the top of his head.

"Good night, kiddo. Love you."

"'Night, Dad. Love you, too."

His father hummed an Elvis song as he strolled out of the room.

Rocky changed the channel to MTV and shut the lamp off.

Cast in the TV's late-night glow, he hoped for a cool video. When the Doublemint gum commercial ended, Michael Jackson's 'Thriller' came on.

He fumbled for the remote control and changed it. He didn't mind scary movies, but that video gave him the creeps. Even just seeing the beginning of it, he had to rub the goose bumps from his arms. Axel always teased him about it. He wanted to know how Rocky could watch Iron Maiden videos but not 'Thriller'. He couldn't really explain it. Maybe the effects were just too good in Jackson's video.

After surfing the channels and not finding anything good, he went to the VHS cassettes and pulled out his copy of *Star Wars*.

As he got ready to load the cassette into the player, something slapped against the outside of his house.

The hairs on his body stood at attention.

His mind told him it was Zombie Michael getting ready to smash through the wall or the window any second.

He pressed the tape into the VCR and stood.

He waited to see if the sound would come again.

His house was perfectly still.

He crept to the window and peeked out, praying gray hands wouldn't reach for him. They didn't.

Instead, he heard something at the front door.

He was slowly edging toward it, checking to make sure it was locked, when the door burst inward.

He nearly screamed.

Julie gasped as she entered the house and closed the door, locking it behind her.

"Jesus, Rocky, what are you doing?"

"I heard something…something hit the house."

"Oh, yeah, that was Derek's dumb friend Kailin. He thought it'd be funny to egg our house." She stepped to him. "Not a word to Mom and Dad. I don't need to give them reasons to hate Derek."

Rocky held his hands up in surrender.

"I mean it. I'll clean it up tomorrow."

"Kailin sounds like a real winner," he said.

"Yeah, no. He's a total loser." She grabbed a soda from the fridge and came back into the room. "What're you watching?"

"*Star Wars*."

Another sound stopped them both in their tracks.

"Oh god, no," Julie said, looking like she was about to hurl.

He turned toward the hall.

"Start the movie. Hurry, and turn up the TV," she said.

A moan came from down the hall, clear as day.

Rocky clamped his hands over his ears.

The final preview ended and the 20th Century Fox logo and music came on.

Julie stepped to the TV and turned it up.

They both sat on the couch and looked at one another. They burst out laughing.

They covered their mouths and tried not to laugh more but that only made it worse.

They eventually settled down. Twenty minutes into the flick, their dad came out singing another Elvis tune in his PJ bottoms in need of another Schlitz. He didn't say a word to them before moseying back off to bed. He just smiled, sipped his beer and sang his way out of the room.

As soon as their parents' bedroom door closed, they both cracked up again.

Julie made them Jiffy Pop and grabbed them each a soda.

They made it most of the way through the movie before falling asleep on the couch.

CHAPTER TEN

"I hope she's at least putting out," Kailin said, as he slowed his Camaro to a crawl. Derek reared back and launched the last egg at old man Russo's house on C Street. It splattered just above the doorbell.

Derek pulled a smoke from the pack of Winstons on the dash. He poked the car lighter and waited until it popped.

"You gonna answer me or what?" Kailin asked.

Derek lit his cigarette and placed the car lighter back in its home beside the ashtray.

"Why should I tell you anything?" Derek said.

"Dude, she's cute but you can't tell me it's fucking serious. I mean, we got the whole summer in front of us. You can't tie yourself down to one chick. That's stupid."

He knew the answer before Derek said a word. He'd never seen Derek with the same girl for more than a month. This was going to crimp their style, for sure.

"I've got a girl. So what? What's the big deal?"

"You're serious?" Kailin asked. "I mean, you're not fucking with me? What's the big deal? How about you're supposed to be my wingman?"

"What? You don't need me to get laid."

"That's not the point, man. We're a team. A damn good team. How many virgins have we busted?"

That got a sly grin out of him. It was Derek after all that came up with the nickname 'The Virgin Busters'. They'd fucked their first chicks in a tent in Kailin's backyard in Saco when they were fourteen. The girls were just twelve and thirteen. Right in the same tent at the same time, followed by high fives and Coors Lights in celebration.

"Dude," Derek said. "We're getting too old to be looking for virgins. Haven't you noticed?"

Kailin spat out his window and grabbed the beer between his legs. "Are you kidding? Look where we live. This is a haven for virgins."

"If you think all these tourist babes are virgins, you're fooling yourself."

"Oh yeah? Come with me right now."

"What? Where?" Derek asked.

"Let's head back to the pier."

"Dude, my house is at the end of the street. I'm fucking tired. No. I'm not going out."

"Lame."

"Yeah, well, whatever," Derek said.

Kailin pulled up to the curb in front of Derek's house and let him out.

"I hope it's not gonna be like this all summer," he said.

"Dude, come on, man. She's cool."

"She's a little bitch."

"You know what? Fuck you." Derek shoved off the car, saluted Kailin and headed to his front door.

Kailin stewed. Even if she wasn't really a bitch, this Julie chick was coming between them, pulling a fucking Yoko act. He was tempted to shout 'Fuck you' back at him. Instead, he did the mature thing – he turned around in Derek's driveway and peeled out, leaving a good hundred feet of black rubber on the road.

*　　*　　*

He was almost back to Old Orchard Street when a black shadow passed before his headlights. When he hit his brakes, the beer between his legs flew to the floor, spilling its contents on the floormats.

"Shit. Ah, fuck!"

The last thing he needed was for the cops to pull him over. The smell alone would get him arrested.

What the fuck was that? he wondered, scanning the roadway, first for any other cars, secondly for the thing he'd almost hit. This end of the street was quiet. The one car he'd seen turned right, heading toward Saco. He could still see some of the lights down at the square lit up, but even the bars would be closing soon.

He was about to let off the brake when a knocking sound on his roof startled him.

What the fuck?

"Hello?" he said.

There was no answer.

He put the car in park and stepped out.

There was nothing on his roof.

From the road, he gave the yards and sidewalk around him a once over. Despite being in a town filled to the brim with people, Kailin had never felt so alone in his life.

Something cold grasped his neck.

He wanted to spin around and beat the hell out of whoever it was, but found he couldn't move a muscle.

"Shhhh," the voice came in his ear. Fingertips caressed his neck, slithering their way over his chin.

Kailin gasped as the hand clamped over his face and his feet came free from the ground. His eyes went wide as he screamed behind the palm of the thing flying him up into the night sky.

CHAPTER ELEVEN

Officer Pete Nelson couldn't comprehend what he was looking at. The Camaro was sitting a hundred feet from the stop sign on Milton Street, engine running, lights on, yet there was nobody in sight. The interior reeked of beer. Perhaps the driver had needed to pull over in a hurry.

After calling in the license plate number, Pete leaned against his Crown Vic, waiting to hear back.

A dark lump in the grass next to the savings bank building caught his eye.

Reggie came over the comm.

"Looks like the car is registered to Kailin Boucher. Nineteen, 6', 155 lbs. According to the registration, he lives at 38 Wilton Road in Saco."

"Well, he ain't out here," Pete said. "And the car is just idling in the middle of the road."

"Want me to send for a tow?"

"Yep, might as well give Jesse a call. He's probably still awake."

"Okay. Roger that."

Pete placed the comm back on the hook and turned his Maglite on. There was a queer sensation running down his back, kind of like a millipede walking across his spine. He didn't like it. He walked over to the Camaro and killed the engine before flicking the hazards on and dropping the keys on the driver's seat.

The light gleamed for a split second over something wet on the blacktop beneath his feet.

He found the spot again with the beam.

Blood. Or at least, that's what it looked like. He bent down and ran a finger along the edge of it. Pete Nelson didn't have a doubt. It sure as shit was blood. He scanned the ground for more, but the drop was the sole specimen.

Great.

Sure, he wasn't concerned about the new AIDS epidemic; he was straight. Not that he had a problem with gays, they were free to love who they wanted, but he really hadn't thought it would be blood. Now, he'd gone and contaminated it with his finger. Chief would kick him in the balls if he fucked this up.

He stood, wiping his finger off on his pant leg.

Maybe the guy was carjacked? He'd never heard of anything like that happening here in town, but you never know. There always had to be a first time for everything.

He waltzed over to the bank and shone the light on the object he'd noticed in the grass. It was a boot.

It was a cowboy-style boot, snakeskin, or fake snakeskin, more likely. He scanned the lawn for the matching boot but came up empty.

Back at his car, he could see headlights coming up the road. Jesse and his tower, no doubt. A warmth flooded his body as the familiar truck pulled up next to him.

"Jesse, good to see you," he said.

"What's the deal with this, Pete?" Jesse asked, chunks of blond hair jutting out from beneath a blue bandana. "We got a drunk?"

Pete had played basketball in high school with Jesse. The guy was good. After his father passed, he wound up smoking dope, getting caught in the trap. Never went to college, never went anywhere. Damn shame. Talent, smarts, good looks, the guy had too much potential to get stuck in a place like this. Yet, here he was at one twenty-five in the a.m. fetching a vacant car.

"Smells like it," Pete said. "Ain't no sign of him though." He made a point of looking around. "Car was right here when I arrived on the scene, still running."

"Dude," Jesse said. "That's fucking weird."

"You don't have to tell me. I've been standing here for twenty minutes. All I found was a boot. Hell, might not even belong to the guy."

"Huh? Want me to snatch her up and bring it down to the lot?"

"Yep." Pete spat a brown stain onto the blacktop. "He'll sure as shit come looking for it tomorrow."

"Unless something happened to him."

Pete had a rush of chills ghost through him. He hadn't mentioned the drop of blood to Jesse. And he really didn't like that the vehicle had been running.

"Jesus, Jessie, don't go wishing harm on the guy."

"It's fucking weird is all. Well, let me get positioned. I'll have it out of here in a jiffy."

Even hearing Jessie talk like a backwoods burnout was a bummer.

Pete slapped the tow truck's cab, gave Jesse a nod and backed away.

He waited until the tow truck drove off with the car before snatching the lone boot he'd found by the bank and heading back to the station to fill out his report.

CHAPTER TWELVE

Gabriel wiped the blood from his lips, watching from atop the bank building as the officer drove away. He'd heard everything the cop and the tow truck driver had said. The officer was afraid. He'd found the man's boot and a drop of blood. Not enough to warrant outright suspicion of foul play, but it had been a bit sloppy on Gabriel's part. He'd have to be a bit more careful going forward. He didn't need the police looking for him before they'd even reached the midpoint of the season. That would be a shame.

He'd dispose of the husk of the young man in the dank basement with the others. He thought of Mother's words from earlier: *"Your scent is ripe with it. Oh, what would your father say?"*

He should go home; there would be plenty of time to feed again tomorrow. A slight tremor moved through his hands. He clenched them and closed his eyes. The hunger only seemed to be growing. Even with the fresh blood flowing through him, tingling every fiber of his being, he wanted…more.

He bit the corner of his mouth until it bled.

He exhaled, feeling the monster within loosen its grip ever so slightly, just enough to allow his mind to clear.

Yes, tomorrow would be fine.

*   *   *

He returned home shortly after two o'clock. He landed in the yard and walked up the steps. Mother was wrapped in a blanket on the front porch waiting. He wanted to tell her not to worry, but she refused to look at him. It'd been foolish of him to think she would not find out. She probably knew every time he'd been out.

A voice in his head reminded him that she, like Father, had a different idea of what constituted a good life. A safe life. Let her be angry. Let that anger fill her. Then, maybe she would understand.

He left her alone and went inside.

The light was on in his sister's room. The music playing from her record player within cut suddenly as he stepped to the door. The light inside went out.

Unappreciative. Both of them. If they would just open their eyes, they would see how much better life could be.

He returned to his room and picked up a book he'd been reading on Maine's history. After trying to get into it for several pages, he set the book aside. His mind was too distracted. Daylight was still more than two hours away.

He paced back and forth for ten minutes before heading back out. A stroll before bed, nothing more.

When he happened upon the paperboy four blocks away, he couldn't resist.

CHAPTER THIRTEEN

Sebago Lake

1985, One Year Earlier

The campground was filling with more people every day. They were drawn to the second largest lake in the state and its seclusion from the rest of the busy little Maine towns. Spending time in the great outdoors appealed to people of many different backgrounds.

Some were in tents, tents that ranged in size from a two-person nylon bubble to canvas mini-homes that could sleep up to sixteen people. Others arrived in RVs, also coming in small, tall and gargantuan sizes, just like the humans within.

For his family, Gabriel had chosen a modest two-bedroom cabin. He would take the loft room upstairs while Mother and November would share the bedroom on the main floor. The five-hour drive from their home outside of Caribou had been long but relaxing in his mind. They'd left just after ten at night and arrived around three this morning. He didn't often take the car, Father's prized 1968 black Pontiac Grand Prix, but enjoyed being behind its wheel very much. It was a powerful, dark beauty, one he felt represented him well. Kept in storage throughout the rough Maine winters, and in pristine condition in Father's care throughout the seventies, the car ran like new.

It was the one thing he truly admired most about his father and the piece of him left behind that also made him feel closest to the man. The car was the loudest, most eye-catching thing about the cautious, docile man. For Gabriel, it shone a light on the inner spirit his father kept a tight lid upon for his entire life. Gripping the wheel, cruising down the black highway in the night, Gabriel enjoyed feeling the vehicle's power and wondered if Father had ever been tempted to just open it up and unleash its full potential. Like many things in their father's life, if he had, he'd kept it private. But the car was a signal to him that maybe there was more to Father than the quiet, hard worker that they saw day and night before his heart gave out.

Staring at the car in the dirt driveway, Gabriel longed to show off what he could do. Not just roaring down a highway behind the man-made classic, but here, in this vacation spot. He could let go, just a bit more, and he could feed his gifts.

Back home, he'd traveled over the border into Canada on bi-weekly jaunts and had given in to the monster within, feeding upon the blood of man. And it was delightful. Father had always preached to take only what you need, stay in the shadows, away from human eyes, but the taste proved too much for him. The immediate rush, the strength and its effect on their gifts was glorious. If his father truly had resisted, had been able to hold back and restrain himself from partaking in the ritual on a regular basis, he had the most powerful will and constitution of any being, man or monster, that Gabriel had ever known. The problem for him now was wondering what he felt more for his father – respect or hatred. To suffocate what you were, and to raise a brood to do the same. Was that not an insult to their kind? Was it not suppressing their spirit? Why muddle through life as a commoner when you could live it like a king?

And unlike the humans and their fantastical stories of vampires and their eternal lives, it simply was not true. They died just the same. They had a limited time on this Earth to discover and live and love and feed....

Maybe if it were the case, if he had an eternity, he could afford the luxury of time and patience and restraint. But that was not the road laid out before him. He could not control what Mother and November chose to do, but he'd be damned, and maybe he was already, if he was going to waste his life never giving his full potential the chance to dine and dance under the moonlight.

No, he'd been tapdancing on the line his father had drawn for them. He knew that soon the time would come for him to step over and discover what he was truly capable of.

★   ★   ★

"Mother wants to go for a walk," November said, stepping up beside him. "She wants to know if you'll join us?"

His beautiful sister was becoming a woman. He'd seen the way she looked at boys. Could see the shape she'd taken on and the way men were now gazing upon her. It wouldn't be long at all before someone tried to defile her. He made it his duty to protect them, but especially her. She was a teenager. Her head full of impossible ideas. She needed watching.

"As tempting as it is, I must decline, sweet little sister."

"Suit yourself."

She lingered.

"When do I get to drive Father's car?"

"Ha," he cackled. "You?"

"What's so funny? I'm nearly old enough. He taught you when you were fifteen."

He couldn't argue with her. But he didn't want her behind the wheel just yet either. More attention was not what she needed.

"That is true," he said. "How about I think about it, and maybe when we get back home, I'll take you out."

"You mean it?"

"We'll see," he said. "Driving takes concentration. An ability to pay attention, which comes with maturity."

"So, you'll think about it."

He rolled his eyes. "Yes, I'll think about it. Now, go fetch Mother and take her out before she comes out and hears this preposterous dream of yours."

★　　★　　★

It wasn't until two weeks later when he caught his sister kissing a boy outside the cabin that something wicked soured his vacation.

He'd come back from Portland having just finished feeding off the drunk little college girl, when he found his sister, at three in the morning no less, in the clutches of the boy.

She didn't even try to stop it. Not even when the Pontiac came growling up the dirt path and pulled into the driveway.

He was out of the vehicle and at their side in seconds, the boy in his grasp, November hitting him, demanding he let the long-haired scoundrel go.

"Gabriel, stop it, he's my friend."

The boy, at first filled with piss and vinegar spoiling for a fight, quickly wilted in Gabriel's presence. Gabriel held him off the ground, the boy's hands clutching at his wrists. The weakling gasped for air, his eyes pleading, until Gabriel tossed him to the back lawn. He hit the ground with a loud *oomph,* held his sore throat and whimpered.

"If I ever see you around here again, I will kill you," Gabriel spat.

"Gabriel, leave him alone," November said, trying to shove him back.

After pulling his gaze from the cretin, he turned upon her.

"And you, I shall expect more of you henceforth."

"You're an asshole," she said.

Before he could stop, he lashed out, backhanding her to the ground. The look of pure hurt that crossed her features weakened his knees.

The boy scrambled to his feet and for a second, looked as though he contemplated defending November's honor. But his tail quickly went between his legs as he ran off through the trees.

"I'm...I...." Gabriel tried to find the words, but his rage cut him off short of apologizing.

His sister scurried inside.

The collision of rage, shame, and hurt made him ill. And a vampire ill is not a pretty sight. Clutched over, he vomited blood until he was too weak to rise.

He awoke the next morning in his casket.

Whether it was Mother or November that put him there, he could not recall.

All was quiet and tense in the house over the next few days.

Mother told him to give his sister space, to trust her.

And he heeded her words.

It was a mistake.

He caught the two lovebirds at it again, this time just outside the boy's camp, necking and groping. Rather than risk the wrath and possible all-out fight with his sister, Gabriel waited. He watched, allowing his hatred and disgust to roil up within as they kissed for what seemed like an eternity. His only solace came when his sister thwarted the blood bag's attempt to disrobe her.

When she finally gave him one last kiss before walking off along the path, presumably heading home, Gabriel made his move.

He appeared along the path behind the boy.

"You know what she is?" he asked.

The boy halted and looked back.

His hands flew up in defense.

"She asked me to meet her," the boy said. "I was going to leave her alone."

Gabriel stepped forward, no longer hiding his vampiric features. His ears and fangs extended, his forehead enlarged, the vein throbbed over his blood-tinted right eye.

"Oh my gah...oh, oh no..." the boy wheezed and whined, stumbling in retreat.

"Leaving her alone would have been a good move for you," Gabriel said.

As soon as the boy's back was to him, Gabriel had his lengthened nails deep in the boy's neck. Airborne, Gabriel and the boy disappeared over the trees until they were on the other side of the lake.

"Puh, puh, please, don't kill me, don't kill me. I-I'll leave her alone, please...."

"Shhh," he said, holding the boy with one arm and placing a nail against his lips to shut him up.

"You see me, yes?"

The boy nodded, tears streaming over his cheeks.

"She is exactly the same. Is this your ideal picture of love?"

The boy shook his head.

"Do you know what we are?"

He turned white as a ghost.

"Say it."

The boy's mouth bobbed like a fish desperate for air.

"Vah...vehm....v-v-v...."

He gripped the boy's neck enough to make him cry out.

"Say it!" he shouted.

"Vampires..." the boy cried, turning into an absolute blubbering mess.

"Was that so hard?"

He was too distraught to reply.

Gabriel began to descend when something jammed through his flesh, causing him to drop the boy into the lake below.

A Swiss Army knife protruded from his ribs.

The boy was swimming for the shore as Gabriel extracted the blade and let it fall.

Overcome with a sense of malice unlike anything he'd ever known, Gabriel swooped down and clutched the boy's head in his hands. In one thrilling motion, Gabriel wrenched the young man's head from his body. A bloodlust coursed through him.

After collecting the rest of the boy from the lake, Gabriel descended upon the campsite, extracted the young man's mother and father from their RV, and drained them.

He disposed of the bodies, packed up their site and got rid of the camper in a dense part of the forest miles away.

By dawn, he lay in his casket, a wicked smile upon his sleeping face.

If his sister suspected him, she kept it to herself.

For the rest of their vacation, she walked alone and kept a distance from others. Being amongst them, but not with them.

For better or worse, his actions had proved efficient.

Only he knew what he had done.

Or so he thought....

CHAPTER FOURTEEN

1986

"Hey, wake up, sleepyhead."

Rocky opened his eyes and wondered what part of *summer vacation* his mother didn't understand. She even had the audacity to pull his shades open, letting the horrible bright yellow ball of gas cast its devilish light spell upon him.

It burns, it burns! his mind screamed.

He nearly chuckled at that one and would have had he not felt like he'd been up all night and woken up far too soon.

"What are you doing?" he grumbled, covering his face with his pillow.

She pulled it away from him and sat down next to him.

"I just wanted to remind you that you told Uncle Arthur you'd help him with that porch today."

"Oh, man, that's right. What time is it?"

"It's almost noon. I just woke your sister up, too. She's in the shower."

He sat up and rubbed his eyes.

"Hey, there's something else I wanted to talk to you about," she said.

Stretching, he said, "What is it?"

She looked serious. Like, scary serious. Her mouth was tight, her brow scrunched.

"Mom, what is it?"

"There's been some concern this morning. On the TV, they said Andy Rice, well, he hasn't come back from delivering newspapers this morning."

He knew Andy. They'd traded tapes a few months ago. Some kids traded baseball cards; he and his small group of fellow headbangers swapped cassettes. He'd just got the first W.A.S.P album in exchange for two Kiss tapes—*Unmasked* and *Rock and Roll Over*. Two for one was always hard, but you had to give extra for what you really wanted.

"What do you mean he hasn't come back?"

"They don't know yet. They think something might have happened to him on his route this morning. His mom and dad are asking around and I guess they've taken off work to do their own search around town."

"Maybe I could help look. I mean, I don't know where he might go, not really, but maybe if I rode around—"

"No, that's the other thing. I want you with Uncle Arthur today."

"Mom, I can ride—"

"No." Her serious face went up a level. Clarise Zukas had put her foot down. There was no one, Dad included, who crossed that line.

"There's another girl being reported as missing. A young teenager from Virginia—"

"Vanesa something, right?"

"Yes, Winslow, I believe. How did you know?" Mom asked, giving him the queer eye, her left eyebrow cocking up.

"I saw a man putting up posters last night on my way back home."

"Well, one missing child is sad and unfortunate. Two in a week is frightening."

He had to agree. Seeing Vanessa's poster had been bad enough for him but hearing about Andy...it made it feel too real.

"I have to work until seven tonight. Your dad will be home at five thirty. I don't want you out on your own for a few days. You get Uncle Arthur or your dad to give you a ride home."

He was about to ask how he was going to get there when Julie appeared in the doorway.

"Get up already. If I'm driving you, the train is leaving in ten minutes."

"Hey," their mother said to her. "This goes for you, as well. Work and home. No stopping anywhere else."

"Well, can Derek at least come here?"

"Sure, but you will behave. I don't need your father coming home to find you two...necking or whatever and giving him a heart attack. Dr. Sewall has him on an Anacin regimen."

"Mom," she said, crossing her arms over her chest.

"Don't Mom me, Julie. A mother knows."

She leaned over and gave Rocky a kiss on his cheek.

"Love you," she said.

"Love you, too."

"Please?" their mom said, stepping up to Julie.

"Yeah, we'll be good."

Mom gave her a hug and a kiss.

"Love you," she said.

"Love you, too," Julie said.

After Mom was down the hall, Julie tossed a pair of mustard-colored gloves at him. "Dad left those for you. Get dressed already."

★　★　★

Julie drove him over to their uncle's and left him at the curb.

He saw the *Portland Press Herald* paper box next to his uncle's mailbox and thought of Andy. He hoped his friend was all right, but he didn't feel good about his chances. A voice in the back of his mind, where the monsters under the bed conversed, where the bad thing in the closet and the creature in the woods played head games, where the nightmare producers in his sleep placed Little House on the Prairie under a heavy fog and infested the family show with zombies, this great communicator told him something bad was happening right here in his summertime town.

★　★　★

"Squirt," Uncle Arthur said.

He'd called Rocky Squirt ever since he could remember. He'd once told him that he'd squirted him with breast milk when Rocky was a baby.

"Hey, Uncle Arthur."

"Oh, wow, I see you got some serious work gloves with you. You really come prepared, huh?"

Rocky slapped the gloves against his palm. "Yeah, Dad left them for me."

"Well, Squirt, let's get to work."

As Rocky followed him around the one-story house, the backyard came into view.

His uncle walked to the lawn chair under the shade of a maple tree and took a seat. Bruce Springsteen sang about Atlantic City from a gray Sony boombox. Uncle Arthur reached into the yellow cooler next to him.

"You want one?" he asked, offering a silver can of beer.

"Ah...."

"No worries, you just got here and it's better to pull shit apart and watch out for nails and shit when you ain't tying one on." He opened the can and took a swig before setting it on his knee. "Offer stands, though. Your mom and dad ain't here, and us working men – old and young alike – are allowed a man's refreshment. You just say when."

"Ah, yeah, cool," Rocky said. He'd never had a beer, but honestly, it was on his list of things to try, right next to smoking a joint and getting laid. "Later," he said, pulling on the gloves.

"You got it, Squirt. I'll make sure to leave you a couple."

"So, where do we start?" he asked, resting his hands on his hips and looking over at the roofless structure.

"Well, Squirt, you see that there sledge?"

Rocky saw it leaning against the wall.

"Yeah."

"Give that baby a heft and start whackin'."

"What are you going to do?"

"I'm gonna finish this beer, have another. By the time that's done, I bet you'll need a rest and I'll take my turn busting shit."

"And I'm still getting paid for this, right?"

"Squirt, you ain't gotta worry about that. Now, get swingin'."

*　　*　　*

Rocky's arms felt like rubber by two in the afternoon, but they'd managed to get the walls down and all the debris in the giant metal dumpster his uncle had rented.

Rocky managed to force down a beer; he worried the nasty taste would stick on his tongue all day. He was checking his watch when his uncle pulled up a second lawn chair and handed him a plate with two hot dogs on it.

"You got a hot date or something?" Uncle Arthur asked.

"What? No, I was just checking."

"Yeah, well, I noticed you checkin' pretty much since you got here."

Rocky bit into the first dog. His uncle leaned into the cooler, popped the top on two more cans, and handed one to him. He took it, even though he was feeling the effects of the first one. He felt fuzzy, and fuzzy felt pretty good. His hot dog tasted fantastic.

After he swallowed his food and took a sip of the beer to wash it down, he said, "Well, there's this girl—"

"Ah, shit. There's always a girl. What's her name?"

"November."

"Hmm. That's different, but I like it. And she's cute, right?"

Rocky nodded.

They ate the rest of lunch to the sounds of WBLM; they were playing Bob Seger's 'Old Time Rock and Roll'.

"So, you supposed to see her today?" his uncle asked.

"Well, we didn't set anything up." Rocky gazed off, his eyelids feeling a little heavy. "My mom doesn't really want me out today."

"Hmm. Because of that paperboy kid this morning?"

Rocky nodded and took a bigger sip from his Coors Light. The taste wasn't so bad now.

"We got a few choices, right now," Uncle Arthur said. "We can get you home, maybe you can meet up with this girl somewhere. We can head inside, watch one of my laser discs. Or we can see if we can get this job done before the night falls down on top of us. Totally up to you, Squirt."

He'd love to find November and hang out with her until she had to leave, but they hadn't set up a date for today. Plus, his mom didn't want him out wandering around alone. His uncle had a great collection of movies, but he knew if they didn't finish this job today, he'd have to give up another day to spend working and not hanging out with November. The choice was easy.

"Let's get this done," he said.

"You got it, Squirt."

★   ★   ★

By the time they were finished, Rocky's entire body hurt. His back was sore, and his legs didn't like him much, either. He could not wait to get out of his back brace and into the shower. His undershirt was drenched at least three different times today. The beer had worn off, and he was starving.

"Come on," his uncle said.

Rocky followed him around the front of the house and over to the garage.

The brown paint on the garage doors was peeling; the cracked windows were all dusty looking. Rocky wondered if his uncle even used the space anymore. His Chevy pickup was parked in the driveway, right where he always saw it.

"So, what's this, like your secret laboratory?" Rocky asked.

His uncle remained quiet.

Rocky half expected the smoke of some toxic gas to come billowing out as the door screeched on its way up.

Instead of a table with a cadaver or beakers or piles of explosives, there set a big, dark beauty of a car. Chrome and metal stared out at him. This ragtopped Buick rested like a dragon in a lair waiting to be called to duty. Rocky stepped past his uncle and ran his hands along the hood.

"Holy Christ, have you always had this hiding in here?"

"No, only since last summer. It's been in storage since I got Betty over there," Uncle Arthur said, thumbing back toward his truck.

"Does it run?" Rocky asked. "It must. I mean, it does, right?"

"Get behind the wheel."

"What? Really?"

His uncle nodded.

Rocky scurried around and opened the driver's-side door. Climbing into the vinyl bucket seat, he held the steering wheel. This was a thing of beauty. Keys dangled from the ignition.

"Turn her over," his uncle said.

Rocky cranked it. And she rumbled to life, a bear up from its deep seasonal slumber, powerful and hungry.

His uncle climbed into the passenger seat and rolled down the window.

"Well, let's see what you've learned."

"You want me to drive this?"

"Listen, if I'm going to pass it down to you, Squirt, I'm gonna have to know you can handle it."

"You're gonna what? Are you serious?" The actual notion that this car could be his.... His teenage mind was blown. He knew his uncle loved him, but this was no mere hand-me-down; the depth of a gift like this was overwhelming.

"This was my first car. Your dad and I enjoyed cruising in this baby, let me tell ya. Nothing broads like more than a cool cat daddy with an even cooler set of wheels."

Rocky thought of November seeing the car. *His* car. He pictured her sitting in his uncle's seat, her brown eyes taking it all in. A smile spread on his face.

"Put her in gear," his uncle said.

He'd never been more grateful for anything, but at the very moment, he was most appreciative that the Buick was an automatic. Easing from the garage, then the driveway, Rocky pulled into the street and nearly clipped John Chaplin.

He slammed on the brake and they jerked to a stop.

"Jesus H. Fuck!" Chaplin shouted from the sidewalk where he'd jumped for his life.

"Damn, kid," Uncle Arthur said. "You okay?"

"No thanks to that dickweed behind the wheel," John said before cupping his hand over his brow and squinting. "Hey, that you, Rocky?"

"Hey, John," he said. He didn't know much about Chaplin, but the kid was okay. He was a year younger than Rocky but seemed much older, and hung out with some of the more misfit types.

John walked around to the driver's side, placed his forearms on the windowsill, and leaned in close enough that Rocky could smell the beef jerky and cigarettes on his breath.

"How come you're driving? You get your license or something?"

"Going for it in a couple weeks."

"No shit?" Chaplin said, cocking an eyebrow and nodding his approval.

"Yeah," Uncle Arthur chimed in. "And when he gets it, this lil' dream is his. Pretty damn cool, huh?"

Chaplin nodded. "Fuckin' rad, man. Just a piece of advice?"

Rocky, with his hands still resting at ten and two, waited for Chaplin's punchline.

"Don't run anybody over, huh?"

"Yeah, yeah, all right, man."

Chaplin snickered as he pulled his pack of jerky from his cargo shorts. "Oh, before I forget. My band is playing a show next Saturday at Jonas Bazinet's garage. Starts at four p.m. You should come see us."

"Is it punk music?" Rocky asked.

"Sure is. Come by, it'll be good for ya. See ya."

John boogied off down the sidewalk.

"Punk music?" Uncle Arthur said, the look on his face like he'd just smelled King Kong Bundy's sweaty asshole.

"He's a pretty cool kid. I didn't know he actually played music."

"Not sure I'd call it *punk* music."

"Yeah, I don't know, but I'll probably check it out."

"You ready to continue?" his uncle said.

Rocky let off the brake and headed toward the beach.

CHAPTER FIFTEEN

November sat in her room surrounded by the voice of Morrissey. Something about his lyrics, cynical and dark as they often were, seemed more human than anything else in her world. Of course, when you live with monsters…. She'd give anything to not be one of them. To be able to survive without sucking the blood of any living creature, to have the simple life. She never wanted to fly or use her strength, not that either ability was particularly strong with her. She chose to abstain from drinking from humans, and thus her monster abilities were less than they could be. It was her rebellion. A middle finger not only to Gabriel, but to their very existence. She could only dream of inviting someone like Rocky over. Sitting here with him now, listening to records together, holding hands, kissing…but that was a dream her brother would invade and devour.

Her door cracked open, startling her.

"Dear," her mother said. "Come. We need to talk."

November got up and joined her mother in the living room in front of the television. The local newsman was talking about two missing children and warned that there could be others. A teenage girl from out of state, and a local fifteen-year-old newspaper boy. The girl had been missing for a few days after not coming back to her hotel. The boy vanished while out on his route yesterday morning. Parents were being urged to keep close tabs on their kids. The few tourists interviewed from just down the road showed minimal sympathy, if any. They seemed more annoyed by the situation.. One man said, "Kids these days take off as they please. I'm sure she'll turn up." A redheaded twenty-something from New Jersey rolled her eyes and said, "I'm here for a good time. This is a bummer, but, like, I hope she's okay." The locals, however, came across as frightened.

"It just doesn't happen here," one middle-aged mom said,

clutching her young daughter to her side in front of the steps of the town hall.

November didn't have to ask her mother her thoughts.

"If it is Gabriel's doing—" her mother started.

"He wouldn't," November said, not quite believing her own words as they left her lips. He'd changed this last year. His broody ways, his nightly outings. With Father gone, he answered to no one. There was no telling what he might be doing out there.

"I know you love your brother. I know you only see the good in him. You two have always been so close," Mother said, taking November's hands in her own.

November wanted to interrupt her and reveal her theories on what happened to the boy she'd kissed last summer, Bobby Colby, but she held her tongue.

"I fear he's...." Mother's old, gray eyes drifted beyond. "I worry about him, at night, when he's out there. He seems distant."

"Do you think he's capable of doing this?" November said, treading carefully, nodding toward the TV.

Her mother backed away and tented her hands over her mouth, staring at the screen and shaking her head. Her watery eyes betrayed her.

A crash behind them caused them both to cry out.

When November stepped toward the bedrooms, she saw the hard-plastic potted plant that had sat upon the bookshelf on the wall had fallen and spilled its spider plant. Soil spread out across the floor.

Mother walked past her, stopping at her own bedroom door before looking back.

"I need rest," she whispered. "I'll think about what we've discussed. You should stay in today. Tomorrow night, we can go for a walk."

Before November could respond, her mother disappeared behind the door.

November tended to the mess, just as she feared she'd have to with whatever Gabriel had gotten himself into. If it wasn't already too late.

★　★　★

She dressed in jeans and a flannel shirt, her sunglasses in place over her eyes as she headed for town. She needed to be around people. She didn't want to think of her brother turning into a full-fledged monster inside and out.

In the main street she noticed the posters on the telephone poles. A teenage girl, maybe her own age, with blond hair: Missing.

A police cruiser passed on her left.

The street where the boy had gone missing yesterday morning. Would they find him? Or the girl? The other question she refused to ask herself was, would there be more? Were there more already?

She was cold, her skin cool despite another hot afternoon. She crossed her arms as she ventured toward the pier.

She needed to see Rocky. Needed to hear his voice, hold his hand. She needed to know that he was safe.

Don't be so foolish, she chided herself. *Gabriel has been glued to his room in the daylight hours. He wouldn't be bothered to venture out into the sun.* Still, she couldn't shake last summer.

She passed Greg's taco truck and saw him talking with a gang of skater kids with spiky hair, holding Santa Cruz boards with neon-green wheels.

She continued, hoping to happen upon Rocky near the arcade or the beach, but he was nowhere to be seen.

She ended up under the pier, listening to the thousands of kids swimming, cheering, crying, woo-hooing while they splashed in and out of the ocean. The waves were standing up today. She watched as they showed the beachgoers the brute, unquestionable strength of the mighty Atlantic. She pictured her life the way it could have been, if they weren't vampires. She imagined her father chasing her into the waves. Her mother calling after Gabriel to go rinse off as he rolled in the sand building sandcastles and moats and pretending there were dragons after his king and queen. Her family had never come to a beach as busy and wonderous as this. They'd stuck to small lakes, campsites where they could easily extract themselves without notice.

A small boy came rushing up to her holding something in his tiny hands.

"Do you wanna see my crabby?" he asked, his voice like a cartoon.

"Sure I do," she said, dropping to a knee and smiling.

The boy un-cupped his hands

A small hermit crab lay tucked away safely in his shell.

"He's asleep right now, but I'm gonna wait until he wakes up. He's real neat, huh?"

"He sure is," she said.

"Okay. Bye."

She stood and watched him run back toward the woman under a dark blue umbrella that she assumed was his mom.

She found herself smiling as a familiar voice called out.

"Hey."

Rocky was walking toward her. He had on the shorts she'd bought him and a Superman t-shirt.

"Hey, Heatstroke, sorry I wasn't here last night," she said.

He stopped at her side and stared out at the sea. She loved the look in his eyes. Like it was the first time he'd ever seen the ocean and all its beauty.

"Do you always look at her like that?" she asked.

"At who?" he said, his cheeks reddening slightly.

"The ocean. You live here all the time, but there's something about the way you look at her."

"Doesn't matter how many times I see it, it's still one of the most amazing things to look at."

He reached for her hand. She took his.

"This is probably going to sound super corny," he started, "but...."

"Go on," she said.

"But I was thinking how you make me feel the same thing."

She leaned forward and pressed her lips to his. They kissed until the rest of the tourists and the pier disappeared, leaving just the two of them and the crashing of the waves.

They found a warmer spot in the sun and settled next to each other.

"So," Rocky said. "You haven't told me about your family."

She didn't feel like going down that road with him. She wouldn't know where to begin with Gabriel.

She gazed up at the Ferris wheel behind him.

"My sister thinks you're pretty cool," he offered.

"She seemed cool. Sorry I didn't hang out. My mom hasn't been feeling very well this summer."

"Oh," he said. "Is she going to be all right? Am I keeping you from her?"

She placed her hand on his. "No, it's not like that. She's not dying or anything."

After a moment of quiet, Rocky smiled.

"What is it?" she asked.

"Yesterday, I wasn't around because I had some work to do with my uncle. And...."

"Yes," she said, urging him on.

"He's giving me a car."

"Whoa, that's great."

She loved the way his smile lifted his eyes. He was the most beautiful boy she'd ever seen.

She looked over his shoulder toward the Ferris wheel. "Hey," she said. "Will you go on it with me tonight?"

"Oh...I, I can't."

"Why not?"

"Well," he said, looking at his watch. "One, I'm supposed to be right back home. My mom's getting really nervous about the missing kids."

"I heard about that," she said, dropping her gaze. She tried to keep Gabriel from her thoughts.

"Yeah, she actually told me to stay home. She thinks I'm in my room listening to music."

"Oh."

He got up. She rose with him.

"Well," he said, "maybe we can meet up earlier tomorrow?"

"I can do that," she said. She gave him another kiss. He smiled again and started to pull away.

"Wait," she said.

"Yeah?"

"You said there were a couple reasons we couldn't go on the ride. What's the other?"

"Oh," he said, looking away and chewing on his lip. "I'm sort of afraid of heights."

She watched him kick at the sand.

"Well, you know what they say. You gotta face your fears."

"Yeah, they do say that, huh?" He nodded. "Maybe tomorrow."

"Maybe tomorrow," she repeated.

She watched him hurry along toward the fountain and the main corner of the square before he looked back, gave her a quick wave and disappeared down East Grand Avenue.

She turned and gazed out at the waves. Rocky was right. It was amazing.

CHAPTER SIXTEEN

Gabriel awoke, his body aching. His hands trembled, and his mouth was dry as hot summer sand. He was sweating like an obese man trying to run his first mile. Disgusted with his body's seeming betrayal, he shoved the coffin open and hurried free. Try as he might, he couldn't still the tremors in his hands.

He left his room in search of his sister. He knocked once on her door before throwing it open. She was not there. He grunted as he made his way to the living room. Mother lay in her normal space on the couch watching more mind-numbing television.

"Honestly, Mother," he said. "Do you not have anything better to do with your time?"

She raised an eye to him, studying him. Her gaze stopped at his hands. He held them behind his back, out of her sight, and stepped between her and her precious programming.

"You have something to say?" he dared her.

"Nothing I haven't said already. Will you please move aside?"

He grimaced, malice seeping over his features as he closed in upon her. "I don't know what you think you know, but I told you I'm fine."

She refused to meet his stare. She leaned to the side and looked past him.

He tried to get her to look him in the eyes, his face no more than a foot and a half from hers. When he realized she wasn't going to give him the satisfaction, he snorted and straightened up.

He walked toward the door, fighting the pangs in his gut as he rubbed his hands together out of her sight.

"Going out again, I assume," she said. Her voice froze him.

"Don't wait up," he said, holding back what he really wanted to say.

I'll do whatever the fuck I please, old woman. It's my business and my life. I'll live it the way I choose. If I want to drain every last blood bag in this town, I will.

And he was off into the night, high above the side streets and in search of the cure to his discomfort.

★   ★   ★

"Come on, Jonas," John pleaded. "You know I wouldn't make you do this if I didn't need you."

"But I'm just gonna sit there like a third wheel. I hate being the odd man out with you and your girlfriends."

"Dude, Sheena. Her name is Sheena." John stopped to light a cigarette. "Like, what are the freaking chances? She's a punk rocker, she's in town for the next couple days, and she wants to make out with me."

"What do you need me for then?" Jonas said, sulking and wiping down his bass with a can of Pledge and a rag.

John got up and sat next to him, slapping him on the back.

"Dude," he said, "that's what I've been trying to tell you if you could stop rubbing that bass like it's your dick. She's got a cousin vacationing up here with her. She promised her I'd bring someone for her."

"What?" he stopped wiping the guitar. "Is her cousin cute?"

"Cute? Dude, she's a babe, I promise you."

"You saw her?"

"From a distance, but she's got big tits, man. I mean, you're gonna just stare at these beauties."

Jonas reddened. "An-and you think she'll like me?"

"Dude, you're in a punk rock band, she's gonna be all over you."

His friend's grin was one of pure delirious hope and joy.

Jonas looked at his watch. "But it's after ten. Are you sure they'll be there? What if...."

John poked out his cigarette and slipped it into the Beefaroni can they kept stashed behind Jonas's bass amp. "Don't even wuss out on me, dude. There's no super creeper out stealing kids. There's no Chester the Molester wandering around the beach. People are just being paranoid."

"I'm not being a wuss,'" Jonas said. "I just...what if the cops see us out. They're gonna send us home."

John clamped a hand to his friend's shoulder. "We'll slink between houses until we get to Old Orchard Street, then we'll hurry down Walnut Street, cross Grand Ave and down the alley beside the Royal Alliance. That's where Sheena said they'd meet us."

Jonas shook his head. "If we get in trouble tonight, I'm gonna kill you."

"Whatever. We got, like, twenty minutes to get there. Let's fucking go already."

As they were about to go out the garage door, Jonas halted.

"Why didn't you ask Brandon to go with you?" Jonas looked down at his shoes then back up again.

"Brandon's older than us," John said. "He gets chicks all the time."

"Yeah, or you just thought Sheena would like him more than you."

"Don't be a dick," John said. Jonas wasn't totally wrong; Brandon could probably steal any girl from either of them, but he didn't even consider Brandon for his wingman. Jonas was a cool kid; he just didn't know it. "I'd rather have you by my side, man. And Sheena's cousin is gonna dig you. Trust me."

"How can you be so sure?"

"Dude, you don't give yourself enough credit. You deserve a girl just like anyone else. More than anyone else."

"You really think so?" Jonas said, wringing his hands. John thought the visible battle between Jonas's self-doubt and hope was perfect.

He put his arm around Jonas's neck and shoved the door open with his foot.

"What did I say? Trust me."

★   ★   ★

Hurrying down Bradbury Street, they saw headlights burst from their right from the direction of the park. Cops always sat around in the dirt lot next to the small park.

"Get down," John shouted.

He shoved Jonas into a thorny patch of bushes. The kid yipped and whined. John wasn't completely silent himself; the thorns were painful.

They crouched as low as they could and waited with bated breath for the car to roll by.

It was a cop, all right. John ducked his head, hoping Jonas would follow his lead.

"Oh my god, that was too close. Maybe we should go back."

"Dude, we're almost there."

John watched as the police cruiser turned left. Perfect.

"Come on. Let's hurry."

They hurried, licking their thorn-inflicted wounds, to Walnut Street, across West Grand and slipped down Boisvert Street between some of the beachside rentals.

"There she is," he said, nudging Jonas in the side.

"Where's her cousin?"

Sheena was there alone, but she grinned from ear to ear when she saw John and jogged to meet him. They wrapped their arms around one another and kissed. He had a feeling they would need to find a very quiet place to disappear.

After making out with Sheena for a minute, John felt Jonas tugging at his shirt.

He turned back. "What?"

"Sorry," Jonas said, "but where's her cousin?"

Sheena wrapped her arms around John's waist as they both turned toward Jonas.

"Tanya couldn't sneak out," she said, her voice husky for a girl. "Her parents are like a couple of hawks. I guess they heard that some kid went missing and decided to keep tabs on their own for once."

John watched Jonas shrink.

"Can I talk to Jonas for a minute?" John asked.

Sheena just said, "Sure."

The two boys walked a few feet away.

"John," Jonas whined. "You can't expect me to stay here and twiddle my thumbs while you two get all...you know."

"Listen, man. It sucks about Tanya. I'm totally sorry, but that doesn't mean I should lose out, too."

"Arrrgh, I knew this was gonna happen."

"Just walk the beach for like twenty minutes. Give me that. Go down past the pier and back."

"No way."

"Please," John said, looking over at Sheena in her cropped Damned t-shirt and striped skirt. "She's, like, the girl of my dreams."

"Go hang out with her, but I'm not staying here or walking the beach like a total loser. I'll just head back to my house."

"Really?"

"Yeah, you know what? Have fun with your punk rock girl. Maybe I'll just see if I can get one of the cops to drive me home."

Jonas stormed off back toward the pathway that led to Boisvert Street.

"Sorry, man," John yelled. "I'll catch up with you tomorrow at practice."

He watched Jonas shuffle down the beach with his hands in his pockets, his shoulders slouched. He felt bad for the guy, but, looking over at Sheena, he didn't feel that bad. It wasn't that long a walk for the kid.

"Is your friend okay?" Sheena asked.

"He'll be fine. His place is only a couple streets over from here. We're jamming tomorrow, so I'll see him then."

"That's so cool," she said.

★   ★   ★

Jonas wondered if the cousin, Tanya, even existed, and now he had to walk home alone.

I never should have come out here, he thought.

He had sand in his sneakers, something most people who lived in a beach town learned to deal with, but he never had. It bothered him to no end. Stopping at the blacktop of Boisvert Street, he pulled off one shoe and shook it free of the beach dirt. He did the same with the other shoe and heard something thud to the ground in the shadows up ahead.

Silence followed.

Somebody in one of the rentals was watching the Red Sox game. The commentators were bickering about Jim Rice. A scream came from another window, effectively getting Jonas's already-on-edge haunches up.

The slim throughway looked to stretch out for miles, growing along with the fear crawling over him. In each dark corner, he suddenly imagined the beasties and ghoulies from his worst dreams.

A one-armed vagrant begging for change as maggots dropped from his mouth, the Xenomorph from *Alien* slipping from a window and descending upon him, and damn it if he didn't think of the movie *Cujo* every time he saw a big dog. He imagined the Saint Bernard awaiting him at the other end of the street, growling and ready to chase him to his death.

Jonas was still holding his left shoe in his hands, staring down the road, when the man appeared up ahead.

"Fuck you doing?" the man slurred.

"I…I was just going home," Jonas managed.

The man turned his back. A second later Jonas heard him pissing against one of the garage doors up ahead.

The man hocked up a loogy, spat, muttered something incoherent and then stumbled to one of the rental buildings to the left. Jonas put his shoe on and began down the dark street, hoping the drunk wouldn't harass him. He reached the triple set of garage doors where the man had taken a leak, when another form emerged from the edge of the building.

Jonas gasped, spooked.

A tall, slim man stepped between Jonas and his view of West Grand Avenue.

This is why I should've stayed home. This is why I didn't want to come out tonight. This is the fiend in the night.

Jonas tried to skirt to the right of the man, but the man followed his movements. He tried to the left, and the man mirrored his move again.

"I'm sorry," Jonas said, his voice revealing the quiver in his lips. "I'm just trying to get home before my parents kill me."

The man stood without saying a word.

Oh shit, he thought. *Just turn around and run.*

To hell with what John and his little punk girlfriend would say or think. Let them tease the hell out of him or swear at him for coming back and ruining their little rendezvous.

Maybe he could make it by the guy if he ran, get right past and run until he was in his own yard. All the Funyuns and Cherry Coke he'd consumed before John showed up at his door were now rising from the floor of his stomach. He imagined them lifting from the ocean floor of his guts like particles of dead sea life coming alive and floating upward. Coldness spread in his veins.

He stood unable to move, let alone run either way.

The man in the shadows stepped forward, his shoes clicking on the tar.

Jonas whimpered where he stood.

The man came closer, one clicking shoe after the other until his shape seemed to swallow Jonas's.

"I just want to go home," Jonas whimpered. He had tears in his eyes, his chin quivering.

The man with the long black hair and long black coat stepped aside and gestured for Jonas to pass.

After a few seconds of uncertainty, Jonas moved ahead. He got about twenty steps when the clicking of the man's shoes started after him.

He glanced over his shoulder and saw the man following him.

His heart sped in his chest.

Jonas broke into a run. West Grand Avenue was just ahead, and with it, the promise of lights and life. Safety.

He was nearly there when he noticed the clicking sounds of the man's shoes had disappeared. Stopping ten feet from West Grand, he dared a look back.

The street behind him was empty.

He let out a small, nervous laugh.

God, I am a chickenshit, he thought.

He exhaled, the tense moments fleeting, and turned to leave.

The man blocked his way again.

"What...wh-wh-where did—"

"Shhh, my little friend," the man said.

"Puh, puh, please—"

The man placed his long, skinny finger to Jonas's lips, leaned to his ear and whispered, "You were very much right to be frightened."

Jonas let out a whining sound. His bladder and its Cherry Coke felt heavy inside him.

Something sharp punctured the side of his neck as the man's hand landed upon him in a blur. Jonas moaned; his bladder let go.

He felt so light that he could no longer feel his feet on the ground.

His back was suddenly against the last building. The man had moved them into the darker shadows at the end of the street. West Grand and its promise of light taunted him.

His thoughts were growing fuzzy as the man was suddenly kissing him on the neck. Jonas heard his own pulse, his own heartbeat thumping in his ears. The chill in his marrow dissipated, encouraging his senseless fears to follow. The corners of his lips turned upward.

What a wonderful night.

The stranger at his neck inhaled sharply, then exhaled in an exhilarated fashion.

Jonas couldn't be certain, but he thought the man's features had shifted. He wondered if he could go home now. He wondered if he still wanted to.

He was so tired.

"Any last words, my friend?" the man said.

"What?"

The man hissed, bringing the sense of dread back tenfold. Jonas hardly had time to think, *He's not human.*

Before the stranger bit a chunk of his throat out and spat it to the side.

He's a vam—

★   ★   ★

John couldn't believe he was getting laid. He moved awkwardly, thrusting himself into Sheena as she moaned and whimpered beneath him.

She sounded like she might start crying any moment. It was all very confusing and fast.

He sensed someone standing beside them before he opened his eyes and saw the dress shoes in the sand.

"What the hell?" he said.

Sheena opened her eyes and screamed.

Her cry cut out as something blurred between them. A thin, dark line appeared across her milky white throat.

Blood seeped from the wound; her mouth opened and closed, her voice lost.

Her hands left John's hips and drifted to the oozing wound.

John climbed from her, his penis shriveling. He pulled free from between her legs, the condom she'd helped him put on clinging to hold on.

He watched in silent horror as the man with long black hair and a dark trench coat buried his face in the girl's wound.

This isn't happening.

He stood and stumbled a few steps backward.

Sheena's legs trembled and then stopped.

Her body was perfectly still while the stranger rose and set his sights upon him.

Blood covered his ugly features. This was no man.

A monster, a vampire had just fed right in front of him.

John stared in disbelief, his pecker out for the world. The creature of the night, its eyes red as the blood he'd just seen running freely from the dead girl in the sand in the light of the full moon above, flew at him.

They were in the sky, rising above the beach when the creature bit into the top of his head with a fury.

John Chaplin felt an immense pain and then nothing else.

★   ★   ★

Somewhere in the night, Gabriel took four more late-night wanderers.

Two were drunk men hiding away, kissing where the last partiers of the night wouldn't see them. He snatched the men and took them below the pier where he'd taken the first man weeks ago. He found another teenage girl in an altered state laughing out loud as she drew flowers in the beach sand with her finger. The last person was an older gentleman smoking on the front stoop of his house on the way out of town.

Gabriel crawled through his bedroom window at their rental cottage, still in full vampire form; he'd been unable to pull back the beast within. No control, no restraint, the blood of his victims had him delirious. His hands trembled. He stumbled into his coffin and tried to close the lid. The bloodlust had him too high to be concerned. Instead, he fumbled with the lid until he finally had it in place.

It seemed an eternity before his body relaxed and sleep finally took him.

CHAPTER SEVENTEEN

"I want you to sit down," Rocky's mother said. Rocky plopped down at the kitchen table with his Pop Tart and a glass of chocolate milk. Her seriousness worried him. He was waiting for her to tell him more kids had been reported missing and that summer was effectively cancelled. He thought of the most awful result– – never getting to see November again before her family up and disappeared from town forever.

She placed a hand on his shoulder as his father came singing into the room.

"Hey, buddy," his dad greeted him before dancing to the coffee machine for a refill. "Did you tell him yet?"

"I was just about to," his mother replied.

"What? What is it?"

His dad slipped an arm around his mother. The man's big grin eased Rocky's worries. Now he was sitting up, dying to know what the big secret was.

"You have your driver's exam on July 9th," his mom said.

"Oh my god," Rocky said, standing up, hitting his leg on the table. "That's awesome. You guys are awesome." He gave his mother a huge hug; his dad patted him on the back. Rocky gave them both a kiss on the cheek.

"Thank you, guys, so much," he said. "I've got to tell November."

"Who?" his mother asked.

"Where's Julia?" Rocky said.

His dad sipped his coffee, gave Rocky's mom a kiss on the cheek and set his mug on the counter. "She's heading to work, which is just where I'm heading, too."

"What? You have to work today?"

"Not real work," his mother answered. "He's going over to your uncle's to start building the new porch."

"You want to come along?" his dad asked. "We could use an extra hand."

Rocky was torn. Part of him did want to help. He felt he owed his uncle all the help he could give with what the man had bestowed upon him, but the thought of sharing his news with November won out.

"I can't, I mean, I totally would, but—"

"It's the girl, isn't it?" his father said. "This...November?"

Rocky grinned and nodded.

"I get it." His dad winked and headed for the door. "Bye, hon."

His mother waved his dad off. "Don't forget to drink some water between beers, please."

His dad smirked and closed the door.

Rocky gave his mom another hug and rushed down to his sister's bedroom.

"Did you hear?"

She smiled as she picked up the can of Aqua Net. "You're going to nail it."

"Thanks."

He hurried to his room, unstrapped the back brace, pulled off the sweaty under shirt and tossed on his *Magnum P.I.*-style Hawaiian shirt and some cut-off jean shorts.

After slipping into his Nikes, he was a blur through the kitchen as his mom called out something about keeping his eyes open for strangers. In all the excitement, he'd forgotten about Andy Rice and that tourist girl, Vanessa. He grabbed his bike from the side of the house, hopped on and pedaled down the street.

He hadn't gone far when he saw the police cars by the Royal Acres.

Boisvert Street was taped off.

Something else had happened.

He coasted slowly, trying to eavesdrop and see if he could pick up any bit of information. He considered stopping and asking, but the beach city cops were pricks, especially to teens.

He saw Officer Nelson. The man reminded him of Barney Fife from the *Andy Griffith Show*. It was one of Dad's favorite shows, but Rocky liked the guy who played Barney more on *Three's Company*. Peter Nelson was usually nice enough, but a little aloof. Only today, Officer Nelson looked super serious.

What if another kid had been taken? Or worse, what if they'd found them?

This was way too close to home.

Rocky pedaled by and tried not to think about the possibilities. He needed to find November and tell her the good news. He needed something positive.

He rode back and forth, passing the main corner, hitting the beach, the arcade, up Old Orchard Street and back, but she was nowhere to be found. Truthfully, he hadn't ever seen her out this early, so it wasn't that big of a surprise. He pulled over at the corner in front of the Good Shepherd Parrish, took his cheap Velcro wallet from his pocket and found eight bucks. Normally, he'd grab some junk food and trade the rest in for tokens for the arcade. This morning, however, he decided to swing into Moe's Diner. He'd left his cereal half-finished at the kitchen table, and his stomach was growling. He had time to kill, and Moe's made the best hash in town. He could eat like a king for eight dollars.

The place was busy, as usual, but he found a booth for two near the back corner. There was a perfect view of West Grand Avenue, the opposite side of Old Orchard Street. This was the direction from town November always seemed to come and go.. Hopefully, if she came around before he was finished, he'd see her.

Kelly Thompkins, in all her braces and goofy smile, came at him and said hello.

"Hey, Kelly," Rocky said. "Can I just get the hash, scrambled eggs, and bacon?"

"Sure, Rocky."

She stared at him dreamy-eyed. He'd known she'd had a crush on him in junior high, but he definitely did not feel the same for her.

"Oh, and some apple juice?"

"Sure," she said, scribbling his order on her pad.

"That's it. Thanks, Kelly."

"Okay, sure. I'll put that in for you, Rocky."

He didn't mind her braces. He had no right judging there; it was more a combination of her weirdness and the fact that she was nearly monosyllabic in every conversation they'd ever had. She'd been that way since she came to Old Orchard in the third grade.

"Rocky," Moe said, coming over and slapping him hard on the shoulder. The old man always did this. Rocky liked Moe a lot. He wore a light-blue short-sleeved shirt with a collar and a bow tie. Dark, caterpillar eyebrows stood prominently above his beady, smiling blue eyes. He always gave you great portions, good food, told stories of the old days and the pier fires, and once in a while, he'd hand out bags of Swedish Fish. The guy was bald, had liver-spotted skin, and smelled of onions, but he was the nicest shop owner around.

"Where's your partner in crime?"

"Axel's in England for the summer."

"England? The old UK, huh?" He rubbed his chin and gazed at the ceiling like he was remembering another time. "I was there, in Manchester, must have been '42? '43? Watching out for Nazis. Real dirty work. I liked the people, though. Food, not so much, but the girls." Moe elbowed him and grinned like a Cheshire cat.

"Girls and Nazis," Rocky said. "Sounds like you had a heck of a time, Moe."

"It was something. Another time, another world." He clapped his hands together. "So, if your buddy's gone, what are you doing this summer?"

"I'm going for my driver's license soon."

"Whoa, look at the big man," he said.

"Yeah, and my uncle is giving me a car."

"Your Uncle Artie?"

"Yep."

"He's a good one. Say, it wouldn't happen to be that old Buick Skylark he's been working on, would it?"

Rocky puffed his chest out and nodded.

"Woo hoo, you are gonna get all the girls."

"There's only one that I care about," he said before he could stop himself.

"Oh, a girl, huh?" Moe patted him on the shoulder again. "A car and a girl. I guess you got plenty of things to keep you busy this summer."

"I do, for sure."

"Well, you be good, huh, Rocky?"

"I will."

Moe moved to the next booth and said hello to the touristy folks there.

Kelly slid his plate on the table and plopped his juice cup on a napkin.

"Hey, Kelly," he said.

"Yeah?"

"Did you happen to see all the cop cars over by Royal Acres this morning?"

"Uh-huh."

"And?"

"What?" she asked.

"Never mind," he said. "Thanks."

She smiled again and headed to the kitchen.

He'd scooped half the plate of eggs into his mouth before he noticed the newspaper on the small table beside him.

Three more children reported missing.

A mouthful of eggs dropped from his mouth to his plate.

He reached for the paper and scanned the article.

Holy bat shit.

The piece was short. It mentioned that Elias Schmidt, a German gentleman renting a nearby condo, found a wallet on the sidewalk during a late-night stroll with his dog. He called the police when he discovered a substance on the wallet. The rest of the front-page story went on about the other missing teens of the last week.

Jesus, Rocky thought. *Mom's never going to let me out again.*

He downed his apple juice and set the paper back on the other table.

For the first time since he'd been gone, Rocky wished Axel was here. The two of them would toss their crazy theories behind these missing kids back and forth. These kidnappings…god, he hoped it wasn't something so sinister. Were there such things as serial kidnappers? Was it someone local? A tourist? They'd get caught, especially if they stuck around. Eventually, no matter how good they were, they always slipped up.

Well, not always, but most of the time.

He thought of the Zodiac killer, the serial killer from San Francisco who seemed to have vanished.

He had to find November. And she couldn't be walking home

alone anymore. He didn't know what he'd do if she wound up missing next.

Of course, she would be gone in a few weeks.

He pushed the thought away. He'd cross that bridge when he had to.

He wasn't as hungry as when he'd come into Moe's Diner, but he wasn't about to throw his money away. He shoveled the rest of the eggs and bacon down his throat and took a giant bite of the biscuit before leaving his cash on the table.

The clouds had rolled in. The wind had picked up and the air had an electric tang to it. A good ol' thunderstorm was on the way. The beach was still packed as he made his way to the sand and scanned the bodies for her. He was going to ask her where she was staying. He'd either walk her home from now on or make sure she had a ride.

By the time she yelled out, "Hey, Heatstroke," the sun was gone, and the first raindrops had arrived. He'd been without his back brace for almost two hours. His mother would kill him if she found out.

November was wearing a black skirt and her Twisted Sister shirt.

"You been waiting for me?" she asked, walking over to him.

"Me? Waiting for you? Nah, I was just kicking some rocks and watching the Canadians in their skimpy swimsuits."

"Even the dudes?"

"Especially the dudes. Have you seen the things they wear? They're hilarious."

She glanced at the sky. "Looks like a pretty heavy storm. Do they get bad around here?"

"Nah, nothing dangerous. I mean, I still wouldn't go swimming or flying a kite on the beach."

"If it's going to be messy out here, I was wondering if we could go to your place and maybe watch a movie or something?"

"Ah, yeah, of course."

"Cool."

She took his hand and they started toward his road.

"Oh shit, wait, my bike is by the diner."

They walked over, and she climbed onto his pegs. She wrapped her arms around his chest as they shoved off down the road.

"Did you hear about that?" he asked, as they neared the police tape. Most of the cars were gone, but the tape remained, along with a couple of local cops.

"No, what happened?"

"They think it's related to those missing kids."

They both fell under a spell, coasting by the tape. This was supposed to be summer, the best time of the year. You only had so many as a kid, and this would surely go down as the one that always stuck. Rocky just hoped it was for something better. He glanced over his shoulder and saw November staring toward the scene. He couldn't tell if she looked more angry or scared.

"Are you okay?" he asked.

"Yeah, it's just...it's just sad. I hope those kids are okay."

Rocky thought about Andy Rice and Vanessa Winslow.

"Yeah, me, too."

CHAPTER EIGHTEEN

It wasn't until later that night on the local six o'clock news that they announced the name found inside the wallet. Jonas Bazinet. His mother reported last seeing him at eight thirty the previous night with his friend John Chaplin. Neither Bazinet nor Chaplin had been seen since.

November clutched Rocky's hand as they watched the report from his living room sofa. His mother had just gotten home and placed a bag of groceries on the table before wandering over behind them. He felt her hand on his shoulder.

A third child, Sheena Wickman, fourteen, of Newberry, Vermont, had also been reported to the police. Her parents thought she had gone to bed early and found her missing in the morning. A cousin of the Wickman girl mentioned that she was supposed to meet up with the boys last night.

"Those poor children," Rocky's mother said.

"I just talked to John the other day outside of Uncle Arthur's," Rocky said. "Their band is supposed to be playing their first show Saturday."

The door opened and his dad came in singing about a West Texas town called El Paso. He stopped just inside the doorway and they all turned to look at him.

"What's going on? Was I butchering Robbins that bad?"

Mom went to him.

"Three more, Dale. Three more kids are missing."

"Jesus," he said. He set his lunch cooler on the table and took Mom in his arms.

"Let's go to my room," Rocky said. November nodded as they got up.

"Excuse me," Mom said. "You haven't even introduced us to your friend here."

Mom had a hand on her hip as she waited.

"Oh, Mom, Dad, this is November."

"Hi," November said.

"Hello," Mom said. "And where do you live? Are you new to town?"

"My family's here for the summer. We have a cottage on Costigan Lane."

"Dear, that's a jaunt from here. Are your parents going to be picking you up tonight?"

"I usually just walk."

"Well, not tonight. Dale will give you a ride home when you're ready to go."

"Oh, that's okay. I'll be fine, really, but thank you."

Rocky braced for a Clarise Zukas all-out insistence.

"I won't hear of such a thing. You just watched that report. I won't have you added to the list under my watch. Dale and Rocky will give you a ride."

Mom stood, waiting for November to agree.

"Yes, ma'am, that would be fine."

"Good. Now, I'm assuming you're staying for supper?"

She looked at him. Rocky gave a crooked smile.

"I'd love to," November said, turning back to Mom.

"Good. Now you two go on, but Rocky—"

"Yeah, Mom?"

"The door stays open."

They were going to his bedroom when he remembered that his back brace was lying on his bed.

"Oh, ah, can you give me just a minute? I just want to straighten up a bit."

"Don't worry about it," she said, trying to push past him.

He gripped the doorframe, blocking her way.

"Please," he said.

She stepped back and smiled. "Okay, if it's that important to you."

"It is. I'll just be a minute."

He went into his room, closed the door most of the way and scrambled to his bed. He snagged the brace and a pair of underwear from the floor and tossed them in his closet. Another scan of the room and he felt comfortable.

"Okay, come on in," he said.

"So, this is where you hide all your secrets," she said, entering and drifting around the room.

His gaze moved to the closet and the brace within. He hadn't had it on all day.

She waltzed by the closet door and went to the TV and the Atari. She picked up the stack of games and looked through them before moving on.

It was a strange thing showing a girl your room. Nothing like having a buddy over. This was like opening a piece of you and exposing your inner world to someone whose opinion you cared about deeply.

He realized he was holding his breath.

He exhaled and joined her by the stereo.

"Remind me to bring over their new record next time." She was holding his cassette of Van Halen's *1984*.

He reached down and picked up Motley Crue's *Theater of Pain*.

"Have you heard this?" he asked.

"No." She held up the new Europe album. "Can you play this one next?"

"Sure, I've actually been listening to that one almost nonstop since I got it. It's an awesome record." He grabbed the Walkman from his bed and pulled the cassette out, setting the tape next to the stereo.

As they settled side by side on his bed, the thought of having a girl not just in his room but on his bed sent a swirl of butterflies cascading through his stomach.

"So," she said.

"So."

"Your mom is pretty serious about you guys giving me a ride home tonight."

"Yeah, she's kind of freaking out about what's been happening. So am I, a little bit."

"I know," she said.

"I was thinking about it this morning," he said. "After seeing those cops and the yellow police tape, I was sitting at Moe's and wondering if you should be walking by yourself, especially after dark."

"That's really sweet, but you don't have to worry about me, Rocky. I can take care of myself."

"Yeah, but what if we really have our own serial killer or kidnapper in town? Doesn't that freak you out?"

She dropped her chin and rubbed her arm. "I'm not like other kids, Rocky," she said.

"I know, but—"

"No, no you don't know," she said, getting up.

He stood and reached out for her.

She walked to his open window and stared out. What was she looking for?

"Hey," he said. "Are you all right? I mean, you always look like you're...like you're expecting someone."

She shoved the screen out.

"I have to go, Rocky," she said. "I'm sorry, but I have to go."

"What? Wait."

She was out the window and running across the lawn before he could chase after her.

Holy shit. He really didn't understand girls. He wasn't sure if she was mad or worried or what. Whatever it was certainly freaked her out. He looked around at his empty room, the Crue still playing on the radio.

All he did was ask if she was expecting someone....

Was someone following her? Had she seen them and that's why she bolted?

He just hoped she would talk to him again when she calmed down.

He also hoped she made it home okay.

He looked out the window and found himself scanning the neighbors' yards and the sidewalk for *who*? He considered jumping out, following her and making sure she got home okay, but he didn't want to upset her more than he apparently already had.

He hoped he'd see her tomorrow. In the meantime, he had to figure out a way to explain to his parents that she literally jumped out the window after promising them they could drive her home.

CHAPTER NINETEEN

Marcy Jackson hadn't stayed awake past seven p.m. since the night she saw the man in her yard. She'd hardly stepped out of the house, only running to the corner grocery to grab milk, bread, and a few other essentials. There was a dark menace in her town. Something not of this world, or if it were, certainly not human. The missing kids were part of it. Poor John Chaplin from next door. Despite all his parents' prayers, their boy would not be returning to them. The Bazinet child was gone, as well.

And the children were not the only ones being preyed upon. The news channels and papers were focusing on the kids, but there were a number of adults vanishing from the beach town, too. She overheard Beth Ann Montgomery and Kayla Dubois talking about Jim and Betsy Seger. How Betsy stopped showing up for work. How one of Jim's coworkers mentioned a trip to a resort off the coast of Florida. Jim's friend couldn't recall the name of the place, but he was certain that's where they'd gone off to.

Marcy knew the Segers. Jim had done Eddie's and her taxes for the last five years. The Segers weren't poor, but they weren't the type to just up and go. They planned out everything. It was in Jim's veins. Numbers and calculations were his world. Betsy wouldn't take a trip to Portland without telling everyone where she was going shopping and in what order she would hit the stores to get the most out of her mileage.

That's why Marcy was planning on breaking into their house. They lived on Bellamy Lane. She would walk right up to the front door and walk right in. The door would not be locked. She'd be willing to bet a dime to a dollar that it was open right now. She just hoped she wouldn't find them…dead.

The B&E was on the docket for tomorrow. Tonight, Marcy was downing three glasses of wine and tucking herself in. She poured the first glass of Merlot and carried it to the back door, where she bolted the new Bregman Lock she'd purchased from Tim's Hardware. The salesman, young Allan Berkoff, assured her they were the best available and most dependable bolt locks on the market. She bought one for the front door, as well. After locking up tight and drawing all the shades, she poured her second glass of wine and cut a big piece of garlic bread for herself. The word *vampire* had crossed her mind more than once. Ridiculous or not, it was there. She also wore her favorite silver necklace, the one with the whale pendant that Eddie had surprised her with for their twentieth anniversary.

Finished with her bread, she skipped brushing her teeth, figuring she'd need every bit of the garlic if the creature should get past her security, and took her third glass of wine to bed. She was feeling flush and smiley. Buzzed, as Eddie used to say. He would have chuckled at her. Eddie always got a kick out of her when she drank. They did their fair share in the heydays of the dance club at the end of the pier before the fire of '72, but when the fires and storms shortened the pier and the town got rid of the dance hall, she and Eddie called an end to their wild nights out, if you called a few drinks and a night of dancing wild, and spent most of their evenings at home. Eddie's community events were the lone exception in the last few years.

Thinking of her dead husband and the past life they'd shared, Marcy smiled and placed the empty glass on the nightstand next to her best silver cutlery. She lay down, closed her eyes and let the fuzzy feeling and sweet memories take her away.

★   ★   ★

Jesse Henderson stared out at the collection of cars and trucks in his back lot. It was getting crowded back there. Just as many of the license plates there read Maine as they did New Brunswick and Nova Scotia. Deep inside, he knew it was wrong. He'd seen the articles about the missing kids in the paper. Six of them so far, but they didn't mention the others. He believed the devil responsible for the children was also at work here taking the folks that belonged to a number of the vehicles filling his back lot. He'd never been superstitious, but these last few nights, he'd felt more than once like he was being watched. Ever since bringing in the Boucher kid's car, he'd been less and less excited about getting a call after dark. Early morning, once the sun rose, he was fine, but the nine-to-five overnight hours filled him with a sense of dread he wished he could puke up and rid himself of.

He reported his suspicions to Pete but wasn't sure whether Pete had decided he was onto something or if the officer just chalked it up to Jesse smoking one too many brain cells from his head. Probably the latter and maybe that was right. Hell, he was high right now, but be it dope-induced paranoia, bad freaking vibes or a case of a real-life serial killer stalking the shores of his town, he did not want to face the night sober. And if he missed a call or two for the next couple nights, he'd be fine with that. Let them call AAA or Red Claw Towing out of Saco.

A call came through just as he was deciding if he was going to close up for the evening. He looked at his watch. Seven fifteen. He had an hour and a half to play with. He had time for one job. Picking up the phone, he felt a tug of regret in his guts.

"Jesse's, what can I help you with?"

He hung up the phone, picked up the bandana from his desk and wiped the sweat from his brow. A call from outside the Black Diamond Pub. Ivan McKenna was hauled off to jail for the night for breaking some Frenchie's nose. Jessie could grab Ivan's tiny Toyota Tercel in less than thirty minutes. Quick and easy money that would see him home before the night fell.

Small miracles, baby. Small miracles.

★　★　★

Derek rode his motorcycle toward Old Orchard Street. The police had found his cousin Kailin's car in this exact spot. He pulled up and stopped at the end of Milton Street. Their last conversation hurt. Kailin was his best friend. He didn't really think he was gone. He couldn't be. Not, like, dead and gone. Maybe he'd got out to piss and wandered off. He felt the pang of hurt. He knew something bad had happened to Kailin. He'd been trying to lie to himself about it all week.

He was supposed to be going to pick up Julie for their date, but he really didn't feel like seeing anyone right now. Revving the bike's throttle, he decided to hit the pier instead. He needed a drink.

He was pulling out when stabbing pains shot through both his shoulders. His hands came free from the bike and he was pulled into the air. He watched in shock as his bike flew to the sidewalk in front of the church and fell over the curb.

What in the hell?

He craned his neck and saw the man who was carrying him over the top of the church.

Man?

Just as suddenly, he was dropped to the roof of one of the businesses along Old Orchard Street. Breathless, Derek barely had time to brace for the impact before he hit the roof and collapsed in a heap. Something popped in his knee as he rolled onto his back and grasped his right leg. Biting back the pain, he watched the man drop from the sky; long black hair, dressed in a long, dark coat and grinning like the devil.

"What do you want?" Derek asked through gritted teeth.

"That's a loaded question, my friend."

"You're the guy, the *thing,* doing all of it, aren't you?"

"Guilty as charged," the man said, his hands behind his back, walking a circle around Derek.

"You killed those kids. You killed Kailin."

The man had his back to him now, looking out over the city. Derek scanned the rooftop for anything he could use as a weapon. If he didn't fight, he was as good as dead.

"Yours is a beautiful town," the man said. "We've hid in the shadows of places like it before. In Virginia, New Jersey, Massachusetts, and now here. People flock to these beachside attractions every year. There are so many that don't belong. So many that won't be noticed. And yet, I've only recently discovered how truly intoxicating it all can be."

There was a broken bottle within Derek's reach. It wasn't much, but if he could surprise this guy, maybe he could get one shot at stabbing the bottle through the sick son of a bitch's throat. He fought past the pain in his leg, stretched out and took the bottle, drawing it to his chest and curling around it. He'd have to wait for an opportunity and since he wasn't sure he could stand, he'd have to wait until this thing came to finish him off.

"I'm what you'd call a creature of the night."

"Are you saying you're, like, a vampire?"

"Yes, my friend," he said, turning slowly to face Derek.

By the light of the Ferris wheel and the multitude of shops and bars and businesses, Derek saw its face clear as day. Piss spread out over the crotch of his ripped jeans. A face as pale as milk, eyes like two black marbles set inside its rigid features. A series of ugly bumps protruded slightly from its forehead, and the teeth.... In the movies, they only ever had the two fangs that bit into the neck to suck their victims' blood, but this was like a mouth full of those fangs.

It hissed at him as it made its approach.

"Your fear is delightful."

"Stay away, please, stay away," Derek cried, the weapon in his hand forgotten.

"I am the fiend responsible for taking your neighbors and your summer devotees of sex and sun and nighttime debauchery. And in return for their sacrifice, their donation of blood and soul, they have given me more power than any creature has ever possessed."

Derek winced as the vampire took flight, hovering above him, gazing upon him from those endless black pits.

Before he could blink, the monster crashed down upon him and made a sharp exhalation of breath before sitting back up and holding a pale hand to the side of its neck.

Derek drew in his own sharp breath as he dared a glance at the bottle in his hand. He'd stabbed it. He'd sunk the broken glass right into the monster's neck.

A crazy grin took hold of Derek's face. A sense of pride and one-upmanship began to course through him. He braced his free hand on the rooftop and sat up holding the weapon.

Blood seeped from between the creature's fingers.

Derek tested his leg and found he could stand. It hurt, but he could do it. He took one hobbling step toward the monster when a smirk creased its face.

"No—"

The vampire's grin fell as it hurled itself full force at him in a flash.

Derek wanted to scream as its mouth of vicious fangs began to tear him to shreds. He had no final thoughts as his death swallowed him whole.

★　　★　　★

After sucking every drop of warm, delicious blood from the young man and dropping the remaining husk, Gabriel found himself crawling on all fours, delirious with the energy pulsing through him. He'd been fortunate the wound this pathetic human inflicted had missed any important arteries. It had punctured the side of his neck, and Gabriel knew he'd need Mother or November to help stitch it up, but the night was far too young and his craving far more overpowering. The wound would wait.

Holding his hand over the gash, he took flight and landed behind a business below. He transformed back to his less-threatening-looking self before stumbling out and going up to the window of the first place he happened upon.

He startled the short greasy kid at the window.

"Jeesh, buddy, what happened to you?"

"I need a bandage. Would you happen to have a first-aid kit back there?"

"Yeah, we got that. Did you get into a brawl or something? You've got blood on your, on your face."

"Yes, a rather rough one at that. Could you help me out?"

"Oh, yeah. Hold on."

The kid disappeared before coming out with a metal box with FIRST AID stenciled across its face.

He handed it to Gabriel, who opened the box and saw Band-Aids and burn ointments among other things he cared nothing about. He took the gauze cloth from the bottom of the box and the medical tape. Pressing the gauze to his wound, he pulled the tape with his teeth and proceeded to wrap the cloth in place. When he was finished, he shoved the box back through the window and thanked the kid for his help.

Gabriel shoved past the people in his way, being sure to keep away from any figure of authority as he made his way to the beach. His eyes scanned for his next possible meal or two. There were visibly fewer people here than on any of the recent nights he'd been out. Despite making sure the bodies weren't found, the count was adding up. People had started to notice, but they would never find out it was him. Not a chance. And too many of these brainless blood bags thought themselves invincible. They wouldn't be scared off until he'd drained half the summer population.

Farther down the shore, he spotted a man pissing in the tall grass, his lady friend lying on a blanket pressing a wet can of beer to her forehead. Gabriel appeared next to the man seemingly from out of nowhere.

"Hey, what the fuck?" the guy mumbled.

Gabriel pulled him into the grass, opened wide and buried his mouth over the other man's mouth, crunching down through the man's lips and gums, breaking teeth. He managed to bite half the man's tongue off before letting him go and spitting it out.

The man was trying to scream but could only make horrible moaning noises.

Gabriel stepped over him and slammed the heel of his boot down on the dying man's throat. The audible *crack* silenced him.

Gabriel came out from the tall grass, wiping the blood from his chin, approaching the middle-aged woman, who was now crab walking away from him in the sand.

"Don't leave me here alone," he taunted the woman.

Just before she could shriek, he flew at her so fast and hard he managed to come away with just her head in his arm. Blood shot up into the night from the stump of her severed neck. With her head tucked under his arm, Gabriel crouched over the spurting corpse with his tongue out, trying to catch the crimson droplets like a child trying to taste a falling snowflake.

As the corpse fell back to the sand, creating a bloody puddle where the head should be, he began to laugh. It nearly scared him how funny the moment struck him.

He was delirious and he loved it.

When he finally managed to stop laughing, he collected both bodies and tucked them away in the tall grass. He would gather his kills later and bring them to his hiding place.

He flew up and dropped to the sidewalk on the closest street over.

There were normally some stragglers out this way just beyond the last of the cheaper motels and seasonal inns, but tonight, the outskirts of town were quiet.

He was high as a kite off the three successive feedings. It was glorious. He strolled out into the center of the street swinging his arms about and singing some old song he hardly knew. Something by The Beatles. 'Hey Jude'. He bellowed out the na-na-na-na's and swirled across the yellow lines until a set of headlights approached.

He stood his ground on the center strip as they tried to pass him, shouting something he didn't understand. He lashed out, shouldering the back end of the car and sending it fishtailing until it stopped down the road.

"Hey, you got a fuckin' death wish, you stupid asshole?" the driver yelled.

Gabriel wanted to attack them. He wanted to teach them about fear and blood and power, but his head swooned.

The driver pulled his head back in the window and the vehicle continued. Gabriel smiled drunkenly and turned back toward home, singing the song from before.

He was just outside the cottage when he realized he hadn't properly disposed of the bodies. He bowed his head. He couldn't afford to be lazy now. He didn't need to give them mutilated corpses.

He took to the sky. The thought of how reckless he'd been tonight was sobering. He'd have to be more careful going forward. As wonderful as it was taking so many, he didn't want it all to end too soon.

After fetching the headless woman and her companion from the weeds, he gathered the man from the rooftop and delivered them all to his temporary mausoleum.

With everything taken care of, he returned home. November and Mother were waiting for him when he stumbled through the door.

"Gabriel," November said. "What have you done?"

He floated across the room, his feet mere inches from the floor, and tucked a strand of hair behind her ear. She swatted him away.

"You're injured," Mother said.

He reached up and felt the bandage on his neck.

"Injured?" November said. "He's covered in blood."

Gabriel pulled the gauze and tape away from his wound and tossed it to the floor before getting lightheaded again and plopping down on his ass with his legs crossed.

"I may need some tending to," he said. "Do be a good sister and help your brother out, hmm?"

Mother was at his side. "Go, hurry," she said to November. "Fetch my needle and thread, some peroxide and something to clean him up with."

November hesitated. He could see the wheels turning in her mind. And that look on her face. Like she was so disgusted by him.

"Don't just stand there looking at me like that," Gabriel said. "Go."

Mother nodded in agreement.

November hurried down the hall.

She returned moments later with the things Mother had asked for.

Gabriel wanted to lie down. He felt like floating, like dreaming.

Before they could question him further about his activities, he closed his eyes.

★   ★   ★

Mother cleaned the wound. November threaded the needle and handed it to her. She watched as Mother stitched the gash in Gabriel's neck. The woman worked in silence, finishing up and rebandaging the wound.

"Help me get him to his room," Mother said.

November took him under the arms.

"What about his clothes?"

There was blood spattered all over his shirt and coat.

"What's wrong with him?" she asked.

Mother said nothing as they carried him to his coffin and hefted him in.

"Go make us some tea. I'll be out in a moment."

She left the room as Mother watched Gabriel resting.

He'd done it. He'd crossed the line again and again. November knew that her brother was responsible for everything bad that was happening to this town. She couldn't lie to herself anymore. They needed to leave before he could hurt anyone else.

She waited at the small wooden table in the kitchen as Mother joined her.

"We should take him now and go home," November said, pleading her case.

"He is a good boy," Mother said. "He's just wrestling with the truth of what we are."

"He's killing people. He's acting like a monster!"

Mother's face grew stern. "You will not speak of your brother that way. We do not use that word."

"He's done awful things, Mother."

"He's a good boy."

"He's a murderer!"

Mother's hand lashed out and left a patch of heat across November's cheek.

"He's your brother. He's my son. We will not speak of him as if he were some common criminal."

November held the tears back. Her mother had never struck her. She bit her lip and got up from the table.

She had so much to say but could not find a single word.

"November," Mother said, reaching out.

November hurried to her room. Behind the door, she burst into tears. Burying her face in her pillow, she cried for herself and for Gabriel.

If they didn't do something now, there would be no saving him. If it wasn't already too late.

★   ★   ★

Pete Nelson entered his apartment, his limbs heavy, his eyelids ready to crash. The night had been fairly quiet. A few fistfights. A flasher, and some creepy kids following a good-looking trio of teens. He had to get Ivan McKenna out of the Black Diamond before he got his ass kicked by a group of tourists, but at least there were no new missing kids.

Not yet, his mind whispered. *Wait until morning. There will be a list of plucked and vanished kiddos that will make your heads spin and put your ass in the unemployment line by the end of the month.*

He climbed out of his pants, folded them and placed them on the chair in the corner of his bedroom. He undid his shirt and hung it on the little hook by the door. There was a nearly full bottle of rum in his cupboard. He poured three fingers into a tumbler, tossed in a few ice cubes and filled it the rest of the way with a half a can of Coke.

Opening the paper he'd brought in from his doorstep, he sat down at the table in the kitchen, relieved that they'd removed the missing kids from the headline. A vote on the Old Ball Park was taking place at the town hall tonight. Locals were trying to stop the rock concerts. Pete couldn't care less either way. He was just happy to not find an in-your-face reminder of the police department's ineptness. They had reports of more than ten people vanishing from the area, half of them local children.

He had thought it was some vacationing pervert out having his way with their open community. It really was the perfect place for a sicko. Somebody like the Zodiac or that twisted fuck Ted Bundy. And it wasn't just kids. It was adults too. Tourists, mostly. Somebody was taking these people right under their noses and it was beating the department's public face to a pulp.

Pete finished his drink and set the glass in the sink.

Turning in, the alcohol just starting to lift the worries from his mind, he thought of the shoe. Kailin Bouchard's one boot, the drop of blood on the pavement that night, the Camaro still idling in the middle of the road.

He pulled the blankets up under his chin and clenched his eyes shut.

The unsettling disappearance of Kailin Bouchard crawled after him into his sleep.

Officer Pete Nelson did not rest well.

CHAPTER TWENTY

November met Rocky at the arcade shortly after noon. She'd cried herself to sleep last night. Seeing her brother turning into the devil and her mother living in denial of it was overwhelming. She knew she had to say goodbye to Rocky. Hanging around with him was far too dangerous, especially if Gabriel saw them together. She'd made a promise to herself to make their last day together special. With the awful condition Gabriel had been in when he came home, there was no way he'd be out in the light today. She couldn't remember the last time she'd even seen him up in the daytime. Despite all her worry that he'd catch the two of them these last couple weeks, he hadn't bothered her once. Whatever hell he was struggling with, it was taking up all his time.

They moved from the arcade entrance to the water fountain that sat just before the beach.

"So, my mom was pretty worried about you last night," Rocky said, sitting on the edge of the fountain sipping a soda.

"Yeah, I'm sorry I left the way I did. It's been a hard week at home."

"Well, I'm glad you made it out today. I thought you might never talk to me again."

Whitney Houston's 'How Will I Know' blared from a boombox being carried by a group of teens on their way to the beach.

"We know this is gonna end sooner than either of us wants it to," November said.

"I know, but…." He let the words die.

Neither of them said anything. It was true and it wasn't fair. Here she was, sitting with a boy that looked at her like she was the most important thing in his world. And maybe, at the moment, she was. She took his hand.

"Kiss me," she said.

He did. It was soft and sweet.

"You're really a great kisser," she said when their lips parted.

"Thanks."

"Come on," she said. "Take me on some rides."

They went on the Thunderbolt twice, the Tilt-a-Whirl enough to make them both queasy, the bumper cars, and the carrousel. Even though it was mostly a kiddie ride, she still made him go with her on it. They grabbed fried dough, orange sodas, and popcorn. After finishing their lunch, they decided the Gravitron would not be a safe idea, opting for the roller coaster instead. It wasn't very big, but it was still fun and had one drop that made her stomach jump.

"That was awesome," she said.

He looked at his watch.

Again with the watch.

"Can I ask you something?" she said.

"Sure."

"Why do you always check your watch? Do you need to be somewhere else?"

He looked away.

"Am I keeping you from somewhere? I mean, I can go home if you—"

"It's not that. I just like to know what time it is."

He was lying.

"I want today to be special," she said. "But I want you to want to be here with me."

"I do, I promise," he said.

"Then prove it." She crossed her arms.

"How?"

"For starters, put your watch in your pocket."

"Okay," he said, undoing the band and tucking the watch away. He rubbed his hands together like he was swiping dirt off them and then held them up in surrender. "Done."

"Good." She stepped to him and gave him a kiss. "Now, take me on the Ferris wheel."

She watched his gaze turn upward. It looked like he'd swallowed something sour.

"Just this once and I won't make you do it again."

"Yeah? And then you'll believe that all I want to do is hang out with you?"

She nodded.

Hand in hand, they got in line for the Ferris wheel.

★　　★　　★

Pulling her Pontiac onto Bellamy Lane, and parking on the curb outside the cozy two-story A-frame house of Jim and Betsy Seger, Marcy Jackson felt the shiver work its way through her body. She shut the car off and stuffed the keys in her pocketbook.

A small Toyota pickup sat in the driveway. The garage doors were closed. Jim's boat rested under a canvas cover just to the right of the drive. Marcy checked her purse to make sure she had her gear. She pulled on the gloves she used for gardening, made sure she had the small ballpeen hammer, the silver fork, and Eddie's old army knife. It was so big it barely fit in the space. She'd also brought the Polaroid camera in case she needed to take pictures for evidence.

Satisfied that she was prepared, she aimed the rearview mirror toward her and gave her disguise one last look over. Sure, it was silly. Everyone in town knew her, and would recognize her car, which is why she parked just down from the Segers' driveway. She wore dark sunglasses and a Red Sox ballcap, her hair pulled back in a ponytail.

Good enough, she thought.

She stepped from the car and hurried across the yard and up the porch. *Welcome One and All* was written in block white lettering on the black rubber mat. Marcy glanced around to make sure there was nobody on the street or out on the porches of the neighbors' houses. The coast was clear. She opened the screen door and gave three loud knocks. After a minute, she knocked again. Peeking in the window by the door, she saw no movement within.

Now, the first true test.

She tried the doorknob.

It turned and the door opened.

She took a deep breath and peeked her head inside.

"Hello? Is there anyone home?"

No answer, but she thought she heard voices. She listened closer;

it was a TV. Maybe one of them was here and hadn't heard her.

She'd come this far; it was too late to turn back. She knew she'd never have the balls to attempt it again.

She entered the home and closed the door behind her.

"Hello? Jim? Betsy?"

She took her sunglasses off and dropped them in her purse. The TV was in the living room just around the corner.

"Betsy?"

She made her way to the laundry room. She lifted the lid to the washing machine. A load sat there, still wet. It smelled like it was mildewing. How long had it been sitting there? She closed the lid and glanced out the window to the empty backyard. There were clothes hanging on the line; a couple of Jim's white undershirts lay in the grass.

Meow.

The cat startled her. Marcy slammed her back against the wall and clutched at her chest.

"Didn't anyone teach you not to sneak up on people?" she said to the scraggly looking feline, a black Himalayan. She reached down and petted the animal as it brushed itself against her legs, mewling. She felt bones.

Marcy knelt beside it and said, "You must be starved? Where did Jim and Betsy go?"

The cat rubbed against her, getting its long hair all over her tan pants.

"Let's make sure you've got something to eat."

The cat followed her to the kitchen.

A cup of tea sat on the table. It was half full. She touched the mug. It was cold.

An open coupon book sat beside it, next to that, a pair of scissors and a stack of cut coupons.

Marcy wondered where the newspaper was that the coupons had come from.

The cat meowed.

"Okay, let's get you taken care of first," she said. She found the bag of Meow Mix in the pantry. She filled the dish on the floor next to the refrigerator and got the water bowl and filled that from the sink.

With the animal taken care of, Marcy went back into the living room. A newspaper sat on the coffee table, a bottle of Schlitz next to it, a half-smoked cigar in the ashtray beside them. She picked up the paper and checked the date. June 18th. Nearly two weeks ago.

There was no way the Segers would leave without having someone take care of their pet. They'd also never leave stuff out like this.

She fetched the camera from her large purse and began to snap shots.

When she'd finished, she put the Polaroids in a pile on the kitchen table and spread them out.

She left them there to develop and started up the stairs to check the upper floor.

Nothing seemed out of order, and there was no sign of the Segers.

She was starting for the stairs when a knock at the door froze her in place.

Shit, shit, shit.

She stepped slow and careful toward the stairs, waiting to see if whoever was out there might try the door as she had and come inside.

The knock came again.

Marcy's heart was racing. She cursed herself for coming here. What if it were the police? How would she explain herself? Would she be taken to jail? The door had been open; did that still count as breaking and entering? The cat, she could say she was taking care of the cat for the Segers while they were away.

There was a thump at the door.

She descended the stairs, careful not to give herself away. She made it to the door and looked out the window.

She could see the mailman's truck outside driving down to the next set of boxes.

Cracking the door, she saw the package and a rubber-banded stack of mail. The package was addressed to Betsy.

She pulled the parcel and letters inside and decided to get out before any other visitors stopped in.

She was in her car and almost home when she realized she'd left the Polaroids and her camera on the kitchen table.

What had she planned to do with them anyway? Take them to the police? Tell them how she got them? She hadn't thought that far ahead. She couldn't go with the pet-sitter line if she was also informing them that the Segers were not on vacation in the tropics but missing altogether.

She needed to go into town today. She'd have time to think up a proper lie. But she would have to get those pictures and her camera back. Her name was on the neck strap.

She'd have to get her errands done as quickly as she could. She didn't want to be swinging into the Segers' when everyone was getting home from work.

A police siren barked once as she pulled onto her street.

Oh god. Someone had seen her and reported her.

She pulled over and hung her head before looking in the side mirror.

A young man she didn't recognize sauntered up to the window.

"Afternoon, Officer."

"License and registration, ma'am."

She dug the papers from her glovebox and pulled her license from her purse.

"You know why I stopped you today?" he asked.

She swallowed hard.

"Not really," she managed.

"You failed to use your blinker on either of your last two turns."

"Oh," she said, relieved that she wasn't going to get handcuffed for a B&E, but sick with the thought that she could have been.

"Sit tight. I'll be right back."

She was not cut out for a life of crime or for being an investigator. In truth, all the improbable possibilities she'd considered this week had turned Marcy into an emotional mess. She wiped a tear from her eye while waiting for the officer to write up his ticket.

★   ★   ★

High in the air, the sounds of summer below them, Rocky clutched November's hand.

"Open your eyes," she said.

"I'm okay."

"It's beautiful," she said. "You have to see your town from up here."

His stomach was doing somersaults, springboards, splits, and twists. He knew if he looked, he'd either throw up or pass out.

He was up here because he wasn't being truthful. He was holding back from her. He cursed himself. He should have just explained why he was looking at his stupid watch. His skin felt prickly. If he didn't say something, he was going to dive into a full-on panic attack.

"Rocky, are you okay?"

"I wear a back brace," he blurted out, eyes still clenched shut, hands gripping the railing in front of them.

"What?" she asked.

"A back brace. It's bulky and ugly and I hate it, but I have bad scoliosis and I'm supposed to wear it twenty-three hours a day to keep my spine from getting any more crooked. I didn't want to tell you because I thought you'd think I was some kind of freak."

He tried taking deep breaths. It felt good to spill his guts, but if he didn't get off this ride, he was going to lose his lunch.

She kissed his cheek and called out, "Stop the ride. Stop the ride! He's having a panic attack!"

He felt the slow-moving wheel slow further.

She sat beside him and leaned to his ear.

"You're going to be all right. It's stopping and we're getting off, okay?"

He nodded but felt dizzy. Black spots came to life behind his eyes.

"Rocky, hey, we're done, okay, come on," she said. He heard the door open. She pulled the lap bar up and they hurried by the woman with the blond mullet running the ride.

Rocky dropped to his knees and barfed by the fence.

November rubbed his back.

"Stay right here," she said. "I'll go grab a water."

He felt the attack slowly let him go, slinking away, leaving him with an empty stomach, sour breath and a case of the cold sweats. One thing was for sure; if November still liked him, he was pretty sure he'd fall in love with her.

"Here you go," she said.

He sipped the water and gave her a weak smile.

"Better?" she asked.

"Much. Thanks."

"So, where's the back brace?"

"At my house."

"You mean to tell me you're supposed to be wearing it now?"

"Yeah, I just didn't want you to see it."

She took his hand. "Believe me, it would take a lot, I mean a lot more than that to make me think less of you."

He climbed to his feet. "Do you want to see it?"

"Sure."

A few minutes later, they reached his house.

He led her to his room and showed her the torture device.

He put the new Europe tape on as she inspected his brace. He cued up the love song, 'Carrie'.

"Should you put it back on?" November asked.

He took it from her and set it on the floor. "In a little while."

She bit her lip as he stepped over, took her hand, and wrapped an arm around her back.

"Dancing?" she said.

"Shh."

She looked disarmed. They swayed together through the song; she placed her head on his shoulder. He knew he'd never be the same after this. He was heading full force into heartbreak but could not even think about stopping.

As the song concluded their lips met. She pushed him to the bed and started to take off her t-shirt.

The front door opened and closed..

He shot up beside November as Julie stormed into her room across the hall and slammed the door.

"Should you check on her?" November asked.

Damn it, Julie.

"Yeah, hold on."

He pressed the front of his pants to help ease the pressure there.

He crossed the hall and knocked.

"Julie? Are you okay?"

"Leave me alone, Rocky. Just go."

"Are you sure?"

"Please, I just want to be alone, okay?"

He returned to his room and shrugged.

"Maybe we should go out?" November said.

He cast a glance toward his bed.

She reached up and thumbed his bottom lip. "Later," she said. "Grab your trunks. I want to go swimming."

★　　★　　★

It was nearly six by the time Marcy got back from Portland and made it to her friend Brenda Hersom's house. She'd promised to bring her the latest Stephen King book from Mr. Paperback. Brenda had broken her foot at the beach a few weeks back, and Marcy had helped her out. Brenda's husband, Gus, worked sixty hours a week at the shipyard, so Marcy had offered to help out where she could. She didn't know what the woman found to like about cheap horror books. This one weighed half a ton and looked bigger than the Good Book. The title, *IT*, creeped her out. The cover featured a child's paper boat floating toward a storm drain. It was absolutely sinister.

By the time she escaped Brenda's she had maybe an hour of daylight left. She needed to collect her things from the Segers', but the thought of getting caught or stuck inside after dark made her want to run straight home, down her wine, and hide in her bed. Let them find her camera. Let them have her arrested. It was a better alternative to roaming the streets with all the shadows and ghouls.

She thought of John Chaplin. Still missing.

Sitting in her car, Marcy saw Brenda wave from the porch, then smile as she opened the cover to her new nightmare.

I'm being silly again. There's nothing out there. She didn't believe it even as she thought it. *I'm just going to rush in, make sure the cat still has food, shut off the television, grab my things, and never go back again. And the quicker I get to it, the sooner I can hunker down at home.*

The other homes on Bellamy Lane were quiet save for the house on the corner. There seemed to be a summer cookout going on, but their front yard faced Willow Street. A few teenagers were gathered at the lawn's edge near the stop sign, but Marcy didn't think they'd notice or care if they saw her. She considered pulling right into the driveway and acting like it was her home but stopped at the curb again. No need to draw any more attention. Nothing good could come from getting overconfident now.

Marcy darted from her car to the porch and hurried inside without knocking.

It was dark in the house save for the light of the television coming from the living room. She scooted into the kitchen. The pictures lay spread out just as she had left them. She scooped them into a pile and set them next to the camera.

"Here, kitty, kitty," she called. The cat did not answer. She saw the food dish was empty and set about refilling it. What little light remained outside was fading fast. She wished she'd brought her flashlight, but she'd left her purse in the car. She wasn't chancing leaving something else behind. She cracked the pantry door open and jumped, doing everything she could not to scream. A bag of potato chips had fallen from the snack shelf. Hand to her chest, she steadied her breathing and took the bag of cat food. A shadow across the room moved.

A trick of the eyes. *Old lady eyes in the dark*, she thought. Still, she was taking more time than she'd wanted to. She filled the cat dish by the fridge; there was still water in the water bowl, so she put the cat food away and moved to the living room.

As she ventured past the laundry room, she stopped dead cold in her tracks. The back door was open. Every hair on her body reached out. Icy tendrils wrapped around her bravery and sense of purpose.

It was here with her.

The shadow in the kitchen....

"I think you have the wrong house," the man's voice whispered in her ear.

Marcy screamed and ran. She was out the back door and down the steps in a heartbeat. She'd never moved so fast in all her life, even in her high school track days, and those days were far behind her. She was at the corner of the house, her car in sight, when her feet came off the ground The sky, a bruised purple on its way to black, was all she saw before she crashed to the ground. Broken ribs and a cracked wrist were the least of her concerns. The creature she'd feared for days stood at her feet. He was tall, thin, with long dark hair, and dressed all in black. His pale face, milky white and all teeth, undulated and changed before her eyes. A monster. A true beast from the movie screen now encroached upon her. She prayed to god for a quick and pain-free release but feared His influence might not touch this malevolent thing's existence.

It had her in its grasp before she could try to rise of her own volition.

Marcy raised her hands, broken wrist and all, to protect her throat.

Her lips trembled at the sight of its teeth. Buried in its shadow, she closed her eyes.

Eddie, dear, I'll see you soo—

Her last thought shattered as the creature crunched its fangs into the top of her skull.

Marcy Jackson's body, broken and bled dry, was discarded down the basement storm doors where it landed beside a number of other husks, the Segers' included.

★ ★ ★

On the blanket beneath the pier, barely out of sight of the few beach stragglers, he watched her discard the bathing suit bottoms and lie down upon the towels. He slipped out of his bathing suit and took her hand.

"Do you have a condom?" she asked.

"Huh? Oh, yeah."

He pulled his wallet from his sneaker and fetched the rubber Axel had given him earlier this year. He'd stolen a box of Trojans from the corner store and gave this one to Rocky. He said they each needed one just in case. Rocky never thought the day would come, but here it was. Good ol' Axel, helping out even though he was thousands of miles away.

Using his total recall from health class, Ricky slipped the condom on and took his place between November's legs.

"Are you sure?" he asked.

She nodded.

He'd never been so nervous and excited in his life. After an awkward start, she grasped his penis in her hand and guided him into her. He felt her warmth around him. She cried out but encouraged him to continue. The act didn't last long, but it was magnificent. Rocky's eyes rolled into the back of his head before he collapsed on top of her. She held him. He returned the embrace before moving to her side.

"Wow," was all he could manage to say.

She took his hand, propped up on an elbow, wearing a grin that stretched all the way across her beautiful face, and kissed his cheek. "I think we should probably get dressed."

Rocky had just managed to get his trunks up when he screamed, "Holy shit!"

"Well, well, well, little sister," Gabriel said. "Look what you've done."

November stepped into her bottoms, turning her back to her brother. "Gabriel, what the hell?" she said.

Her brother had Rocky by the throat. He must have been over six feet tall, dressed in black like some sort of vampire or modern-day ninja.

"You will not see her again," he said.

"Ah, eh, ah," Rocky wheezed, trying to breathe past the man's grasp.

"Leave him alone, Gabriel. It's my fault. I came to him."

He shoved Rocky to the ground, where he landed flat on his back, the wind knocked from his lungs.

Gabriel spun and smacked November so hard it sent her twisting to the sand.

Rocky watched as the psycho went to her and lifted her from the ground by her hair.

Rage simmered up within. Rocky rose, fists clenched, ready to attack.

Gabriel let go of November and turned to face him.

"Do it, boy. See what happens next."

"Rocky, no!" November cried, jumping between them and pushing Rocky back. "Don't. He'll kill you."

His anger slipped.

She was in tears, shaking her head from side to side.

"But—" he started but didn't know what to say.

Gabriel leered over her shoulder.

"Go home, Rocky. Go, please," she said.

He couldn't speak. All the words mashed into each another.

"Will…will I see you—"

"Go now!" she said, dropping her chin.

He picked up his sneakers and towels and slowly backed out from their spot beneath the pier. Above, the sounds of people living it up, alive and happy, having the times of their lives, seemed a cruel juxtaposition to the deep heartache and bitter loneliness pulling him out with the tide and swallowing him whole.

"If I see you near my sister again, my young friend," he heard her brother say, "I will kill you."

Rocky stumbled into a run at the first path he found and bolted all the way home in tears.

After bursting through the front door, he headed straight for his room.

"Hey, hey," his father called. "Get back here, now!"

He stopped before his bedroom door. Julie's door opened. She appeared, her eyes red-rimmed and tired looking as though she'd been crying, as well. Her melancholy expression matched his own.

"Get. Over. Here," his father said.

He couldn't remember his dad ever sounding so threatening.

Julie closed her door.

He chewed his lip as he joined his parents in the living room. His mother was fighting back tears.

"Where the hell have you been? Do you know what you put your mother and me through?"

Shame elbowed its way into his overwhelmed state.

"There are kids being taken, people are missing, possibly dead for Christ's sake and you just disappear for hours without letting anyone know where you were going? Do you understand how stupid and thoughtless that was?"

Rocky's shoulders hitched as he broke down again.

His mother got up and pulled him to her chest.

He wrapped his arms around her, holding on for dear life.

His father joined them.

The Zukases shared their pain, but none of theirs quite reached the depths of Rocky's.

CHAPTER TWENTY-ONE

He was grounded for two weeks. His driver's test was cancelled. And it all happened two days before his sixteenth birthday no less. He was certain he'd never see November again. Her brother would probably pack her and her mother up and leave town. He'd had a horrible dream last night about her brother. Rocky had woken up this morning feeling the man's hands on his throat, squeezing the life out of him.

Julie plopped down on the couch next to him.

"I'm sorry about your test," she offered.

"It's...I deserve it."

"And about your girlfriend."

He turned to her. He would have shed a tear, but he was all cried out.

"Thanks."

"They think Derek..." she began. "*I* think something's happened to him."

"What do you mean?"

"I think the killer got him."

"What? Why?"

"He was supposed to pick me up two nights ago and never showed. His mom said she's not sure if he's been home since he left."

"Julie, what the hell is happening here?"

"I don't know, but I'm really scared."

They embraced.

For the next two days, none of Rocky's family went anywhere alone besides work. Julie called out of work. She said her boss had a crush on her so she wouldn't lose her job. She stayed home with Rocky and the two of them tried their best to distract one another from their pain. It didn't work, but it made them both feel a little better having each other to lean on in their first post-relationship days.

The whole family was gathered around the television, TV dinners on their trays when Dad switched to the news.

"Old Orchard police are urging residents and tourists alike to stay in pairs and to be on alert. If you do decide to go out tonight, remain in well-lit areas, be aware of your surroundings at all times, and if you think you're being followed or see anyone suspicious, locate the nearest officer or enter the closest shop or bar, get around others and phone Old Orchard Police. Police Chief Michael Donnelly says his crews will be out on patrol in full force borrowing extra help from Saco and Scarborough police departments, even placing two officers on the beach until sundown.

"A strict ordinance was voted into place by the town council in an emergency gathering yesterday afternoon. The ordinance renders the beach off limits after dark and will be in place until further notice. Police still have no suspects in the disappearances but have some clues and evidence that they're hoping lead them to the responsible party or parties soon.

"I'm Peggy Block, WGME Channel 13 news."

★   ★   ★

It was like a movie Rocky had seen last summer at Axel's, *The Town that Dreaded Sundown*. Only, this wasn't Texas, and none of the bodies had been found yet. It seemed surreal. His birthday was tomorrow, and it had gone from being possibly the greatest week of his life to the worst. His Salisbury steak no longer looked appetizing.

"Can I be excused?" he asked.

"Sure," his dad said.

His mother glanced at his father, but she let it go.

Rocky was glad. The last thing he needed was to start a fight. He slid his TV tray in the space between the fridge and the wall, emptied his plate in the garbage and left it in the sink. In his bedroom, he put on his headphones and hit play. November had given him a copy of *Purple Rain*. He never thought Prince would be his cup of tea, but 'The Beautiful Ones' and the title song were really hitting him in the right spot. He was also pretty sure 'I Would Die 4 U' couldn't be truer. As upset as he was about losing out on the driver's test and the Buick from his uncle, he'd lost the only girl he'd ever loved.

Staring at the window, he wished she would appear and call him outside. He envisioned them slipping away and being together again like they were under the pier. What had her brother been doing there? How had he found them? And why was he such an asshole? Had they left? Were they miles away now?

The first verse of 'Purple Rain' played in his headphones as he felt the tears in his eyes. He put his hands over his face and cried. He didn't care if he was being a baby. There was no one to see him, and even if they did, to hell with them.

Did she feel like this? Did her heart keep falling to pieces every few minutes?

When the song ended, Rocky rewound the tape and played it again, wallowing in the hurt. By the time he'd rewound it and played it a third time, he was asleep, caressing his pillow.

★　　★　　★

He woke up with a start. His mother sat on his bed, stroking his head.

"Hi, Mom."

"Listen," she said, "I don't want to ruin your whole summer. I called this afternoon and rescheduled your test for Tuesday morning."

"What? For real?"

She nodded. "And if we can come to an agreement, I'll let you out of being grounded."

"Anything," he said.

She poked at his stomach, hitting his brace. "You wear this like you're supposed to. I don't want to find it hiding in your closet again."

"Okay."

"And you let one of us know where you're going and who you're going with for the rest of the summer. No ifs, ands, or buts."

"Yeah, of course."

"And I want you home and inside by nine o'clock every night. Deal?"

"Deal."

She hugged him and he squeezed her good.

"We haven't really talked about this girl, this November."

He looked away and shrugged.

"Do you want to tell me about her? Or is something wrong?"

"I don't think I can see her again."

"Why not?"

"Her older brother caught us...together. And he said he doesn't like me and that he'll beat me up if he catches me around her." He left a lot out, like what he meant by 'together' and how he'd not get beat up but 'killed'. That the guy was a total psycho.

"What were you two do—" Clarise Zukas went tight-lipped and averted her eyes.

Rocky felt his cheeks get hot.

"Oh," she said.

"We...we were careful."

"I hope so."

He didn't know what else to say.

And she got up, apparently out of words, as well.

His mother slipped out of the room.

Rocky wasn't sure he should have admitted anything, but he hated lying to his mom.

He expected his dad to pop in any minute, but he didn't. He'd given Rocky 'the talk' two summers ago.

Rocky got up and shut off the light.

He was about to lie down when something zipped past his window.

He crossed the room, his heart beating faster, and pressed his face to the screen.

"Hello?" he whispered.

There was nothing there. He pressed his face onto the screen so he could see to the right and left better.

Satisfied that it was just his hyperactive, nervous brain, he went back to his bed.

Lying down, he wondered if he'd see her tomorrow. And if she'd be alone or even willing to talk to him.

He didn't want to give himself any hope, but he couldn't help it; it was all he had left.

CHAPTER TWENTY-TWO

The time dragged. November's records offered comfort. While her wounded heart absorbed every lyric of melancholy and pain alongside the ones of love and devotion, she fought back the urge to run to Rocky. Gabriel had spoken. And his threat was real. She'd expected him to barge in any moment to tell her that they were leaving. Yet, in the two days she'd spent mourning, yes, mourning the loss of whatever she and Rocky shared, she hadn't seen or heard her brother once.

After they'd arrived home from the beach, he'd forced her to her room. On the other side of door, November heard him tell their mother to stay clear of the room, that November was to be left alone to consider the danger she'd placed the family in.

Not even Mother had come to her door.

A horrible thought twisted like smoke in her brain.

What if he'd done something to her? To Mother?

She rose from the bed, took the needle from the record, and placed the arm carefully into its cradle. The silence beyond her door was worrisome. For once in her life, she wished her powers were enhanced. After drinking blood, she could hear a pin hit the floor from two rooms away. She hadn't even feasted on vermin in days. And her sun exposure made it worse. She needed to feed. She turned the knob and opened the door.

Poking her head into the hallway, she could see that Gabriel's door was shut. Mother's was, too.

Tentatively, she crept down the hall and found the living room void of life.

She scooted across the floor and out into the yard.

It was near dark. The moon sat above the treetops wide and brilliant, lighting up all below. Stepping through the grass, she wandered over to the small cemetery that sat between their cottage and the forest. She felt energy here. She'd always felt it walking amongst graves. She thought of Rocky. Tomorrow was his birthday. She should be there with him. She should celebrate with him and kiss him.

Something bolted through the grass and over a nearby grave.

November sprang and snatched the opossum by the tail. Ugly little critter, but it was a better feast than a rat. Without hesitation she bit into the thing's back and sucked it dry.

Tossing its desiccated carcass to the edge of the graveyard, she felt the normal flood of ecstasy and warmth that accompanied fresh blood. The darkening world around her brightened. The soundtrack of nocturnal life filled her ears as she stood there with her eyes closed, breathing in the salty air of the sea. It truly was remarkable, this curse. It wasn't all bad, but it was the other side that always coalesced with the good and soiled these feelings like rotten earth. Reminding her that she was a creature of ruin.

Shame, like a great wave from the blue, rose up and swallowed her where she stood, dropping her to her knees to wallow among the dead. She looked at her hands and at the blood that remained on them. All she ever wanted was to be human. To be normal and not this thing. She'd wanted them to move here, for Gabriel to give up his old ideas and his hatred for the beautiful people of this world, and to just realize that they could live freely among everyone else.

Even as she circled the track she'd tried so desperately to create in her mind, the blood on her hands refused to give in to her fantasy, dragging her clawing and screaming back to reality. Her reality. She imagined Rocky, foolishly but romantically sneaking out of his house, finding his way here and catching her with the animal in her mouth, feeding like a beast in the wild, the blood dripping down her chin, the monstrous look that adorned their faces while in the act of feeding. Their true face.

She pictured Rocky's look of utter terror before Gabriel descended from out of nowhere and placed his hands upon the boy's shoulders. His mouth jutting to Rocky's throat.

November cried out in the night.

When her voice died, she was utterly and totally alone.

She didn't want to think like a child, but only one thought repeated in her mind: *It's not fair.* The childish mantra, the crux of every moment or incident perceived to be against them, in her time of sorrow and frustration, seemed impossible to push away.

She stood slowly, heartbroken, riddled with the awful truth – Gabriel was right. No matter what she wanted to believe, they were not like everyone else. They were something much worse.

Once she was back inside the house, she decided to check on Mother. She stopped at her mother's door and placed her ear against it. She could hear her labored breathing coming from within. The old woman's condition seemed to be worsening. Whatever illness sat with her was unrelenting.

She opened the door and whispered, "Mother?"

She could make out the woman's shape beneath the blankets on the bed. Unlike Gabriel, who decided to give in to the myths and legends of their kind, building his own coffin wherever they landed, November and Mother simply closed their curtains and chose to rest in comfortable beds.

She sat at her mother's side and placed a hand to her shoulder.

Leaning to the old woman's ear, she repeated, "Mother?"

She knew she wasn't dead, but for the briefest of moments, as she sat there watching her unresponsiveness, the thought crawled into her belly.

Mother's lips parted as her eyes fluttered open.

"Yes?" she said, her voice weak and raspy.

"Mother, are you all right?"

"I'm tired, dear."

"It's time to rise. Will you join me in the other room? We could watch some TV."

"Your brother's not well."

"Now you believe me?" November said.

"I'm so sorry," Mother said. "I wasn't ready to believe what I knew to be true."

"Then we should leave here," she said.

"I fear it won't matter. I fear he's too far gone."

Her mother's words stifled the air in the room.

November didn't need validation of her fears. She wanted lies, beautiful, comforting lies, especially from her mother.

"That's why we need to go home. Get Gabriel away from here and back to seclusion."

Mother shook her head.

"Yes," November cried. "We'll just pack up our things and go. And if he doesn't want to go, together we'll make him."

Tears slipped from her mother's eyes.

November lay down beside her and held her tightly.

★   ★   ★

Blood coursed through him as he watched the boy's window from above. His little sister's lover – the thought filled him with rage. He'd seen this pathetic human copulating with her. To the weakling's credit, he had heeded Gabriel's warning. The boy had not sought out his sister since. His sister, who pined away in her room. The anger released him momentarily as a grin crossed his face. Whatever bond they had forged in the past weeks could not compete with his word, his law.

Oh, and the delicious thought of his own intentions made him shiver in anticipation. Severing the young couple's relationship was only the beginning. He would make the boy pay. And it was not going to be quick. It was not going to be nice. There would be fear. There would be blood.

Hell was coming.

CHAPTER TWENTY-THREE

Rocky woke up wincing. The pain in his hip used to bring him to tears, but over the last year and a half, he'd grown used to it and even learned to sleep with it throbbing away at his side. Some mornings, it was a little sharper than others.

He got out of bed and released the straps on the brace, taking in a deep luxurious breath with the contraption's release. He placed it on his bed, stripped off the sweaty shirt, grabbed some shorts, underwear, and a clean t-shirt from his dresser, and headed for the shower.

Sixteen and ready to try his best not to let his birthday be a complete pile of garbage. He wondered if he'd see November. He allowed hope a shot. No sense spending the day beating himself up and being miserable. There was plenty of summer left for that.

Showered and ready to see what the day would bring, he found his first surprise on the kitchen table – a card from his parents featuring a dog driving a Trans Am, and a handwritten note from his mom with the new date and time of his driver's test. The note also contained instructions to be home no later than five p.m. and had a twenty-dollar bill taped to it.

He pocketed the cash and stuck the exam notice on the fridge under a *Bob's Propane and Gas* magnet.

Julie was in the living room putting on her shoes.

"Happy birthday," she said.

"Thanks."

"I'm heading to work but I only have a four-hour shift, so if you want a little more practice, we can do it when I get home."

"Yeah, that'd be cool."

"I'm sorry about November."

He picked up the other half of his sister's Pop Tart from the coffee table.

"Thanks. Sorry about Derek. Have you heard anything?"

"No."

"This is kind of a messed-up summer," he said.

"We can only control our own actions, right?" she said. "Like, whatever is going on here, it's out of our hands, but we can keep our chins up and our eyes open."

Rocky nodded.

She got up and ruffled his hair. "Let's just try to make sure you have a good birthday. I think we can do that, don't you?"

He thought of November.

"As long as we have some pizza and I get some sweet presents, I think we can do that."

"Right on, little brother," she said. "I hope you get to see her today."

"Me too."

With that, his sister was out the door and he was left to his own devices.

He was on his bike and on his way to the square when he sensed somebody watching him. Glancing around at his surroundings, he saw cars, vans, trucks, and motorcycles galore piling into the local parking lots. Every year, more of these lots seemed to open, the owners making a daily killing packing tourists and out-of-towners as tightly as they could to turn the maximum profit.

As his eyes passed George's Parking, one of the only lots with a bathroom/changing building and one of the longest-running spots along East Grand Avenue, a dark shape caught his attention.

"Hey," a man shouted.

Rocky turned and came inches from running into two men walking straight at him. He yanked the handlebars and almost took out a woman and her baby.

"Jesus Christ, kid, get off the fucking sidewalk," one of the men said. "Pay attention!"

"Sorry."

The man grumbled as he and his friend continued in the opposite direction.

Rocky, now stopped and resting out of the way just off the sidewalk, scanned George's lot for the dark shape he'd seen, or thought he'd seen.

Satisfied that he was being paranoid again, Rocky pedaled on, moving into the road so as not to get caught in the middle of the crowded sidewalk and piss off another asshole who might do more than yell at him.

He could smell the yummy goodness as he rounded the corner onto Old Orchard Street. He had a pocket full of money and could have anything he wanted. Normally, that would be easy. A slice of pizza and some fries from Lisa's. But today the fried dough stand called out to him, a beacon in the middle of the storm of summer folk.

And maybe the chances of running into November there were greater.

As he hurried across the street, a little green Ford honked at him, but he snaked through and reached the entrance to Palace Playland. He found himself looking for her among the throng. His throat went dry when he spotted the dark man again. Dressed in black, and standing at least six feet tall, the creep stood out like a dead body at a birthday table. Was it possible? It couldn't be. He'd just seen this man over on East Grand. He'd have to be faster than a speeding bullet to get over here already.

A set of five beefed-up, jock-looking douchebags wrestling in front of the mystery man blocked Rocky's view of the shape. When they finally got out of the way, he was gone again.

Cold tendrils of fear slithered down his back.

The man looked like November's brother, Gabriel. But why would he be out following him around? Rocky hadn't seen November in days, no thanks to him. The size and build of the guy looked like Gabriel, but it could be anyone, plus it wasn't even the same guy in both spots. That was impossible.

He thought of the shadow at his window last night.

Somebody's watching me.

It wasn't just the name of that song with Michael Jackson; it was an all-too-strong feeling closing in around him.

His focus was captured by the wall of Missing posters on the side of the front ticket building to his right.

What started with just Vanessa Winslow was now a bulletin board's worth of photos from one of those thriller movies where the detectives are trying to catch the movie of the week's version of the Zodiac.

Rocky stared in shock at the flyers, which easily numbered in the double-digits. John Chaplin, Jonas Bazinet, Sheena Wickman, Andy Rice, and another kid from school. He was a sixth grader named Ryan Soucy. The kid was well-liked. Rocky had seen him and his friends in the arcade hundreds of times over the last two years. He looked so small in the photo. He had a head of short, curly black hair. An aw shucks smile that looked too big for his face rested under smiling brown eyes.

Rocky searched his surroundings for the man in black. What if it wasn't Gabriel, but the creep? The kidnapper wandering around in broad daylight and looking for his next victim?

Instead of grabbing his dough and heading straight home like he wanted to, Rocky found himself skipping his lunch and actively seeking out the man he'd seen watching him.

What if he could spot him, follow him, maybe find out where he was staying or what he might be driving? Something he could give to the cops.

He was coasting through the crowds, keeping an eye out for the black shape, when he spotted her, a look of pure sadness upon her perfect face. November. A picture that did not belong in this or any other world. He wanted desperately to call out to her, but did she even want to see him? What if she looked and then turned away and left? Or if she did talk to him but only to tell him to get lost? He wasn't sure which would be worse.

"Rocky?" she said, her voice loud, clear, and lilting like an angel in his ear.

She scanned the crowd around her, looking for Gabriel no doubt, and then hurried over.

She rushed up to him so close that their lips almost met. He opened his mouth to kiss her, but she placed a hand to his lips and bowed her head.

"We can't," she said.

His heart dipped in the flood of emotions.

She had a small brown paper bag with a handle in her other hand and brought it up to him.

"I know it's your birthday. I was hoping to see you so I could give you your present."

He reached for it before seeing the dark shape behind her duck behind one of the carnival game booths.

"What is it?" she asked, looking over her shoulder.

"Nothing. I thought I saw someone I knew."

"I'd better get going," she said. "Here, take it. I want you to promise me something."

He took the bag. "Anything."

"Promise you'll give your gift a fair chance."

"A fair chance?"

"Just promise," she said.

"Okay. I promise."

"And please promise…" she said. She bit her lip and averted her wet eyes.

"What? November, please," he said, reaching out.

She backed away. "Promise you'll always remember me."

"I love you," he said, blurting it out without thinking.

"I love you, too, Rocky. Goodbye."

Tears fell from her eyes as she turned away and hurried into the crowd.

"November!" he shouted. But she was gone.

His own tears dropped to the brown bag in his hands. He wiped them away suddenly, all too aware that he was crying in public. He sniffled and opened the bag. He pulled out a brand-new cassette copy of Van Halen's *5150* album.

He placed it back in the bag and headed home. He didn't stop, he didn't look around at anyone that might see him crying (and he did cry), and he didn't keep a lookout for the man in black.

But he should have.

CHAPTER TWENTY-FOUR

November crashed through the front door and made a beeline for her brother's room. Head of the family or not, he couldn't do this to her. It wasn't fair. Childish mantra be damned. It was the truth. It wasn't his choice and it wasn't for him to decide how she should live her life. She wasn't a baby and she wasn't careless. Knowing that she'd just broken Rocky's heart was more than she could bear.

She burst through Gabriel's bedroom door and gazed at his coffin. God, he was such a dramatic asshole.

Whatever he was going through, he needed to leave her out of it. She reached for the lid and threw it open.

It was empty.

Oh god.

She stepped back, her hands steepled over her nose and mouth. The sun was high in the sky and far too many hours away from giving up to the night. Her brother, who always preferred to stay at full strength , was never out at this time of day.

Rocky.

Rocky was in danger and she'd brought the devil right to him. November found her mother covered in sweat, lying tucked away in her darkened room. Her breathing was raspy, and her complexion was taking on a gray tint. November closed the door without disturbing her.

Was it possible Gabriel was manipulating their mother's health? She didn't want to believe him to be that sinister, but at some point, she had to face the fact that he was changed. Denial wasn't going to do any of them any good.

She wished she had some place to turn to, someone to speak with who would be familiar with their condition and the varying behaviors that could occur depending on their blood intake. It wasn't like there were magazine articles on the subject. If there was a book somewhere, she didn't know about it or have access to it. Father never spoke about the negatives that were possible from within, and Mother seemed content sitting in denial.

November knew it was up to her. It was all on her to confront Gabriel and his activities.

First, she had to make sure he didn't get to Rocky.

She hoped she wasn't too late.

★　★　★

Dressed in a long-sleeved dress shirt, khaki pants, and comfortable loafers, an ensemble he'd purchased just this morning for this specific assignment, Gabriel followed the boy, watching him from behind cheap sunglasses and a dark gray fedora. It had been a long time since he'd willingly subjected himself to the sickening effects of daylight. He didn't know how his sister did it on a near-daily basis. Her desire to be like *them* never ceased to disturb him. And now she'd put him in this position. He thought she'd learned from last summer's experience. Well, this time, he would not spare her the truth. He would give her every grisly detail of what he was going to do to the boy.

He'd seen them an hour ago. All the tears and sentimental bullshit. They had no idea what they were doing. What did they think awaited them? Some sort of romantic future? What could they possibly think would come of their brief abomination of a relationship? His sister was far more to blame for the despicable situation, and it was her penance that Gabriel made his concern. Unfortunately for the boy, her hard lesson was going to be one of pain and death for him. November had to learn, and she had to learn now. Their safety and their family's future depended on it. He'd made a mistake not presenting her with the truth last year, but he'd learned much about many things in the past twelve months. Where he'd been lenient and careful, he now would rule with a ruthless authority that would have zero chance of being misunderstood.

The boy was hiding away in the bedroom where Gabriel had watched him last night. Music poured out through his open window, and although it was slight, Gabriel detected the hitch and sobs of heartbreak. He smiled. The hurt the boy felt now was merely the first wave of what was coming his way. It was also the least vile of the things that lay ahead.

It wasn't long before the beige car pulled into the driveway. The boy's sister. Gabriel leered as she made her way from the car to the front door. Before reaching the door, she glanced over her shoulder.

He stepped out of his hiding place behind the neighbor's fence and waved. He watched her shrink away and disappear into the false safety of her home.

★   ★   ★

"Hey," Julie said, peeking her head into Rocky's room.

He wiped the tears away and turned down the volume to his radio.

"Sorry," she said. "Can I come in for a second?"

"Sure."

He sat up and reached for the soda on his nightstand.

She crossed his room to the window facing the street and peered out.

"What's going on?" he asked.

"Not sure, really. I just saw a guy across the road that kind of creeped me out."

Rocky straightened and hurried off the bed to join her side at the window. "What'd he look like?"

"He was wearing a hat and sunglasses. Black shirt and dress pants, but the strange thing was that it looked like he came out from behind the Mills's fence. Like he was being a weirdo over there. I don't know, it gave me real Michael Myers vibes."

"Did he have long dark hair? Tall?"

"I don't know. I guess he could have been tall. I didn't see his hair."

Rocky scanned the sidewalks, front yards and trees. He studied the fence by the Mills's yard but didn't notice anything out of the ordinary.

"Well, he's gone now," Rocky said, stepping back. "Are you sure it wasn't Mr. Mills?"

"He didn't look like Mr. Mills. He looked younger. And he waved at me."

"Sounds like Mr. Mills."

"Well, it wasn't. I would have known if it was Mr. Mills. This was no one I'd ever seen before."

After a brief minute to sit with her thoughts, Julie said, "What if it was the killer?"

He watched the hysterics begin to rev up in her. She was dancing on her heels, fidgeting with her hair.

"Hey," he said, reassuringly, placing a hand to her arm. "It wasn't him."

"How do you know? How can you be sure?"

"The psycho only strikes at night. Every one of the people that have gone missing has disappeared after dark, right? Why would he risk being seen or caught in the daytime?"

The line was meant to alleviate his own fears as much as hers.

"I don't know. I guess, but what if...." She contemplated for a second. "What if he finds his, his, his targets in the day and he follows them?"

It was completely possible, though he wouldn't say so out loud.

"I don't think he works that way. I think it's more about opportunity...." He rubbed his chin, thinking on it. "He's on the prowl and finds the right person at the right time in the right place."

He thought suddenly of November's brother.

He'll kill you.

"You're probably right, but I don't like it," Julie said. "Derek and Kailin have both disappeared after being here. What if he's staying at one of the hotels or inns on our street?"

Now that was highly probable. East Grand was full of places for travelers. There must have been at least twenty hotels, motels, and sleazy little inns running up and down the road. It was totally the perfect place for a serial killer, especially a seasonal one.

"That's what these sick guys do," Julie continued. "They find someone and learn their patterns. When they go to work, when they come home. Who they go with."

"How do you know all that?"

It did make him think of the scene in *The Town that Dreaded Sundown* when the girl in the red car gets followed home by the Phantom Killer.

"It's what they do in the movies. Where do you think the writers get that stuff from?" she said.

"Well," he said, peeking out the window again, "what do you think we should do about it?"

"Call the police."

"It couldn't hurt, I guess," he said. "Mom and Dad are gonna freak out."

Julie went to the living room to make the call. Rocky went out on the front porch to get a better view. What if it had been November's crazy, overprotective brother? Maybe he'd followed her to town this afternoon and caught them talking. Then he followed Rocky home.

Great, now the dude knows where I live.

He wished he had a way of touching base with November, getting her to find out. He'd much rather know that it was Gabriel and not someone worse.

Julie joined him on the porch.

"They said they'd send someone over," she said.

"Hey, at least my birthday hasn't been boring."

"Oh, Rocky, I'm sorry you have to deal with this. We could still go out for a practice drive after the cops leave. If you want to."

He did want to. He wished he knew where November was staying, so he could drive by. What had she said? She must have dropped a clue at some point.

"Thanks, sis. At least if we go out together, there'll be two of us if Michael or Jason pops out of the trees."

She punched him in the shoulder.

"Don't tease me. You won't be laughing if I'm right."

She was right, of course.

The police took Julie's statement, searched the area, and came up empty. They made their notes, told her and Rocky not to hesitate to call them again if the man came back around. They also offered to do a few additional passes at this end of the street for the next couple days.

Julie thanked them and told Rocky she felt a little better. He'd relaxed a bit, too, though he wasn't keen on the idea of being home alone tomorrow.

"So where are we going?" she asked him.

They'd decided to go for the drive rather than sit at home like a couple of paranoid androids for the rest of the afternoon.

They'd crossed over to West Grand Avenue, passing the Seaside Inn, when something November had said about the cottage her family rented hit him. *A cemetery.* She'd said it wasn't far from the beach, and that they had a graveyard next door. That she walked it at night.

"November mentioned a graveyard by the place they were staying. The only one I can think of that's close enough to the beach to walk to and from is the one out here. I can't remember the name of it, but Axel and I messed around there last Halloween on a dumb dare from Dale Keene."

He recalled the stupid challenge from Dale. Dale was a year ahead of them. A tough metalhead who would kick anyone's ass who didn't know who Iron Maiden or Motorhead were. He liked to tease Rocky and Axel for their love of bands like Foreigner and Journey. But last Halloween when Dale and Dale's girlfriend Mary overheard them talking about how the dead could rise on Halloween because the veil was thinnest between the spirit world and our own, the headbanging couple decided to make them their holiday project. Dale and Mary dared Rocky and Axel to walk among the graves just before midnight. They'd have to walk from the road to the crumbling fence at the back of the cemetery and then back to the road without pussying out. Rocky instantly wanted to kick Axel in the shin for bringing that damn Samhain book from the library; instead, they agreed to take on the challenge. The graveyard was old and spooky as hell. No one had been buried there since something like the 1950s. That's when they ran out of room and started burying their dead in either of the neighboring towns, Scarborough or Saco. And that night, the fog was rolling in hard from the ocean just like in one of Axel's favorite movies that he made Rocky watch at least once a month. Had it not been for Jamie Lee Curtis being in the flick, he'd have thrown a fit. But she was gorgeous, so he dealt with the ghost pirates, creepy music, and nightmares. He remembered thinking how if the veil theory was true, this was the night it would be proved. They made it to the back fence and were halfway back when Dale's buddy, Craig Easley, jumped out of a tree near the center of the graveyard dressed in a hockey mask and swinging a plastic machete. The prank scared the piss, literally, out of both Axel and Rocky. Their high-pitched shrieks would have challenged even Ms. Curtis's best. The story was now engrained in the school's Halloween lore. At least it was a short season.

As Rocky cruised with his sister down West Grand Avenue, the old cemetery came into view. Clear and sunbathed, not a hint of that All Hallow's Eve touch. On the contrary, the tall weeds and fully bloomed sapling at the heart of it all were striking in their natural beauty. Rocky watched the grass sway with the slight breeze, a constant from the great Atlantic.

"Is that it?" Julie asked.

He saw a quaint cottage with gray siding, a tarred roof, and white shutters. The yard matched the wildness of the graveyard next door. No one had mowed in weeks, maybe months. The windows on this side were all covered in dark curtains.. A black Pontiac Grand Prix rested in the dirt driveway.

He'd found her.

Rocky accelerated, letting the home drift behind them.

"Don't you want to stop and see if you're right?" Julie asked.

"I don't need to. She doesn't want to see me anyway."

Watching in the rearview mirror, Rocky saw a curtain fall.

He had his own plans.

"I just want to have fun tonight," he said.

After turning around and driving back to town, followed by two more successful attempts at parallel parking and a stop at DQ for vanilla cones, they arrived home with fifteen minutes to spare before Mom came rolling in.

★   ★   ★

November slunk around outside Rocky's house, ducking through the backyard just as Julie and Rocky drove into the driveway. She hadn't seen Gabriel, but she had a feeling he'd already been and gone. She'd wished for visual confirmation but settled with what she felt in her gut to be true. He'd been here. And that wasn't good.

She needed to confront him. If she couldn't see Rocky anymore, then neither could he. There was no need to bother Rocky when it was her fault to begin with.

November was halfway home when Gabriel appeared at her side.

He looked...wrong. His skin was still pale, but now it clung tighter to his features. Behind his horrid smile, his teeth seemed to be somewhere between human teeth and monster fangs. They were a bit longer than they should be and each came to a point. This was not a good sign. Even his forehead hinted at the bumps that protruded when they changed. She was willing to bet that behind the shades, his eyes would hold another vampiric trait, or at least the glimpse of one.

"You can't tell me to stay away from him and then go over there yourself," she said, doing her best to sound confident.

He snatched her arm hard.

"You do not worry about what I do with my time. You just do as I say. We wouldn't want any harm to befall your precious human."

"Let go of me," she said, trying to pull away.

"He found us."

She'd seen it too. She'd been looking out the window when Rocky and Julie drove by, slowing slightly as they passed the cottage. She was sure he'd stop, but he didn't.

"I know, but he doesn't dare return," she said. "Not after meeting you." The words spat out like venom and she didn't care.

Gabriel let go of her and gave another grin.

God, it was awful to look at.

"There's something wrong with you," she said.

"Whatever do you mean, little sister?"

"Have you seen yourself?"

"That's my concern."

"Not if you turn into a monster and ruin everything we have going."

He lashed out, smacking her so hard her feet came off the ground. November crashed into the sandy gutter off the shoulder of the road. A truck approaching them slowed to a stop.

Her jaw hurt. She sat up and spat blood..

The truck pulled over and two guys climbed from the back, two more from the cab.

They looked like factory workers with their matching coveralls, hardened faces, and dirty hands.

"Is there a problem here?" asked the driver, a guy with stern eyes and salt-and-pepper hair cropped tightly over his ears.

"Please, leave us alone. Everything's all right," November said, getting to her feet and stepping between the men and her brother.

"This fella just hit you, ma'am," said one of the tall guys, with a deep voice and greased-back hair.

"He's my brother."

"That ain't no excuse where I come from," the deep-voiced giant said.

"Please, guys, I'm fine, really."

"You've got a bloody mouth," the driver said.

"And what about you?" the tall man asked Gabriel. "You got anything to say?"

"Hell with it," the driver said, "I'm gonna wipe that fucking grin right from his face."

"No!" November cried.

Gabriel moved faster than anyone she'd ever seen. The driver's throat splashed blood first. Before he could fall to his knees, the tall man came off the ground and crashed into the gutter, his entire face missing. The other two attempted to run, but Gabriel was on them before November could react. She didn't even know what to do.

"Grab that one and place him in the back," Gabriel ordered, one of the men limp in his arms.

November looked the other way and saw a vehicle coming.

"Do it now or we'll have to explain this to the authorities."

She could be disgusted with her brother later. First, she needed to help clean up his mess. She snatched up the driver and lugged him to the truck bed, where Gabriel had already placed the two runners. They were both staring into the void as she shoved the driver on top of them.

Gabriel flung the body of the faceless tall man in last. She almost vomited then and there when he chucked the bloody flesh that had once been his face in next to the bodies.

"Get in," he said, grabbing her arm and guiding her to the passenger-side door.

She climbed in while he shut the door and walked around the front end. She was in shock, totally thunderstruck by what she'd just witnessed. The callousness. The efficiency. He even waved at the two cars that passed as he climbed behind the wheel and started the truck.

She sat in silence as he drove them home and parked in the driveway.

She couldn't move. But even in her shock, something stirred inside. A thirst. She'd never been so close to so much blood.

"We have much to discuss," Gabriel said. "For now, you may run inside. Unless you want to help me take care of your heroes, that is."

Her hand moved to the door lever, trembling as her fingers curled around it. The lure of blood was very strong. Much more so than she ever imagined.

"What's the matter, sis? Hungry?"

No. She wouldn't. She couldn't. She'd never be like him. He had become a beast.

She opened the door, hurried around the truck and went inside.

She shut the door and heard the truck pull out and peel away.

She looked at the blood on her hands.

A series of quick thoughts raced to the front of her mind.

Gabriel wasn't about to stop. Rocky wasn't safe.

She went back outside and sought out a rabbit. When she found one, she sunk her fangs in and sucked it dry.

Gabriel had to get rid of the vehicle and dispose of the bodies. That should give her time to warn Rocky. She needed to come clean to him about everything. He had to know what he was up against.

CHAPTER TWENTY-FIVE

"Thank you, Uncle Arthur. This is way too cool," Rocky said. His dad and uncle stood on either side, Schlitz bottles in hand, and each one admiring the way Rocky looked at the Buick.

"It's a wonderful gift, Arthur," his mom said, "but I really wish you would have talked to Dale and me first."

"I'm sorry, Clarise," Dad said. "I've known the whole time. I've been helping Artie get her fixed up for the last couple months. Hell, you didn't really think I was over there drinking the nights away, did ya?"

"Dale Zukas," Mom said, slapping Dad's arm.

"Ow," he feigned.

"Oh yeah, right," Mom said. "Ow."

After a moment, she crossed her arms and gazed at the car. "It is a beauty," she said.

"Hey," Julie shouted out the door. "Rocky."

"What?"

"There's a phone call for you. I think you're gonna want to take it."

"Ohhh," Dad teased. "Is it that cute girl from the other day?"

Mom slapped his arm again. "Leave him alone."

Rocky ignored them and left them in the driveway.

"It's November," Julie said when he reached the door. "She says it's urgent."

"Thanks," he said, slipping past her and picking up the phone. "Hello."

"Rocky, I need to see you. I have to tell you something... something...."

"Just tell me."

"I can't do it over the phone."

"Where are you?" He could hear vehicles and loud voices in the background.

"I'm down the road. Can you meet me around the corner?"

"All right."

★   ★   ★

He met her just down the street on the corner of East Grand and Boulet.

He thought he'd be angry or heartbroken when he saw her; instead his heart went out to her. She looked frightened.

"Are you okay?" he asked.

He saw the bruise on the right side of her face and the cut on her lip.

"Listen to me. I had to come here. I have something that's going to sound crazy, but you have to believe me."

"Did someone...did your brother do this?"

"That's what I came to talk to you about."

Rage boiled up within him. The adrenaline made his clenched fists shake at his sides. He paced in front of her. A dog in the next yard over was yipping up a storm as a couple of Harleys roared by.

The last of the daylight had faded away. He was lucky it was his birthday; his parents would never have let him leave the yard this late. Not now. Not after all the scary stuff happening.

"You shouldn't make excuses for him. Julie had a boyfriend who smacked her once. My dad went straight to his house and threatened to knock the shit out of him."

She took his hands in hers. Her brown eyes tried to capture his own.

"I need to tell you this. And it isn't easy."

"What. What is it already?"

"My brother is dangerous."

"Yeah, I figured."

"He's a...we're...."

"Yes. What? Whatever it is, November, just spit it out."

"We're not like you. We're...."

God, what was she going to say? The idea suddenly hit him that she was going to tell him that her brother was the killer. He was sure of it.

"We're vampires."

"What?"

"I told you you wouldn't believe me. And I don't have much time to convince you."

He pulled his hands from her. "I don't know why you'd rush over here to tell me something lame like that. I mean, what the hell, November? Just tell me to get lost and that you guys are going home. God."

He turned his back and started to walk away.

She grabbed him by the arm. He tried to pull away but couldn't. They were behind the old utility shed when she let go and rose into the air. Rocky watched as her feet came free from the grass. Stumbling backward, he crashed into the building, unsteady on his feet.

"Wh-wh-what...are you?"

"I told you." She landed and reached for him.

"No, no," he cried. "Don't touch me. Jesus, don't fucking touch me."

"Rocky, please don't look at me like that."

He started toward the road. "Stay away from me."

She was in front of him again.

"How'd you—"

"My brother is dangerous. You have to watch out for him. I don't trust him."

"What the fuck do you want me to do? Throw garlic at him?"

"Rocky, please...."

He went around her. "Do me a favor. You and your brother can both stay away from me and my family. Go back to wherever you came from."

Rocky didn't wait for her to respond. He didn't want to hear anything she had to say. He broke into a sprint and didn't stop until he came panting up his driveway.

His uncle's truck was gone.

"Is everything all right?" his mom asked as he came through the door.

She was sitting with Julie, playing Yahtzee at the kitchen table.

He couldn't think straight. He couldn't speak.

He held up a hand as he passed them by and went straight to his room.

She'd said it. She'd said the word. *Vampire.*

She'd flown. She'd pulled him to the utility building like he was a toddler.

They were real. She was real. Monsters. *Monsters are real.*

He nearly collapsed, stumbling to his bed and burying his face in his trembling hands.

He'd fallen in love with a monster. She'd lied to him. She'd hid this from him.

But honestly, would you have talked to her if you knew? he asked himself.

He'd done more than talk with her. They'd kissed. They'd had sex. What if he was infected? No, he'd worn a condom, but did that work against vampires?

None of it made sense. She was almost always out in the daytime. Vampires weren't supposed to be able to be out in the sun. They were supposed to burn up or explode. They weren't supposed to come to beach towns and play in the ocean, make boys fall in love with them and then crush their hearts.

All the pain and sorrow he'd felt these last couple days bled away. It was far worse than a case of a broken heart. Old Orchard Beach had a family of vampires among them.

All those missing kids, all those missing tourists.

He didn't want to picture November attacking anyone. He couldn't. She wouldn't. But Gabriel.

He's dangerous. I don't trust him.

Rocky looked toward the open bedroom window. The shadow from the other night. The stranger across the street.

He got up and closed and locked the window.

CHAPTER TWENTY-SIX

"Artie, I really can't thank you enough for what you did for my boy."

Arthur raised his beer to Dale's. "Cheers to Rocky. Maybe he'll enjoy even a fraction of the good fucking times we had in that old car."

"Cheers," Dale said.

Arthur finished his beer and reached into his cooler for another. He grabbed two, tossing one to Dale.

"You really didn't mention any of the work we were doing to Clarise?"

"Not you, too, man," Dale said, popping the can open. "I didn't think she'd go for it, or at least that she'd just say 'Oh, that's a wonderful idea.' You know how women are."

"Well, I know you didn't give her that chance."

"Oh hell, you're probably right, but she did come around pretty quick. You gotta give her that."

"Well, we can thank that old beauty for that. No woman could ever resist the presence of the Buick."

They laughed together. Arthur wasn't surprised Dale hadn't said anything to Clarise about them working on the car to give to Rocky. It would have been a battle for sure, but Arthur liked to give Dale hell when he could.

"When's his test?" Arthur asked.

"Tuesday morning."

"Wow. He'll pass."

"Yeah, I think so."

"Well, shit. If you don't mind, I'm gonna go take a whiz."

"What do I care unless you need me to hold it for you."

"You wish," Arthur said, grabbing his crotch and laughing his way out of the room.

He entered the bathroom and waited for his stream to kick into gear. One of the wonders of being over fifty, you have to piss all the time, but it took forever to get it going, and when it did, the damn stream was so weak it took a lifetime.

A loud crash in the other room startled him, making him piss outside the bowl.

What the hell was that?

He finished up and opened the door.

"Dale? What the hell'd you do out there?"

He stopped cold in the entryway of the living room.

The chair was empty. Dale's beer sat spilling onto the floor beside his chair.

"Dale?"

Arthur stepped into the room and saw the front screen door smashed in and lying on the floor.

"Dale!"

Dale was lying face down on the porch. Arthur was about to go to him when a man stepped before him. Only it wasn't a man. His chin was pointy, matching the awful mouth of sharp teeth. His eyes were black as coal.

"Hi there, Artie," it said. Its voice was gravel and death. "Or do you prefer Arthur?"

"What did you do to Dale?"

"I'm afraid he hasn't the *heart* to join us."

"What do you want?"

"Oh, that question is so blasé. Don't you fools have anything worth saying?"

The monster flew forward, taking Arthur by the throat and pinning him to the wall.

Arthur could see Dale still not moving behind this thing.

"Is…is he dead?"

The monster looked over his shoulder before turning back to Arthur.

"He will be soon. Too bad, too. If you called him an ambulance right now, he might make it."

"Please," Arthur said. "Let me get him help."

"I'm afraid we've got other plans. We just can't afford to hang around. You understand?"

"Please."

The monster pulled him forward, and then snapped his head back. The back of Arthur's skull smashed against the wall, and everything faded to black.

★   ★   ★

November was sitting in the cemetery crying when she heard the door to their house slam shut. Gathering her courage, she rose and flew toward the cottage. Barging through the door, she called out to her brother.

"Gabriel!"

He appeared from the hallway, fully vamped out. She faltered.

"You called, little sister?"

"What did you do?"

He walked around the sofa. She circled away from him, heading toward the kitchen.

"Why, whatever do you mean?"

"You need to stop...whatever it is you've been doing."

He pushed on; she continued to circle, not wanting to be in his striking distance, even though she'd seen him in action earlier and knew he could get to her if he wanted to.

"And what do you think I've been doing?" he asked.

They circled the room.

"Just cut it out. All those people. All those kids on the Missing posters in town. You...you did that."

"Guilty," he said, raising his hands. She saw the fresh blood on them.

"Where were you just now?" she asked.

"I could ask you the same thing."

Oh no, don't let him have been following me.

"You first," she said. "You tell me where you went."

"If you must know, I went to see a...a friend of the family, I guess you could say."

She stopped. "What do you mean?"

"Well, after I took care of your hero friends from before, I was heading home when what should I see but you and your little Romeo."

"You didn't. Tell me you didn't hurt him." She stiffened. Ready to strike.

"No, no. I wouldn't waste an opportunity such as this to simply kill that pest."

"What did you do?"

"Come with me and I'll show you."

"I'm not going anywhere with you."

"Oh, you'll change your mind. You and I have some business to take care of tonight. And whether you like it or not, you're going to help me."

"I will do no such thing." She stood tall. It was high time she quit being afraid of him and letting him walk all over her and their mother.

"We'll just see about that," he said.

He flew past her so fast her hair danced in the wind.

She moved to the kitchen and looked for a weapon. The kitchen knife should serve well should she need to wield it.

She turned around and was not prepared for the sight before her. Gabriel had an unconscious man bound to a chair.

"Who's that?" she asked, hiding the knife behind her back.

"You don't recognize the family resemblance?" he said, placing a hand on the back of the man's head.

"Should I?"

"This is Arthur. Artie to his friends. Uncle Arthur to your little Romeo."

This was the one giving Rocky a car for his birthday. She'd never met him, but Rocky had told her about him.

"You have to let him go," she said.

"Let him go? Oh no, no, no, little sister. I'm afraid not."

"I'm telling Mom." She felt like a stupid child saying it out loud, but she had nothing else to threaten him with.

"Mother?" His brow furrowed. "Let me tell you what we're going to do tonight." He wrenched the back of the guy's neck as the man's eyelids fluttered open. He tried to cry out, but it came out muffled behind the rope wrapped around his mouth.

"Shut up, blood bag."

"Gabriel, don't do this."

"Oh, I'm not going to do anything." He straightened up and gazed at her with the eyes of the devil. "You are."

"I don't know what you have in mind, but I'm not doing a damn thing."

"You will. You will get your hands good and bloody. You will quench that thirst I saw in your eyes earlier today. You will feast on this human or—"

"Or what? You'll kill me? You can't frighten me anymore, Gabriel." She hoped it didn't come out as weak as it sounded to her.

"You'll do as I say," he said. His voice grew louder and nastier, coming out as a near growl. "If you choose to disobey me again, your precious boyfriend is dead. Now join me."

"No," she said.

"I will kill the boy and his entire family. Now, you get over here and do what you were born to do."

She clenched the knife in her hand and shook her head.

"No." She stepped into the hallway. "Mother?"

"All right then. You want to bring her into this?" He stepped to her. "Have it your way."

"What are you doing?" she asked, following him down to their mother's room.

"Get up, Mother," he shouted.

"Gabriel?" November said, reaching for him. "What are you doing?"

He swatted her away and stomped to Mother's bedside. He snatched her blankets and tossed them to the floor.

"Get up, *Mother.*"

"What? What's…Gabriel? November?" Mother's weak voice said.

Gabriel clenched her by the arms and hauled her out of the bed.

Mother groaned.

"Leave her alone," November yelled as she launched at him, sinking the blade into his shoulder.

"Arrrgghhh," he cried, dropping their mom to the floor.

He spun fast, took the knife from November's hand, and stuffed it in the back of his pants.

November dropped to the floor next to her mom.

Gabriel shoved past her, scooped their mother up, and carried her like a dying bride out of the room.

He slammed her down on the living room floor next to the man in the chair.

November rushed into the room, tears in her eyes, fear eating her alive.

"Now, you will suck the life from this man, or I swear to you here and now—" Gabriel pulled the knife from behind him and placed it to their mother's throat. "—I will start with our lovely, dying mother."

She wanted more than anything in the world to believe him incapable of such a vile thing, but this was no longer the brother she'd adored, the brother she'd trusted. The brother she'd loved. This was a monster in its truest form.

Mother whimpered as he pressed the blade against her throat, drawing forth a crimson teardrop that traced its way down the pale white flesh.

"Do it, little sister. Take him now."

Deflated and broken, November joined the three of them.

"Drink."

Mother looked so weak. Tears spilling from her eyes, November put one hand on Arthur's head, the other on his shoulder, and said, "I'm sorry."

She took a deep breath, took on her vampiric form, and sunk her teeth into Rocky's uncle's neck.

The power of the blood hit her hard and fast, pulling her in and taking her over. She felt possessed by its magic. She sucked and drew in his life's blood, latching on to him like a starving creature given a golden feast.

She was lost in the moment until she saw the flash and heard the camera.

Pulling free of the drained soul, she looked at Gabriel shaking the Polaroid picture he'd taken of her in the middle of her feeding.

"No," she groaned, her voice unrecognizable to her own ears.

She looked to her mother. She was lying on the floor, but outside of the nick on her neck, she seemed to be relatively fine.

It'd been so long since she'd fed on a person, and even then, it hadn't come close to the amount of blood she'd taken here. She was dizzy, her stomach queasy. She felt wobbly, like she was going to faint.

"That's a good girl," Gabriel said. "You're going to thank me later. But for now..."

He knelt beside her. "You're going to rest like the dead. And you're going to love every second of it."

And she fell into his waiting arms.

CHAPTER TWENTY-SEVEN

Rocky woke up to the sound of crying. He rushed out of his room and down the hall to the living room. His mother and sister were clinging to one another. Officer Pete Nelson stood next to them.

"Rocky," Julie said.

"What's wrong?" He looked from one person to the next. "Where's Dad?"

"Rocky, honey," his mother said. "Your father had a heart attack last night."

"No."

"Someone attacked him at your uncle's. He didn't make it." His mother's voice collapsed on the last word.

Rocky backed up, shaking his head.

"No, that's not true. Dad's at work."

Officer Nelson stepped forward. "I'm sorry, son. Your father's gone and we haven't located your uncle."

"What? Uncle Arthur? What do you mean you can't locate him?"

"As of now, it looks like he bolted the scene," Nelson said.

Rocky ran back to his room, slammed the door, and threw himself onto his bed.

★　★　★

The funeral was held three days later. Rocky skipped his driver's exam and didn't care if he ever went for it. He didn't care if he ever went anywhere or did anything again. His soul had been demolished. In a matter of days, this summer had turned from the greatest of his life to the worst ever. One that he'd look back on as a grown man and be able to pinpoint where and when it all went to shit.

At the viewing the night before, he'd been numb. The body in that casket hardly resembled his father. He was all puffy, his face all wrong. It was like pure cruelty looking at him. It was some form of blasphemy. This wasn't his dad. This was some horrid wax figure, some horror movie dummy meant to appear like the man who had taught him how to ride a bike, how to fish, how to tie his shoes....

He couldn't hold any of it back as they lowered the casket into the ground. Julie held him tight and he soaked the shoulder of her dress as he clutched to her like a life preserver in a swell that would surely swallow them all.

When it was finished, Mom held his hand and walked him to the car waiting to take them home to the post-funeral reception.

He got in the car and sat next to the window.

His itchy eyes stared off at the brilliance of the sun's golden beams filtering through the maple leaves and casting shadows on the freshly tarred road. It was almost like another hateful trick, this beauty when his heart felt completely deflated. He looked out at a world that had decided to turn against him. His sorrow twisted like thorn bushes, drawing blood.

The car rolled up behind his father's truck and the simmering rage within him demanded release.

He got out of the car and started toward the sidewalk.

"Rocky, honey," his mom said. "Where are you going?"

"I'm going for a walk."

"Rocky, get back—"

"Mom," Julie said. "Let him go. He needs it."

Their voices faded as he power-walked away from town, toward Scarborough. His breathing quickened. He gritted his teeth and wanted everyone to know how mad he was. He wanted to put his pain on the world. An eye for an eye. He wanted to break something. Kick something.

There was an old shed set back from the road just over the town line. He and Axel had smoked cigarettes in there last winter. They'd also smashed out the two remaining panes of glass in the crappy place. He stormed off the road, picked up one of the moldy two-by-fours left to decay beside the building. He screamed as he swung it, slamming it against the side of the building. He swung it again and again until the board snapped in half. He chucked the piece in his hand and walked around to the door. He kicked it in and entered the shack. There was all kinds of loose junk on a worktable, rusted screws, nails, clamps, and old tin coffee cans filled with washers. He picked up a coffee can and launched it against the wall, where it exploded and shot its contents everywhere. He grabbed the edge of the worktable. It wobbled in his hands. He began to jerk it back and forth, determined to snap it free and flip it over.

Every time it refused to give, he pulled and pushed harder. He felt the stabbing of more than one splinter puncturing his palms and fingers, but he didn't care.

He wanted the wood to break. He wanted it to fall to pieces. He wanted it to hurt.

He wanted his father back.

As the acknowledgement came to him, he let go of the table and dropped to his knees, becoming a puddle of emotions. He couldn't breathe. He felt the goddamn back brace trying to suffocate him. He grabbed the front of his dress shirt and ripped it open, sending buttons cascading everywhere. He wrestled out of the shirt and reached back, clawing at the Velcro straps of the brace. He undid all three, pulled the hard plastic shell off and threw it as hard as he could across the small room. He wanted it to shatter, but it bounced off the far wall and tumbled to the floor. He didn't want to cry anymore. He didn't want to feel this pain, but at the same time, there in that old shed, he let himself crumble again and again. Out of sight and out of reach, he mourned.

CHAPTER TWENTY-EIGHT

Pete Nelson hadn't been out to the bars since this nightmare began. All the missing, and still no answers. And no bodies. It was getting to the point that he was ready to start searching the night sky for UFOs. Close encounters of some goddamn kind. How else do so many vanish without a trace?

That all changed this morning.

They'd received a call from Scarborough Police. A truck was pulled from the marsh. Four dead bodies. One without its damn face. The flesh had been torn off and discarded. They'd found it all right, though. It looked like some gruesome Halloween mask.

Discovering the bodies changed things. If indeed it was the same person or persons responsible for the other disappearances, the perpetrators had switched things up. Could they be upping the ante? Daring the police to find them? Or there was the other possibility. This was the work of someone else. A completely separate case. It didn't feel like it, though.

Pete needed to get out for a bit. So, he went to the only place he thought might relax him. He walked up the pier and stepped into Duke's.

The place was alive. Summer might be affected out there, the streets were a little quieter after dark, but here on the pier, in the company of so many others, the people of his beach town were doing like he was – they were all trying to forget.

"Officer Pete, mahalo," Duke said. "What can I get for you?"

"Hey, Duke," he said, taking a seat at the bar. "Good to see you're still getting some business."

"Yeah, well, I can't say it's as good as it has been with all that's going on."

"Look, I'm sorry. We're doing our best—"

"No, you misunderstood," Duke said. "I'm not blaming you. You guys are experiencing this madness with all of us."

"That's good to hear, Duke. Truly. A Jack, straight. Leave the bottle?"

Duke nodded, tossing his rag over his shoulder. "You got it, boss." He poured the whiskey and slid the tumbler to Pete, placing the half-full bottle next to him.

Leaning on the bar, Duke asked, "Any connection with the truck you guys found in the marsh?"

Pete never talked shop with Duke. Maybe Shannon or Thomas did. They were up here all the time, but Pete didn't come often enough. He thought he'd wanted to be left alone when he set out this evening, but Duke's was far from a dive in the town. There were plenty of other dark corners he could have sneaked away to, but he landed here.

He downed the drink. Duke reached across and refilled it for him.

"Thanks," Pete said. "Honestly, we don't know yet. Seems likely, I mean, we go thirty-something years without multiple homicides and then we wake up one sunny morning and find a bloodbath on our hands. Only, we ain't found no bodies."

"Until today?"

"Yeah, until today."

He thought again of the faceless man. Zack Walters. Good guy. Hard worker from the shipyard. Family man. Wife, three kids. Same went for Lenny Crates. Pete had met Lenny and his wife, Miranda, last winter at the police charity ball over in Saco. Lenny's brother, Lyle, was married to Miranda's sister, Jewel. Both Jewel and Lyle served on the Saco force. All of them had camps here in Old Orchard. The other two bodies dragged from the marsh belonged to two locals, Jim Coniglio and Richie Duncan. Single fellas, but Pete had never heard a bad word on either of them.

How the hell had the truck ended up in the marsh? Well, that was easy. The killer drove it in. Why? None of it made a damn bit of sense.

Duke patted Pete's arm. "You got a lot on that mind, Officer Pete. I'll leave you in peace. I'm here if you wanna talk."

Pete tipped his glass to him. He was beginning to understand why Shannon and Thomas frequented the place.

The luau-chic joint – tiki torches, hula-girl waitresses, bamboo-dressed tables and chairs, ukulele songs pouring from the jukebox – made him feel like he was on the set of a television show or movie. He thought of that Elvis flick where he's in Hawaii. He glanced around. The place was nearly full. Another paradise within a paradise.

★   ★   ★

Pete had to check his watch when he saw the first wave of people begin to vacate the bar.

It was only ten p.m. and at least half the place was now empty.

"This is how it's been. They keep leaving sooner and sooner," Duke said.

"Jesus," Pete said, trying not to slur his words.

"Yeah, it's not good, but this is how it stays until closing time."

"Sir," a woman called from the other end of the bar.

"Duty calls," Duke said, before shoving off.

Pete left two twenties on the counter and drifted toward the door.

Outside, he watched the mass exodus from the pier. Must have been at least a hundred people leaving and only a few, in twos and threes he noticed, coming up. While he was inhaling the salty air, trying to clear his head, one of the comers caught his eye.

He was tall, slicked-back black hair in a ponytail, dressed in black and wearing sunglasses at night. He most certainly was not Corey Hart. It gave Pete the willies just looking at him. He rubbed his arms, feeling the goose bumps spread like wildfire over his flesh.

Not wanting to stare at the guy and look like a weirdo himself, Pete moved next to a group of longhairs spouting about the Judas Priest concert coming this week to the Cumberland County Civic Center. Heavy metal. It wasn't Pete's cup of tea, but right now, he'd just as soon go along with these degenerates than stay here and get caught alone with this fella.

After checking his watch again, he looked up and lost the man in the shades.

Shit.

He looked down toward the end of the pier but didn't see him. When he turned to look the other way, the man was standing next to him.

"Lovely town you have here," the man said. What a voice – it sent chills up his spine and turned his stomach. Like the sound of metal scraping metal. The wrongness of it resonated after his last word.

"Ah, yeah, we-we like it all right," Pete managed.

"Quiet out here tonight," the man said.

"Well, yeah, it's been an interesting season to say the least."

The man grinned. It was awful. Pete thought he saw teeth, two rows of canines, but more jagged.

Too much whiskey.

"You-you from around here?" Pete asked.

"Just visiting with my family."

"Oh? And wheren' might they be?" Pete asked.

"We have a rental nearby. Say, are you feeling all right?"

"I'm fine," he said, sounding more and more drunk by the second. "Say, you got a name?"

"It was nice chatting with you, friend," the man said. "I believe I'm ready for a drink."

Pete didn't like the evasiveness. He jumped when the man reached for him, long fingernails coming straight for his neck.

"You have a spot of something there," the man said, contacting Pete's neck with his sharp fingernail.

"Ow," Pete said, stepping away and clamping his hand to the spot.

"Got it," the man said. "Good evening, sir."

Pete watched him disappear among those leaving.

He pulled his hand away from his neck and stared at the blood.

He suddenly didn't feel like walking home alone.

He couldn't explain the sensation, but it was set like stone in his mind and soul.

He'd be all right if he never saw the stranger again.

CHAPTER TWENTY-NINE

Rocky awoke sometime after noon. He'd been awake until nearly four in the morning thinking about his dad and uncle and November and Gabriel until his brain felt completely fried. He still couldn't believe what he was dealing with and that he was the only one who knew that Old Orchard Beach had a family of bloodsuckers taking up residence. That the good kids like Andy Rice, John Chaplin, and Jonas Bazinet and all the others were not the victims of some pedophile or psycho killer, at least not in the traditional sense. Almost more than the others, Rocky was sickest over Vanessa Winslow. Seeing her poster that first night, and the man he came to verify later from seeing him on the news as her father hanging those posters up, made it all real. Rocky remembered the unease that slid through his insides at the sight of Vanessa's poster.

He'd made up his mind last night to do his part. He would go to the police station and spell it out for the cops. He knew they would probably laugh him out of the building, but at this point with the number of missing growing exponentially with each day that passed, they would at least have to consider the vacationers out on the edge of town. It ate him up to think November might have a real hand in any of this. Monster or not, he didn't believe her capable of killing anyone. Yes, she was a vampire. Maybe she had to kill or feed off someone every so often. He was just guessing here; all the other movie stuff seemed to be wrong, and maybe that was, too.

Even though his heart believed her to be innocent, his mind always brought him back to the facts. She'd lied to him from the very start. Betrayed him. She never told him about how crazy her brother was or that he could be in trouble messing around with her. If she knew Gabriel was a fucking psycho killer, why would she put him in the line of fire? And if it was just her brother doing all this killing, what happened to the bodies? Did he bring them home for the family to feast on? Rocky couldn't help but picture her with her face buried in Vanessa Winslow's neck.

If she turned out to be the angel he'd made her out to be in his mind, well, then that was great for her.

If the cops followed his far-fetched lead and discovered the truth, that could mean many different things.

First things first. He had to spell it out for them and let them make of it what they would.

The first person he bumped into at the police station was Officer Todd Shannon. Shannon was a prick. He'd busted Rocky and Axel for stealing two summers ago at Hector's Hi-Fi records. It'd been bad enough to get banned from their favorite local record shop for being a couple of stupid thirteen-year-olds, but the way Officer Shannon made a full-blown drama out of it was more than he could take. He'd cuffed them on the sidewalk and chose to stop traffic on Old Orchard Street. This was during the drive home, five o'clock traffic mixing up with all the tourists, not to mention their parents each coming home at that time. Shannon brought them across the street and walked them up to the station, where he made them sit in an otherwise empty jail cell while he called their parents.

He'd never forget Mom's look of disappointment when she came through wiping the tears from her eyes as his dad talked to Shannon. Rocky had gotten an ass-whipping that night. His father almost never hit him, but that night he'd spanked his bare ass raw. Rocky learned the lesson. He hadn't stolen from a store since. A yard sale or the school book fair was a different story, but he didn't have the brass to try at a shop ever again.

Walking up to Shannon with his story was not going to be easy. He glanced around for someone else, anyone else, but saw no one.

Hell.

He made his way up to the desk barely able to meet Shannon's judging gaze.

"Oh, Mr. Zukas, gee, it's been what? Two years since you've walked through them doors?"

Rocky already regretted this.

"What can I help you with this early in the morning?"

Where to start? He'd thought about how he would lay it out

for them all night, but he pictured Officer Nelson or maybe even Chief Donnelly.

"Well? Speak up, Zukas."

"I think I might have some information on the killer." The words were hardly more than a whisper coming from his mouth.

"Come again? What did you say, Zukas?"

He sighed.

"I said, I think I know where the killer lives."

Shannon sat back in his chair and crossed his arms over his thick chest. "Is that so? Well, you want to tell me how it is that you came upon information that five PD stations' worth of hard-working, competent officers haven't been able to even catch a whiff of, huh? You want to tell me how a little thieving punk like you just happened upon the answers to the crime of the century?"

Rocky wanted to both run and punch Shannon in the face simultaneously in equal amounts.

"Well, Zukas? Enlighten us all with your a-ha Sherlock Holmes moment."

"The man's name is Gabriel. Gabriel Riley. He's renting the cottage out by the old cemetery on outer West Grand Avenue. My sister called you guys a few days ago to report him acting like a creep across the street from our house. He's also personally threatened me."

Rocky held back the bit about Gabriel being a vampire. He wanted to at least be listened to first.

"What proof do you have that this... Gabriel Riley, was it? What do you know about this guy that tells you he's responsible for the abduction of over fifteen people and the possible deaths of four more?"

This was the tricky part.

"He's the man that broke into my uncle's house and attacked my father. I don't know what he did to my uncle, but I bet you'll find all the proof you need at that cottage."

"Listen, kid, I'm real sorry about your dad. I am, but if this is some sort of sick way of placing the blame...." To Rocky's surprise Shannon sighed. He seemed genuinely empathetic.

"Morning, Todd," a voice said from behind Rocky.

"Morning, Pete, you look like hell."

Officer Nelson looked like he hadn't slept in weeks. The bags beneath his eyes were like bruised craters.

"Can I talk to you for a minute?" Shannon said, standing up.

"Sure." Nelson nodded at Rocky. "What's this about? Everything okay?"

"Let's talk first," Shannon said, before looking Rocky in the eye and tapping his desk. "Stay right here a minute, okay, kid?"

Rocky nodded and folded his hands over his lap.

Shannon and Nelson went all the way across the room to what Rocky assumed was Pete Nelson's desk by the window.

He couldn't make out a thing they said, but he took note of each and every glance they threw in turns in his direction. Neither one laughed.

He'd gotten this far in each of last night's imagined scenarios. The next part was the make-or-break part of the conversation.

"Kid," Shannon yelled. "Come on over here."

Rocky got up and headed around the front desk and joined the officers at Nelson's desk.

"I remember the phone call from your sister. Julie, right?" Officer Nelson said.

Rocky nodded.

"Some tall weirdo in sunglasses...." Officer Nelson trailed off as he said it. Rocky thought it looked like something clicked in his mind.

"Pete," Shannon said, "what is it?"

Nelson opened a drawer and shuffled through a number of files. He found the one he was looking for and pulled it out, placing it on the desk. He opened the folder and lifted the handwritten report.

"Tall, pale, sunglasses, hat, maybe ponytail."

That was Julie's description of the man that waved to her from across the street. The man Rocky already knew was Gabriel.

"And you say you now know who this man is?" Nelson asked.

"Yes."

"And how's that, if you don't mind telling me."

"I've been seeing his sister since almost the start of summer vacation."

"And do you have any reason to think he means you harm?"

"He caught us together on the beach a couple weeks ago and told me if he caught me around November, that's her name, that he'd kill me."

Nelson appeared to think on it.

"I don't know, Pete," Shannon chimed in. "I mean, I guess the guy could have a grudge against Zukas here, but that doesn't make him a killer or even a bad guy in my opinion. I have a younger sister. Sometimes you have to scare punks away."

"Did you see his teeth or his fingernails?" Nelson asked.

"What?" Rocky wasn't sure how to respond. "I mean, I didn't see his teeth...or his fingernails, I guess."

Shannon barged in again. "Zukas, have you guys seen this Gabriel guy since that day your sister reported him?"

"No."

"There you go. Maybe he wanted to scare you away from his sister. Looks like it worked like a charm."

Nelson looked at Rocky. There was almost a sense of acknowledgement, what it meant Rocky had no idea. "Shannon," Nelson said. "Can you give me and the kid a few minutes?"

"Sure, Pete, but I think—"

"I know what you think, *Todd*. Thanks."

"All right, whatever." Shannon shoved his chair back, agitated. He ran a hand through his short blond buzz cut and started back to his desk.

Nelson squinted. "Is there something you're not telling me about all this?"

Here was his opening. Here was his chance to say it.

Say it.

"Why? You don't believe me?" Rocky said instead.

Nelson picked up a pencil from a black pen holder on the corner of his desk and began tapping it on the desktop.

"This man who threatened you. You're certain he's also the fella your sister saw?"

"Yes."

"But you haven't seen him since."

"No."

"How about the sister?"

Rocky saw her floating off the ground.

We're vampires.

"Yes."

"When?"

"Twice," Rocky said. "I saw her at Palace Playland on my birthday, the 4th, and she gave me a present right before telling me we couldn't see each other anymore. That it wasn't safe."

"It wasn't safe for you?"

"Yeah, I think so."

"And the second time?"

"She called me later that night. After nine. We were celebrating my birthday at my house and my sister said I had a phone call. It was my friend, November, and she asked me to meet her down the street."

"And did you?"

"Yeah. She...she warned me that there was something different about her brother. That he was dangerous."

"Those were her exact words?"

Rocky nodded.

"I'll tell you what," Nelson said. "I'm interested in having a talk with this Gabriel."

"So, you believe me?"

"I'm not so sure about tying the guy to all that's happening around here, but I bumped into a fella last night on the pier. Matches the description of your guy. Tall, ponytail, and sunglasses even though it was well after dark. Now, that can fit plenty of people floating through town, but this guy spoke to me. And I didn't get a real good feeling from him. Between you and me, he managed to give me the creeps."

"That sounds like him."

"Well, you have that address for me?"

CHAPTER THIRTY

Pete sent the Zukas kid home and told Shannon to stay put. Damn, he felt bad for the boy. He'd seen him fall to pieces right before his eyes when he had to tell him about his father. Heartbreaking. Pete had lost his older brother to the Vietnam war. Freddy had been enlisted for two years when the shitty conflict began. Made it through three tours before getting blown up a week before he was set to come home.

Shaking the memory free, Pete stepped into the parking lot and saw the newbie, Matt Martin, getting ready to take off.

"Martin," Pete said.

"Yeah?"

"I need you to run out to see someone with me."

"Yeah, sure," he said. "I'll follow you?"

"Yep."

"Officer Nelson," Matt said.

"What'd I tell you, Martin? Nelson or Pete is fine. What is it?"

"Is this anything to do with…with the killer?"

"I don't think so, Martin, but you've got to be prepared for anything."

The kid swallowed hard.

Pete felt bad for him, almost.

He remembered the case of the heebee jeebees this Gabriel fella had left him with last night. Nightmares and everything after he finally convinced himself the guy wasn't coming through his window.

Five minutes later, they arrived at the cottage the Zukas kid described. A black Grand Prix sat in the driveway, only now it had a U-Haul trailer attached to it. The kid hadn't mentioned that. Pete didn't doubt that it hadn't been there the other day.

He pulled in behind the trailer and watched as Martin pulled his cruiser up on the shoulder before the rental place.

They stepped to the door and knocked.

It was just before eleven in the morning. To Pete's surprise, the man, Gabriel Riley, answered the door.

The sunglasses were gone. It looked as if the man's pupils had swallowed the rest of his eyes. Two onyx orbs bore into him.

"Hello, *Officer*," Gabriel said. "Why, look at you, all dressed up. Ah, and the nick on your neck looks much better this morning, if you don't mind me saying."

Pete's hand found the Band-Aid. "Can we come in, Mr. Riley, is it?"

"Why yes, of course, but you must excuse the place. Our vacation is coming to its end here in your lovely little town." He moved aside and ushered them in.

The place looked nearly empty save for the stock furniture the renters probably supplied. A blue sofa, wooden coffee table, little stand with a small Zenith television, a Formica table in the clean kitchen across the way.

"Are you the only one home?" Pete asked.

"No. My sister and mother are in their chambers."

Chambers?

"Is there a problem, officers?" Gabriel asked.

"We received a couple reports about a gentleman that fits your description," Peter said. "A couple of harassment complaints. Had your name and address even."

The smile on the pale man's face with the midnight eyes faltered slightly.

"I assure you, officers, I have harmed no one."

"I didn't say anything about harm," Pete said, pulling the little notebook from his front pocket. "When did your family arrive in town?"

"I'm not sure I need to answer your questions."

"I'm quite certain you do, Mr. Riley. We take harassment charges very seriously in this town."

"I see," he said. "Well, then, we arrived here June 3rd."

"So, you've been here just over a month then?"

"Yes. I suppose so."

"Do you know a Rocky Zukas, Mr. Riley?"

"No, I'm afraid that name doesn't ring a bell."

"Is your sister a November Riley?"

"Yes."

"Were you aware at any time over these last few weeks of her relationship with a local boy named Rocky Zukas?"

Gabriel took a deep breath. Pete noticed the man's nostrils flaring. His eyes squinting.

"I do not meddle in my sister's affairs."

"Did you know she was seeing someone here in town?"

"What she does is not my business, so long as she doesn't get herself into trouble."

"And did you think this boy, Rocky Zukas, was trouble? Did you threaten him on the beach after catching him with your sister?"

"I…I may have told the boy she was with to find someone else to aim his hormones at."

"Did you threaten to kill Mr. Zukas if you caught him with your sister again?"

Gabriel seemed to unravel ever so slightly. He was rubbing his forefinger and getting visibly agitated.

"I told him what I had to, to protect my younger sister. If I used that sort of language then forgive me, but it worked. For goodness' sake, officer, it was just to scare the young man off. You know what these boys have in mind nowadays with their heavy metal music and their drugs."

"Did you ever go to the boy's home?"

"What?"

"The boy's sister called to report a man fitting your description last week standing outside their home."

"When did it become a crime for someone to wave to someone else?"

"I never said anything about you waving to her."

"What is this all about?" Gabriel asked, his voice rising.

"May we take a quick look around the premises?" Pete asked.

"Fine. Do as you wish, but may I please ask you not to bother my family? My mother has been very ill this summer, I'm afraid she's been laid up for most of our vacation."

"Sure. May we see your room?"

"Of course," he said, stepping past them and leading them down the hall.

He opened the door to a very basic, barebones bedroom. A simple full-sized bed, a dresser, and nightstand with a lamp upon it. The lamp was lit since a very heavy black shade covered the lone window.

"Afraid of the sun?" Pete asked, motioning toward the drawn shades.

"I'm a bit of a night owl. I'm usually just waking up at this hour, but with the preparations to head home, I'm up early."

"Hmm," Pete said, walking in and opening the closet. Bare. "Wow, you either packed very lightly or that U-Haul outside is already filled."

"Yes, we are hoping to head home within the next couple days," Gabriel said.

"Does this property have a basement?" Pete asked.

"Why, yes it does," Gabriel said, his lips curling upward at the edges.

The butterflies in Pete's stomach began to take flight. Everything about this guy was telling him there was something more to him. He didn't like it. The disappearances began precisely in line with his arrival. He'd threatened a local boy, and inadvertently admitted to harassing the kid's sister. Though none of that was enough to charge him with anything.

As he and Martin followed the man to the door in the dim hallway, Pete's hand moved to the pistol at his side.

"I'll have to warn you to watch your steps, officers. The stairs are a bit creaky and weak in spots. There's but one dim bulb at the bottom."

Pete looked back to Martin and nodded at the gun on the boy's hip. Martin gently undid the button over the flap to his sidearm. He looked nervous but otherwise showed no signs of weakness.

Good, Pete thought. Being scared kept you on your toes.

They began their descent behind Gabriel.

The scent of earth told Pete it was a dirt-floor basement. Probably not more than the size of the living room above it, maybe the living room and kitchen.

As they reached the bottom, Pete grabbed for his flashlight. If Gabriel was in front of him, he couldn't see him. He didn't even hear the man over his own blood thrashing in his ear.

He was about to flick his flashlight on when the dim bulb at the center of the small cellar bloomed to life, revealing nothing but a few mostly empty shelves featuring some paint cans and a small toolbox. There were two wooden pallets leaned up against the far wall.

"Satisfied?" Gabriel asked.

"Yes, thank you," Pete said. Relief flooded him; the adrenaline rush subsided, leaving him shaky but able to breathe again.

"I'll stay down here with the light until you gentlemen reach the top step."

They turned and made their way back up and to the front door.

"Should we talk to the sister?" Martin asked.

"Let's just head back," Pete said.

Gabriel was right behind them. Both officers jumped.

"Sorry, did I frighten you, officers?" That devilish smirk crossed his odd face again.

"One more question," Pete said. "Where were you on the night of July 4th between the hours of, say, nine and two?"

"I believe I watched your town's wonderful fireworks display from the beach before retreating home."

"Really? You just went home? I thought you said you were a night owl?"

"Not that night," he said, the smile gone, his dark eyes intense.

"And your mother or your sister could verify your whereabouts during those hours?"

"They surely would."

"Mr. Riley," Pete said, "I may need to check with them on that. I won't disturb them at this moment, but you can count on my coming back later, unless they'd be willing to come down to the station this afternoon."

"Of course. If you truly think you need to speak with them, I'll be sure to let them know."

"Thanks much," Pete said, heading toward the porch steps.

"Say, you wouldn't want to show me the inside of that trailer, would you?"

"I'm sorry, Officer," Gabriel said, a scowl on his face from where he stood in the doorway, his voice a low growl. "But is there something you want to charge me with?"

"No, but I would ask that you and your family stick around for the next forty-eight hours or so. At least until I can check on a few things," Pete said, raising his notepad. "Now, you have yourself a nice afternoon, Mr. Riley."

Gabriel went back inside, slamming the door.

Pete eyed the trailer as they walked by.

"Sir, is there something you need to tell me?" Martin asked.

"Let's get back to the station. I think we need to see what's inside this trailer."

CHAPTER THIRTY-ONE

Officer Nelson had sent him home, but Rocky's hands trembled as he reached his uncle's house. Part of him expected to see his uncle come bouncing out the front door or laughing around the corner welcoming him to come out back and have a drink. Neither happened, of course. Rocky stared at the front door, looking through the small porch where they'd found his father. Where Gabriel had left him to die. But if Gabriel was responsible for killing his dad, why had his body been left when no others had?

His father's official cause of death was a heart attack. Maybe vampires couldn't drink from someone who was dying. An accident, maybe?

Another reason came to mind. It was a message. A message meant for him.

Bastard.

Rocky stepped to the porch and stood at the busted door. Looking around the entryway, he saw so much of his uncle. His trusty red Coleman cooler, his waders hanging from a nail on the other side of the door, and of course, the babes in bikinis from his *Hot Rod* magazines plastering the limited wall space, a true tits-and-ass wallpaper, and probably part of the reason his uncle never had a girlfriend. Well, that and the fact that his uncle seemed content drinking beer and puttering around the yard and garage at will. Before meeting November, Rocky could have easily seen himself enjoying a lifetime of solitary comforts, wrapped up in music, movies, and a few burgers and drinks with Axel. Had Uncle Arthur ever met someone like her? Well, not just like her. No one was like her. Maybe there had been women. How well did he really know his uncle in his personal life? Rocky couldn't recall a time when he'd ever asked his uncle about his likes and loves outside of cars or bands. Standing next to the porch's broken screen door, picking at the splintered wood where the hinges had come off, he spotted a jackknife on the floor in the corner. Simple brown handle with a tarnished brass end. He picked it up and pulled out the blade. Tracing its edge with his thumb, he saw it was still sharp. He closed it up and slipped it into the pocket of his shorts.

He made a trip out back and gazed at the newly built porch he was supposed to have helped with. His uncle had known better than to wait for him and had finished it himself. Behind him sat the lawn chairs where they'd sat and drank after tearing the old porch down together. Turning back to the porch, he felt both a sense of sadness and accomplishment. Uncle Arthur was gone, most likely dead, but this was still here, standing like some kind of monument to him. Even when the house was sold to someone else, they'd use *this* place. Put tools or furniture out here. Sit out here in the warm mornings and drink coffee or tea. Maybe an old couple, talking about their past or their plans for the day. An old man and his garden out back by the blackberry bush. The old lady dead set to knit a new blanket for the sofa or tending to the flowers she'd put in every open corner of the house inside and out.

Someone would make something of this place.

Rocky smiled, just a little.

He headed to the street and started back to his house. He knew no one would be home. His mom was at Grammy Jan's and Julie had decided to try and go back to work, which meant he'd have to find something to do until they got home. What would they say when he told them that he'd gone to the police? That he'd pointed the finger for all the killings and disappearances at November's brother. They wouldn't be upset with him, he knew that. He figured he had about the longest leash of any teenager anywhere after what he'd gone through. He had no intentions of taking advantage of the situation, but it was nice knowing that he could make mistakes.

He'd intended to take the side roads home, but found himself drawn to the center of town, to more people. The sun and the sounds of summer, still alive and well, at least in the daylight, surrounded him at every turn. Girls in their summer clothes, guys with their tongues wagging after them, parents and their children in bright colored shirts and shorts, Polaroids or disposable Kodaks in their hands. Little kids with their faces painted in melted ice cream, at least half a dozen dragging behind crying about being tired and wanting to go home. The heartbeat of his town seemed to be taunting him.

The beach and the waves were where they always were, crashing and splashing on an ocean so cold it made your ankles numb to walk into. That would change near the end of August; by that time, the Atlantic would have warmed up to maybe sixty degrees, which would feel like a hot tub compared to what it was right now.

He was almost home when he found himself wondering what may or may not have happened at the cottage. Officer Nelson seemed to believe Gabriel was responsible for something. Kidnap and murder? Maybe not, but Rocky had sensed the man's fear. Like his own when Gabriel stood in front of him. Would November get in trouble?

He reached the end of his driveway and grabbed the mail. More letters from family he hadn't heard from in a million years. He sifted through the envelopes, reading the return addresses. Aunt Joan and Uncle Allan up near Augusta, Great Grandma Lilian and her boyfriend Stan in Monmouth. Dad's friend Gary and his wife, Ruth, from work. He grabbed the letter and a Welby Superdrug flyer and stopped cold at the door. There was another envelope taped there.

Rocky – For yours eyes only.
   -G

His heart began to hammer in his chest. He spun around, scanning his and the neighbors' yards for any sign of movement. Cars continued to whiz by and a slew of people made their way to or from town along the sidewalks, but he couldn't see Gabriel anywhere.

He set the mail under his arm on the stoop and sat down with the letter addressed to him.

Holding the plain white envelope, he felt a familiar shape within. It was a picture. A Polaroid. He was afraid to see it.

Carefully, he slid his finger in the corner of the envelope and swiped across under the flap, opening it. He reached in and took the picture in hand, letting the envelope fall to the ground.

He raised the Polaroid and felt the world begin to burst at the seams. He couldn't breathe; he knew he was going to throw up.

He turned to the side and vomited in the grass.

The image pummeled his insides.

When his stomach was empty, he sniffled the snot from his nose and wiped his eyes, the picture still clutched in his hand.

He looked at it again and the river of deceit and disbelief flooded him all over.

November, lips overrun with blood, had her mouth buried in Uncle Arthur's ruined throat.

Rocky hugged his legs, burying his face in his knees, and grieved.

His uncle was most certainly dead, and his girlfriend was a fucking liar and a killer.

CHAPTER THIRTY-TWO

"What have you done?" Mother asked, moving on Gabriel like a lioness on an unsuspecting elk. November trailed behind her feeling much as she did in her childhood when something posed a threat outside their old home in the woods. November had only seen her normally soft-spoken and tender mother's aggressive side twice that she could recall. And it was just as shocking then as it was now.

Mother, with her nails extended, teeth bared, and vampiric form on full display, had Gabriel by the throat and pinned to the front door. Gabriel, eyes wide, mouth agape, tried to speak but barely got out more than a squeak behind Mother's death grip.

"You have brought the *authorities to us*?"

November had sat in her room, curled up in the corner, unsure of what was going to happen, while the police officers walked the house with her brother. Would they pull their firearms and start shooting? Would Gabriel react first and drain them where they stood? And how many more would come before they could get away? Would they escape? She was terrified. She was no longer innocent. Gabriel was not the only monster to have taken a life in this gracious little town. She could still taste the blood from Rocky's uncle. She'd been sick over her actions ever since. She'd hardly slept and done nothing but loathe herself. But that despair, shame, and guilt were only topped by the immense hatred that now burned within her for Gabriel.

Watching him suffer at Mother's hand now offered a small sense of vengeance.

"I sat by, admittedly unable to act due to my condition, but I will stand aside no longer. Whether I'm ill or not, your actions have consequences. For decades, your father led this family, fed this family, kept this family well and safe in a world that would just as soon set fire to us and watch us burn for what we are. He killed only to secure our well-being. He fed only to sustain his strength. Not for himself, not for lust or for power, but to defend our way of life.

"You think your crimes have gone unseen. You thought your nightly adventures back home, sneaking out, going to different towns to quench your growing thirst were somehow out of my sight?"

November stood at the edge of the hallway, slinking back step by step, uncertain how far Mother intended to take this. And worse, wondering what would happen if she let Gabriel go. Part of her hoped she wouldn't.

"This monster inside you is not your friend. Your gifts are not a right to take lives. Do you hear me? This thing will swallow your soul if you let it. It will only lead to one destiny. Death. The legends are all lies, my son."

Tears rolled over Gabriel's cheeks. November's resolve trembled. She hadn't seen her brother cry since their father had passed. And that had been for a matter of minutes before he stiffened and accepted the role as head of the house. When he was twelve and November was five, they'd had a pet cat Gabriel had named Thomas after Tom and Jerry. They'd kept Thomas as an indoor cat for the first four years of his life but eventually, Gabriel began to take the cat with him out in the woods around their home. Thomas followed Gabriel, a loyal friend. The two were nearly inseparable. When Thomas disappeared one early evening, Gabriel searched and searched for hours. He looked for the cat for three days until Mother told him to stop. The cat had surely been attacked and eaten by a larger predator. The pain in her brother's eyes then was with him now as he wilted in Mother's grasp.

Gabriel's arms reached out. Mother let him go and pulled him to her. His sobs were heavy and deep.

"You are a good man, Gabriel. This sickness clutching you now is not permanent. As with any addiction, you alone can defeat it, but you must acknowledge it for what it is. You must accept the truth and you must decide that you want to change. That you want it to stop, to release you, to return you to us."

"Mother," he said.

"Yes, my son?"

"It's so powerful. I feel it coursing through me, even now. Standing here, I want to taste it. I want to feel the power that makes me forget."

"This bloodlust has its claws in you," Mother said, stroking his hair as they sank to their knees.

He looked like a boy, his head on her shoulder.

"You have me, son. I will be right here with you every step of the way." She pulled him back so she could look at him. "But you have to decide whether or not you want it. Whether you are ready to confront the monster and lay it to rest."

She wiped the tears from his eyes. Her monstrous form receded.

"I love you, no matter what. Your sister loves you—"

"No!" November stepped into the room. "You can't let a few tears excuse what he's done. What he's brought upon us. What he's made me do."

"November," Mother said. "Please, go."

She saw Gabriel as he was the other night. Ruthless, hungry, vile. "He—"

"November!" Mother said, craning her head back to look at her. "Leave us."

And in the split second between when their eyes met and Gabriel's face transformed and shot forward, November's world shattered.

Blood seemed to explode from Mother's neck, spraying like a broken fountain into the air, over her shoulder, onto the floor, against the wall. And as heinous a sight as the crimson burst was, it was the devastating hurt in Mother's eyes that made November's knees weak, and the light that went out of her mother's forever sympathetic eyes that felt like a stake in her heart.

She watched, feeling separate from her own body, as Mother's dead, violated form slumped to the floor and Gabriel rose, a demon crowned and unleashed. His face and neck covered in blood. Mother's blood. His eyes, black as a starless midnight, turned to her.

"Little sister," he said. His voice was like dirt shoveled on a fresh grave, gritty, cold and filled with a sense of finality.

November fled straight to her room and smashed through the bedroom window. She took flight, hurling herself through the air without hesitation. Without worry of consequence of being seen. She flew away. Away from him, away from the nightmare her brother had become.

She feared there would be no stopping him.

Not now. Not ever.

CHAPTER THIRTY-THREE

Rocky jumped when November appeared, a mess of tears and shakes at the foot of his bed. He couldn't navigate between the mash-up of fear, anger, betrayal, and even love colliding in his soul. He couldn't speak.

She raised a hand, gesturing for him to give her a minute. "Please, you have to listen and listen close. Gabriel...Gabriel is coming... he's...."

Rocky's gaze moved to the Polaroid picture on his nightstand. Her words faded beneath the scream forming in his mind.

He grabbed the photograph and held it out, rising from his bed and bringing it inches before her tear-streaked face.

"Oh my god, Rocky...I—"

"You killed him. *You*. How could you do this?" He couldn't hold back his sobs.

She reached for him.

He smacked her hands away and shoved the photo in her face again. "That's you. That's the real you. Killer. Liar. Monster."

"Rocky, I know it's...I can't take it back, I wish I could, but you don't understand—"

"No, you don't understand. You're a fucking vampire. You're a murdering...horrible...."

"Gabriel is something worse. I know it won't matter to you now, but he made me do that. He gave me no choice. He was going to kill you, your family, my...my...mother."

Rocky stepped back, shaking his head. He crumpled the picture in his fist. "No, I can't...I can't trust you or anything you say."

"Rocky, please, I just watched him kill my mother. The police showed up and he walked them through our house, but, but he packed everything up. Everything, anything, and I thought we were leaving. But when the officers left, Mother confronted him. I thought she'd gotten through to him, but then...but then he...."

Tight-lipped, sniffling, Rocky swallowed hard and tossed the Polaroid to the floor.

"Rocky, he's going to come for you. You have to hide."

"Get out," he said, not able to look at her.

"What? No. You have to get as far away from here as you can. You and your family."

"Get out of my house! Take your lies and just go away. I never want to see you again. Get out!"

She backpedaled to the window.

"Rocky, please," she whimpered.

"Haven't you done enough? Leave me alone."

She opened her mouth to say something more, but he pointed at the window and she clamped up. She was still crying when she slipped over the windowsill and vanished.

Let him come, Rocky thought. *Let that bastard come here and try to kill me.* Rocky reached into the pocket of his shorts and pulled out the jackknife he'd picked up at his uncle's. He opened it and stabbed it into the wall next to his window. Monster or not, Gabriel could be killed. November had said so or alluded to something about how they weren't like the indestructible things in the Hollywood movies. They were not eternal creatures.

Night was still a few hours away.

Rocky figured he still had time to prepare for Gabriel's attack. As big and bad as he was, the vampire still only took his victims at night. And if Officer Nelson had been there to see him once, Gabriel had to know his time in Old Orchard Beach was through. Dead or alive, Gabriel was done after tonight. There was a chance he'd take November and leave now, but Rocky didn't believe it. The vampire would make time for one last kill. He'd make time for Rocky.

Rocky spent the next hour preparing. He hoped his mother would stay late at Grammy Jan's house again as she had the last two nights. If Julie came home, he'd find a way to make her leave. Make her go to one of her friends' houses. Say he needed the place to himself, cry or swear or break things until she finally gave him space.

He grabbed his knife and hurried out to his bike.

Wait a second, I have a car.

They'd moved his car into the garage next to Mom's. The only problem, well, besides the fact that he didn't have a license yet, was that his dad's truck was blocking the way.

When he looked at his father's Chevy, the thought was there. *Drive it.* He laid his bike down in the freshly mown grass. One of Mom's work friends, Debbie or Kimberly, had sent their son over to cut the grass this morning.

Rocky ran into the house and found his father's keys in the basket on the kitchen counter where his family kept them. Holding them in his hands, with the big silver Chevy symbol, Rocky remembered how proud his father was of his Chevy. He'd even had a hat made at one of the custom design screen-printing shops in town. The hat had *My Chevy* printed over a photo he'd brought in of his truck parked on the front lawn. Rocky remembered the day he'd taken the photo. He'd helped his dad wash the truck. He was happy to get to spray the hose and even got his dad and Julie wet during the process. They'd feigned anger with him and by the end of it all, the truck was clean and the three of them were soaked.

He made his way outside to the truck. When he opened the driver's-side door, it all came rushing at him. The smell of the pine tree air freshener hanging from the rearview mirror, the hint of stale cigarettes clinging to the fabric seat cover, the working smell of oily tools hiding behind the bench seat; he imagined his old man there behind the wheel, aviators, slicked-back pompadour he wore well past its in-style times of the fab fifties. Marty Robbins crooning about El Paso from the truck's cassette player.

He shut the door. He couldn't do it.

Thinking it over, traffic would be terrible in and out of the square. He'd spend way more time inching his way to town than he would cruising through on his bike and he didn't feel like wasting another minute.

He thumbed away the tears from his eyes and brought the keys to his dad's truck inside.

Two minutes later, he was on his bike and pedaling up Old Orchard Street, heading for St. Margaret's Church. He dropped the kickstand and rushed in through the front doors. A number of white-haired men and women were scattered about the pews. He made a beeline for the little cream-colored fountain holding water Rocky hoped was blessed or holy or at least touched by the hand of the Lord somehow. Turning to position his body between the water fountain and the parishioners, he pulled out the jackknife and placed it at the bottom of the little pool of water and knotted his hands in prayer.

Not sure whether he believed in god, Rocky took a deep breath and whispered a prayer anyways.

"Please, lord, I…I need you. I need your protection. I need your strength, your power. Help me stop this…monster."

Reaching for the knife, he paused.

He raised his chin and stared at the giant cross high on the wall ahead of him.

"And if you can't be bothered to watch over me…well, to hell with you."

He snatched the knife closed as he turned to find Moe from the diner sitting in a pew next to his wife.

"Rocky," the diner owner said.

"Hey, Moe."

They stared at one another a few seconds more. Rocky thought Moe understood the quiet passing between them, like the man knew Rocky had something massive to do.

Moe gave him a nod. Rocky gave one in return and hurried to the doors and back out into the light.

He considered trying to find garlic or wood to make a stake, but something told him he had the right weapon for the fight. He could feel the knife thrumming with energy against his ribs from the inside pocket of his jeans jacket. He knew that couldn't be right, could it? It felt electric, alive.

When he reached the corner of Old Orchard Street and West Grand Avenue, he pulled up to the fountain and stared out past the pier, to the wide open Atlantic, which stretched out seemingly forever. He'd shared that view with November. He'd shared everything with her. Had she planned it out from the start? Had she targeted him? He didn't think so. The moments they'd shared and the time they'd spent together seemed too real.

Regardless of whatever feelings he had lodged inside, he couldn't forget or forgive her for what she'd done.

He closed his eyes. The roller coaster from Palace Playland rumbling down its tracks, the children giggling and babbling on the carrousel, the hoots and hollers of punks in the arcade cheering one another on or claiming dibs on the next game, the cars, jeeps, motorcycles around him, all fell into the background to the cries of the starving seagulls circling overhead. The sound of the screeching birds pierced his mind, making him feel weaker. His hand slipped inside the jeans jacket and clasped the knife. Slowly, the birds quieted.

He truly hoped god was up there and that he'd spare a couple hours to help him face down a devil. Either way, Rocky shoved off and headed for home and a showdown not only for his soul, but for every person he'd ever cared about and for those taken by this beast.

CHAPTER THIRTY-FOUR

"Pete," Todd Shannon said, holding the phone to his chest.

Pete Nelson handed Martin a stack of files on the men, women, and children who had vanished from town since the arrival of the Riley family out on West Grand Avenue.

"Man," Shannon said, "you're going to want to take this."

Shannon was white as the snow that blanketed the beach in the midst of winter's clutches.

Nelson took the phone. "Hello, this is Officer Nelson."

"Pete, it's...it's Bill Scholz."

Pete knew Scholz, one of the postmen in town. They always talked football. Scholz was a staunch Jets fan, which drove Pete crazy, being a Pats fan. Bill would never let Pete live down the ass-beating the Pats suffered at the hands of the Bears this past January in Super Bowl XX.

"What is it, Bill?"

"I was doing my route over here on Elm and Central. And it's, well, it's the Segers' place."

"Damn it, Bill, what about the Segers?"

"They haven't been collecting their mail. And they haven't placed a stay on delivery. I thought I'd put their pile up on the porch, where it wouldn't be bothered so much by the weather."

Nelson held his tongue.

"The Segers have this bench that lifts up. Jim showed it to me one time. Contains all his and Betsy's outdoor tools and such? Anyways, I thought I'd stick the mail in there until they got home, and that's when I smelled it. Something off. Something bad. Something dead."

★　★　★

Nelson and Martin arrived to meet Bill Scholz at the end of the Segers' driveway in less than ten minutes. The smell of decay hit Nelson as soon as he reached the front steps of the home.

Knocking on the door, he called out to Jim and Betsy Seger but received no reply.

He kicked in the door, pistol at the ready, then he and Martin worked their way from the entry to the kitchen, living room and to the laundry room in the back. The smell only grew worse.

"Martin," Nelson said. "Check upstairs."

Within a minute, Martin was back at his side next to the basement door.

"All clear, sir," Martin said. "There's no one up there."

Nelson knew the source of the stench awaited them on the other side of the basement door.

Goddamn basements.

"You ready, kid?" he asked.

"Not really, sir," Martin said.

Nelson appreciated the kid's honesty. If he made it past whatever they were about to discover, the kid might make a hell of a peace officer for some time to come.

He turned the knob and pulled the door open.

The door made a pop sound as it belched out the rot and a flurry of houseflies held within.

Both Nelson and Martin backed away, swatting at the buzzing pests. They covered their mouths, gagging as they pressed on.

Nelson covered his nose with the crook of his elbow, found the light switch just inside the door and nudged it with the butt of his pistol.

"Shine your light down," Nelson said to Martin.

As soon as Martin's Maglite beam hit the basement floor both men cried out.

Piled at the foot of the steps was a stack of shriveled and desiccated forms that hinted at ruined flesh and bones. The only movement was that of the maggots and flies undulating over the husks of the bodies.

Martin held his lunch. Another notch on the kid's belt; Nelson managed to hold his until he made it to the kitchen sink.

Outside, composed as he could be at the side of his car, Nelson paced in the yard.

"What the hell are we dealing with?" Martin asked from the front steps of the Segers'.

Pete didn't believe the word that passed through his thoughts: *vampires*.

His hands trembled. His mouth went bone dry. He faltered against the vehicle. Fear. Fear of the impossible was rushing over him like a swell from the sea.

"Sir?" Martin said. "Are you okay?"

Nelson stumbled toward his car, fumbling for the door handle.

"Sir?" Martin said.

Nelson felt the entire world flatlining. Heaven and Hell, fairy tales and scary stories told around the campfire, truth and the consequence of that truth prickled his skin, a thousand needles puncturing holes in everything he'd ever believed.

Ignoring Martin's concern, Pete climbed behind the wheel, started the cruiser and bolted from the house of the dead. He glanced back in his rearview mirror and saw Martin throw his hands in the air.

You're already a better cop than I ever hoped to be, he thought.

He was across the Scarborough town line and out by the marshes where they'd discovered the shipyard workers' truck and bodies when he finally pulled over and killed the engine. He could hardly breathe. His clammy hands clutched the steering wheel as he leaned his sweat-covered forehead against the rubber cover.

He took deep breaths trying to calm his nerves, but his mind showed him the maggots and flies. The putrid bodies and the scent haunted him even here by the sulfur-scented marsh. Bile burned its way up his esophagus. He threw the car door open and emptied his guts again in the dirt.

When he thought it was over, he got out of the car and paced behind it. Traffic was steady both ways. He waved off a couple of vehicles that slowed near him.

He was still wrestling with his urge to get in the car and drive until he was so far away they'd count him among the vanished, when something thumped down in the grass behind him, followed by a second thud. A familiar voice crawled into his ear like the cold casing of an earthworm.

"Miss me?"

Nelson knew it was Gabriel Riley, the murderous creature of the night that a few hours ago he thought he might take down.

When he thought Riley was a mere mortal. A creepy, disturbed, but *human* monster.

He knew better now.

He realized it all much too late.

With a speed that would appear to the folks driving by as nothing more than a strange blur in the scenery, if anything at all, the vampire hauled Pete Nelson down to the ground beside his patrol car facing the marsh.

"Officer Nelson," the monster said. "I simply couldn't wait for you to come back to my home. I hope you don't mind, but I cannot tolerate loose ends."

"They, they know about the house...they know where you put them," Pete said.

"They might find what's left of the bodies, but there's no one to tell them about me."

"M-Martin will have called it in."

"Ah, yes, the young officer you just left behind. Well, I don't believe he'll be sharing anything...ever." Gabriel leaned out of the way and pointed to the tall grass behind him.

Pete saw the dead open eyes of the young kid that he'd inadvertently fed to this creature.

I'm so sorry, Martin.

"I couldn't have you two snoops giving me away just yet."

"You were there...inside the house, weren't you?"

The fiend's smile said it all.

Pete closed his eyes as the vampire snatched his head, palming the back of his skull.

There were no more threats or whispered promises. There was a quick, horrid screech from the thing before it tore Pete Nelson's throat to shreds and drained him.

★　★　★

Gabriel tossed Officer Nelson's corpse into the marsh before snatching up Officer Martin's. He had plans for this one. He shoved Officer Martin's body into the back seat of the patrol car.

He ignored all the crooked eyes made by looky-loos as he got behind the wheel and drove to the first parking lot he could find, an empty church lot, and left the patrol car there for someone else to discover later. Whenever they found the vehicle it would be insignificant. He and his sister would be long gone.

But first, there was one last thread to sew.

He would make the boy suffer. Like father, like uncle…and soon, like sister and mother.

Taking to the sky, with the body of Officer Martin in tow, a dark blur in the fading summer sun, he used the fresh blood coursing through him to steel him against the effects of the daylight. He would need to get inside soon. Not for fear of weakening; with the amount of human blood in his veins, he was far beyond the old Kryptonite of his kind. No, he was not afraid. But anyone who saw him would surely scream at the sight of the nightmare he'd become.

His teeth refused to retract; his vampiric features were prominent and fixed for the moment.

He landed in the Zukases' side yard just as Julie Zukas's yellow Beetle pulled into the driveway.

CHAPTER THIRTY-FIVE

November battled fatigue as she emerged from the cottage. Everything was gone. All of it. The last of their belongings, the U-Haul trailer, Gabriel's Grand Prix. Worst of all, she couldn't find Mother's body. Gabriel had even taken the responsibility of burying her away. She couldn't save her mother. Now, she couldn't even say goodbye.

She didn't have time to wallow in pity or grief.

If Gabriel wasn't here, she knew right where she'd find him. And that's exactly how he'd meant it to be. He wanted her to come to him. He wanted her to witness the last act of this menacing play.

Rocky wouldn't be dead. Not yet. But if Rocky didn't allow her to try and help him, he would be before the end of the day.

Nightfall was coming fast.

CHAPTER THIRTY-SIX

Gabriel watched Rocky's sister enter the home; she hesitated briefly at the door. She sensed danger. All creatures did, it was instinct. When a predator was near, no matter if you were a rat or a man, you felt it. It started as a hyper sense of awareness that something, an unknown variable, wasn't right, causing one to proceed with caution, checking dark corners, turning on lights and trying to convince one's mind and body that everything was okay. Gabriel loved this dread-riddled anticipation. He had watched it in a great many of the people he'd killed these last few weeks. It thrilled him and acted as a sort of appetizer before the main course. Of course, not all the recent kills had come that way. There had been others he just moved on with little to no notice. And those too gave him exceptional gratification. In one blink life is full and their own, the next it is his and they are no more. That power to snuff out a soul in an instant was the power of a god.

He moved along from window to window, daring her to see him. She draped a teal sweater over the back of the sofa before striding down the hall. Through the boy's window, he watched her duck her head into the darkened room. Once she left the doorway, he let himself inside.

Gliding toward the hallway, now an alley of shadow in the day's fading light, he placed himself on the ceiling of the girl's bedroom. From above, he listened to her move around the room, the floor giving out quiet moans as she did. He was certain she and her family knew the spots that made sounds well and had grown accustomed to hearing them. For some, it was the high-pitched hiss of a metal heating radiator; for others, the soft creak of a house that shifts with the changing of the temperatures or humidity.

For all her worry upon arriving home, he sensed she had relaxed, assuming she was safe.

She came out of the bedroom and moved down the hall to the living room. Gabriel crawled on the ceiling above her, trailing slightly, smelling her scent, a slight musk covered by hairspray and a fruity perfume. Gabriel bit back the saliva cutting loose in his mouth and punctured his bottom lip with one of his teeth.

Julie Zukas picked up the telephone's handset and began to dial when a single droplet of blood from Gabriel's lip dripped onto her milky-white wrist.

She began to tremble as she stared at the small crimson blotch against her flesh.

She slowly raised her chin.

Gabriel, done with pleasantries, hissed and put his fangs on full display before descending upon her.

★   ★   ★

Ten minutes later, he was leaning against the kitchen counter as Clarise Zukas came through the front door. He watched, silent and still, while she ventured to the living room without noticing him. She stopped at the sight of her daughter lying motionless on the couch.

She leaned down to see if Julie was all right then she shot bolt upright, hands to her mouth.

"What in Heaven's name?" she said aloud.

Gabriel was behind her when he whispered into her ear, "What do you say the three of us take this party somewhere else?"

She slowly turned her head.

Her eyes bulged from their sockets as she took him in.

A scream roiled up from the depths of her bruised soul.

He cuffed her behind the ear, rendering her unconscious before the shriek could escape.

There would be plenty of time for screaming.

CHAPTER THIRTY-SEVEN

Rocky approached his house half expecting to find Gabriel or November waiting for him. Julie's car sat in the driveway. He would have to convince her to leave. He shoved through the door and was met with silence. It wasn't fully dark out yet, but inside, the house was cast in malevolent shapes and shadows. He turned on the tall lamp in the living room and glanced around, glad not to find any unwanted guests.

"Hello?" he called out. "Julie? Mom?"

His mother had been picked up by Aunt Betty and taken to Grammy Jan's early this morning. Her car was in the garage next to his. She could be home anytime if she wasn't already, although last night she'd been out until nearly one in the morning. He was praying for the same tonight. Convincing his sister to leave was one thing; telling Clarise Zukas what to do, well, that would take a Herculean effort that even the gods would have trouble achieving.

He moved to the hallway, his fingers reaching out to flick on the light. He told himself he wasn't afraid of the shadows growing there, just like he wasn't afraid of the thing on the wing of the plane in the *Twilight Zone* movie.

His trembling fingers found the switch and flipped it.

The light bulb halfway down the hall flickered, refusing to come to life, twisting the dread in his stomach and raising the fine hairs on his arms and neck like the dead. Finally, the light bulb stopped its spasming and buzzing and bathed the hall in all its sixty-watt glory. Rocky breathed a sigh.

Down the corridor, both his parents' door and Julie's door were closed.

The bathroom door was also closed, although he could hear the shower running.

He placed an ear to his sister's door and listened, hearing nothing.

It seemed logical to assume Julie was the one taking a shower.

He moved slowly to his parents' room and gave the door a slight knock. "Mom?"

His heart flew into his throat; his hand went to the knife in his jacket.

If Gabriel was here, well, now was as good a time as any for victory or death.

He opened the door just enough to reach inside, fumbling around for a light switch and certain a cold hand with dagger-like fingernails would snatch his wrist and pull him in.

He found the switch and flicked it upward.

He shoved the door open, grateful to find another empty room. His gaze landed on his father's crate of records sitting atop the bureau. He was tempted to walk in and pick them up. Go through them. Sit with them. Instead, he bowed his head and shut off the light.

Walking toward his room, he thought the place felt too quiet. He suddenly wished he'd turned the TV on, even if just for background noise.

He stopped at the bathroom door and gave it a knock. "Julie?"

She didn't answer, but there was no way he was opening it and looking in on her.

His bedroom door was open just a crack. He went in. The summer breeze was making his half-open shade dance. The window behind it was wide open.

I left that open, he thought, uncertain whether it was true or not.

The light coming in from the streetlights outside gave him a good look around.

No beasties or bloodthirsty fiends in here.

It wasn't until he flicked his light on that he saw the note on his bed.

His legs were like two wet noodles trying to hold up an air conditioner. Wobbly and sick to his stomach, Rocky stepped to the bed and gazed down upon the white lined paper. There was a message written in blood.

Want to see your mother and sister again?
Meet us at 2 a.m.

Beneath the two lines was a crude drawing of the Ferris wheel.

He looked at the alarm clock by his bed. It was only 9:02.

He dropped to his knees and swatted the bloody note to the floor.

It was his fault. All of it. They'd all be alive and well if he hadn't fallen head over heels for November. All because he fell in love with a monster.

His eyes welled up with tears. He was ready to throw himself to the lions. He deserved it. He'd gotten his uncle and his father killed. Now, Mom and Julie were next if they weren't dead already.

No.

They were all right, but probably not for long.

Climbing to his feet, he pulled out his holy jackknife.

Uncle Arthur's Blade of the Gods, he thought.

He wanted this to be like a movie. He wanted the steel blade to glow with the power of the Lord, but it didn't. Still, it felt good and right in his hand.

"You can't fight him alone."

Rocky jumped, dropping the knife as he spun to find November standing in the doorway dressed in the Twisted Sister t-shirt he'd first seen her in and a pair of ripped jeans. Her black hair was drawn back in a ponytail. He'd never hated her beauty so much in his life. He was angry with himself for being attracted to her even now.

It was probably some vampire trick, a spell. She'd said they weren't like the creatures depicted in movies. She never said they didn't have some of their powers. He'd seen her fly, for god's sake.

He bit back the urge to cast her out again; he might actually need her.

"He's got them," he said.

"I know."

"Did you help him? Tell me the truth."

"No, but if you want them back, you're going to have to let me help you stop him."

"How do you propose we do that?"

"I told you, we're not like the movie monsters. We can...." She looked away, fidgeting with her fingernails. "We can kill him."

"You'd do that? You'd kill your brother?"

"I told you what he is. I told you what he's become. He killed my mother right in front of me. I won't let him do that to you or to anyone else."

He believed her. He saw it in her eyes. There was a simmering sadness and rage working inside her, just like it was inside him.

November stepped toward him.

"I know what you're thinking, Rocky. You're thinking this is because of us. Because of what we did. Because we fell in love."

Maybe she could read minds, too.

"It's not," she said. "This all happened because Gabriel is sick."

"You mean like your mother?"

"No. He's in the grip of this thing, this...addiction. A vampire can't indulge in human blood day after day. It increases our abilities, but that sensation, that draw can also become too strong to escape. The cravings can become all we think about. The high is so good, it very quickly becomes far more powerful than anything else in our lives."

"So, it's like, a drug...but you said it boosts your powers?"

"That's right."

"But if he's been doing this since you guys got here, he must be like the Incredible Hulk by now. How the heck are we supposed to stop him?"

"We do it together."

She reached out and took his hand.

"I know you hate me," she said. "But what we had was real. And I wouldn't take back a minute of it."

He pulled his hand from hers.

He didn't know how it was possible, but he wanted her. He wanted to kiss her here and now. But he wouldn't allow it. Not after everything.

"He left me a note. I don't know where he took them, but the note said to meet him at the Ferris wheel tonight at two a.m."

"That makes sense," she said. "He's been out in the daylight. He probably wants to rest up. The Ferris wheel fits his style too. He's always had a flair for theatrics."

"You don't know where he might have taken them?"

"No," she said. "He's been gone every night since we got here. Now we know what he's been doing, but I don't know where he's been putting the bodies."

Rocky threw his hands up. "Well, what the hell are we supposed to do for four hours? Just wait?"

"We rest."

"Are you kidding me? Rest? While he's got my mom and Julie, doing who knows what to them?"

"Yes."

He was flabbergasted, pacing around the room.

"He won't kill them, he wants you."

"How do you know?" he asked.

"Look, we don't know where he is, but he'll be at Palace Playland when he said he would. We're going to need all our strength to take him on."

He hated the thought of just sitting here while they were out there somewhere, but he really didn't have a clue where to find them. He just hoped they were okay.

"Okay, we rest," he said.

He didn't think he'd be able to, but after lying on his bed for half an hour the weight of this entire summer crashed down on him. All the rage, the sorrow, the betrayal, the anxiety. His eyes grew heavy, and he closed them.

He was shocked when November shook him awake.

"It's time," she said.

* * *

They were on their way toward the square. Glancing at all the buildings, he'd never been out this late at night, long after all the hellraisers on Harleys or cruising in muscle cars had gone home for the night. Even the hotels, motels, and crappy little roadside inns were quiet. It was calm, and he did not trust it.

"We're not immortal," November said, breaking the silence. "We die just like you, but Gabriel is riding a storm that I don't think he can handle."

"What do you mean?" Rocky asked.

"When we're in control, I mean, like, total control, we can stay looking like this, looking normal."

"What do you look like when you're not *normal*?"

"It's…it's ugly. I hate it," she said. "But right now, Gabriel is not in control. This bloodlust has done something to him. I saw it when he had my mother, he kept changing back and forth. And a few nights ago, he couldn't even turn back to normal. Something's wrong. I'm hoping whatever it is, it gives us a shot at him."

"We have to make it work," Rocky said.

"We will."

They stopped when the darkened Ferris wheel within the gates of Palace Playland came into view. Its outline in the moonlit sky sent a chill down Rocky's spine.

As they got closer, he could make out two shapes in a bucket at the tippy-top.

He pointed.

"I see them," she said. "But I don't see my brother."

"I don't think I can get to them," Rocky said. His stomach was doing somersaults. The mere thought of—

"You might have to climb up there," November said.

His body went numb when he imagined making the ascent.

"You can't fight Gabriel one on one," she said. "He'll kill you, but I can maybe at least keep him distracted while you get them free."

"There's got to be another way."

"If we can get in there without Gabriel jumping us, we'll look for the controls and see if we can get the machine to operate."

"Oh god, I hope so."

They reached the gate to the amusement park.

"Here we go," November said.

"Victory or death," Rocky muttered.

"What?"

"Nothing. Let's do this."

CHAPTER THIRTY-EIGHT

"It's locked," he said, tugging at the chain on the amusement park's fence.

"Let me," November said.

Rocky stepped back in awe as she grasped the lock and broke it off in her hand.

She tossed it to the side and let the chain slip free. Rocky flinched at the sound of the heavy metal links clinking to the tar like the intestines of a Transformer spilling to the ground.

November turned to him. "He already knows we're here."

"Yeah, but maybe we can at least get inside before we alert him to our exact position."

"Come on," she said.

Rocky pulled the holy knife from his pocket and flicked it open. He imagined it glowing again and wondered what would happen if he touched November's arm with it.

He reached out and placed the blade up to her skin.

"Hey," she said, pulling her arm away. "What are you doing?"

"Did it burn?" he asked.

"Did it burn? What? No. Why, what'd you do, bless it or something?"

Rocky felt like an idiot.

"Something like that, yeah," he said.

"Well," she said, holding her arm up to show him there was no damage. "I told you, this isn't a movie. Now, come on."

He scanned the closed vendor booth, waiting for Gabriel to attack at any moment.

When they reached the base of the Ferris wheel, Rocky gulped, following its metal jungle gym of arms all the way up. His skin felt too hot, too tight.

"Over there," November said, pointing to the control podium.

"They haven't even tried to call out," Rocky said. "Do you think they're still...*alive?*"

She hesitated. "I'm not going to lie. He probably hurt them. They might be bound or gagged, but I don't think he'd have killed them without...."

"Without what?"

She looked him in the eyes and said, "Without you watching."

He glanced back up. If that monster had hurt them....

"Let me see," he said, charging past her and walking around to the side of the podium with the controls. His heart dropped. The wires leading into the control board were hanging out and shredded.

"Shit," he said.

"If it isn't my two favorite lovebirds." Gabriel's voice came from a distance somewhere behind them.

November grabbed Rocky's forearm. "Look at me," she said, a fierceness in her eyes that made him focus solely upon her.

"You need to get up there and free them. There should be handles to climb in the middle. Get up there—"

Rocky chewed his lip, turning to gaze up at the height of the damn thing.

"Look at me. Listen."

He did.

"We're not going to get any second chances. You have to do this."

"Wha-what about you?"

"I'll try to keep my brother busy."

"He'll kill you. You said he's been feeding for weeks."

"We don't have any other choice."

"What if...."

An idea came to him.

"What if you drank some of my blood?"

"No. For one, I don't know that I could stop."

He gulped.

"Plus, if I did there's no way you'd get to them. You'd be too weak."

"I'm going to have to suck it up," he said.

She nodded. "You better go."

"Yeah," he said.

Gabriel still hadn't shown himself.

Rocky slinked away into the shadows, staying low to the ground as he moved toward the edge of the Ferris wheel.

★   ★   ★

She strode to the open space between the Ferris wheel and the vendor booths.

"Gabriel, you don't need to do this," November said. "Let's just leave. We can go home. No one will ever find us."

He snickered from somewhere to her left, deeper into the park.

She tried to see him but couldn't.

"I'm the one you're angry with," she continued. "Rocky didn't do anything."

"So romantic," Gabriel hissed from the shadows. "So pathetic."

He stepped from the center of the carrousel, winding his way around the painted horses and stroking each as he passed until he reached the edge.

"You should have listened," he said.

"*I* should have listened?" she said. "What about you? You ignored everything our father taught us. You betrayed every oath, every rule he set to keep us safe."

His vampiric face was on full display.

She could see the rage settling in. She was getting to him.

"Little sister, you don't have a clue," he said. "Do you know why our father died? Do you know how weak he was when he passed?"

"I know he died a good man."

"You know nothing," Gabriel seethed.

"He was a kind and gentle man. You're...you're a monster."

He stopped ten feet from her and laughed. Cold, reptilian laughter. "Finally you understand. You're already smarter than either of our parents. This," he said, moving closer still, "is what *we* are. Dark, glorious creatures so powerful, and without equal."

November saw the madness in his dark eyes. Total and unchangeable.

What small amount of hope she'd held inside for him was snuffed out.

This night could only end one way.

She flew at him.

★　　★　　★

Rocky discovered the twin metal A-frames, one on either side of the ride that peaked at the giant wheel's center. Service ladders climbed up the side of each frame. The real anxiety waited at the top of this ladder where the steps discontinued.

He inhaled the cooling night air between his teeth, listening to the gentle crashing of waves from the ocean just on the other side of the fence and across the sand, the heartbeat of the sea.

It's now or never, he thought. *Victory or death.*

He began his ascent, and was nearly at the top when he heard the battle cry from below.

He hoped November lasted long enough for him to help.

Rocky was halfway up when a wave of nausea rolled in. He closed his eyes, clinging to the rungs, and waited for the awful feeling to pass. He thought of his mother and sister, of November putting herself in harm's way standing up to her murderous brother. The least he could do was climb.

He urged himself forward, taking it one step at a time, not looking down, not looking anywhere but to the next one.

All was well until he reached the end of the ladder. His resolve fell to pieces when he realized he'd have to climb the fifteen feet to the bucket holding his mother and sister.

Just move, he told himself. *Just get it over with.*

He reached up and his fingers slipped.

He saw himself falling to his death; cold sweat broke through his pores as he regained his balance and reached around the ride's metal arms, trembling and clutching on for dear life.

"Oh my god, oh my god, oh my god," he murmured.

"Hello?"

"J- J-Julie?" he said.

"Rocky? Oh my god, Rocky. Where…where are you?"

"Ah…I'm below you."

"It got you too?"

"No, I'm re-re-rescuing you."

"What?"

"Is Mom okay?" he asked.

"I don't know. He took her someplace else. My hands and feet are tied."

"What do you mean Mom's not up there? I, I thought I saw someone next to you?"

"It's a cop, but he's…he's dead. Oh god, Rocky please get me out of here."

Officer Nelson. It had to be. He'd told him about Gabriel and now he'd gotten him killed, too.

He had to get himself together. What's done was done. He could add it to the pile of guilt trying to crush him later. If he didn't move now, he and Julie were both going to die up here.

"Are you injured?" he asked.

"No," she said. And he heard her start to cry.

"What is it?" he asked.

"That thing…it…it touched me."

Rocky gripped the rungs, this time with anger instead of fear.

"Did he…did he…."

"I can still feel its hands on me."

"Listen to me, Julie. I'm coming up. I have a knife with me. I'm going to cut you free and then we're going to have to climb down."

"What?"

He wished he was half as confident as he was trying to sound.

"Once we get down the arm under the basket, there's a ladder built into the frame. The workers use it to climb when they have to fix parts, or like, if it gets stuck, like now."

He could hear her getting hysterical.

"Julie, I'm coming."

Victory or death. Victory or death. He repeated the mantra in his head as he loosened up enough to move.

Trying like hell to block out how high up they were, Rocky clenched his arms and legs around the metal arm and inched his way up like climbing a fireman's pole or the ropes in gym class.

When he reached the next series of cross bars, he was able to step on one. Standing on the thinner beam placed him just below the body of the white bucket, maybe four feet across. He could see the closed door on the side where you step into the bucket.

In a calmer voice, he said, "Julie, is there any way you can get the side door open?"

"I...." She hesitated. "I think I might be able to kick the latch handle thingy."

He sucked in a breath as the bucket began to sway.

He heard her kicking at the door.

There was a *clank*, and the door swung inward.

He moved before he could chicken out. He held the metal arm with one hand and stretched out as far as he could with the other, his fingers gripping the edge of the opening.

"Julie, can you hold the door open, so it doesn't come back and shut on my fingers?"

He was beginning to sweat like crazy.

"Got it," she said. "Rocky?"

"Yeah?"

"Please be careful."

God, if you're really up there, don't let me fall.

Zeroed in on the door's edge, Rocky let go of the wheel's arm and swung his other hand up over the side. His feet came free of the crossbeam. He felt panic scuttle up his body as the bucket swayed. His breathing quickened. There was another crossbeam an inch below the bottom of the bucket. He'd need to try and wedge his foot in the corner where it met the main frame all while not losing his damn grip. He swung his foot for the intersecting metal arms. He had it for a second, but his foot slipped free.

"Rocky!" Julie called.

He held on tight, his legs and feet swaying with the bucket.

He used the slight momentum to try again.

This time he got it, wedging the toe of his sneaker in good.

Slowly, he extended his leg, letting go with his left hand. He searched the inside of the bucket for something else to hold and found a cylindrical metal grip from the latch system.

"You got it," Julie said.

He pulled himself up, gripped the upper side of the doorway, climbed into the bucket and put his back to the bucket's wall in front of Julie's legs, then he shut the door to catch his breath.

He looked at the dead cop. It wasn't Officer Nelson but some young guy he didn't recognize.

He sat up; the bucket swayed slightly. To their right the shore carried on as if nothing were wrong. Waves washed up, lapping at the sand. The pier was dark and empty. To their left he could see Old Orchard Street leading up to Saco Road. Where were the police? How come they weren't combing the streets looking for the killer? He turned back to the poor dead cop. What if Gabriel had killed them all?

"Rocky," Julie said.

"Oh, sorry," he said. He pulled the holy jackknife from his coat pocket. Julie leaned forward as he sawed through the rope around her wrists.

"There," he said as it dropped free. "Now, the scary part. Are you ready?"

"No," she said, rubbing the dark marks around her wrists. "But I guess we don't have a choice."

He told her where to find the steel crossbars and where to hold the lip of the door's edge. He held her arm as she got down on her stomach and lowered her legs out the door.

"I've got you," he said. "Feel around with your feet, there's a spot to wedge your foot. Then you can lower down to the next one and shimmy down."

She whimpered but he held on to her, reassuring her.

"I've got it," she said.

She began her descent.

Rocky needed something to keep the door from closing and cutting off his fingers.

He looked to the dead cop.

He didn't want to touch the guy, but he needed to. He dragged the body over and positioned him against the inside of the door.

The name tag over his right breast pocket read *Martin*.

"Thanks, Officer Martin."

He dropped to his stomach and lowered his feet over the edge.

Climbing out and down was much less stressful than the ascent had been. Julie was waiting for him on the ladder.

"Rocky, how did you get past that monster?" Julie asked.

"November."

November's cry echoed through the night.

"Hurry," he said, motioning for Julie to keep moving. "I have to help her."

As they hurried down, November's cries were cut short.

Please be all right.

★   ★   ★

November couldn't breathe. She tried hitting at her brother's arms, but his death grip on her throat would not relent. Her right eye was swollen shut, her mouth and nose bloodied, but she'd managed to rake him across the face before he got a hold of her.

Lying on the metal grate walkway of the Tilt-a-Whirl, Gabriel pressed his weight upon her. She felt lightheaded and ready to either pass out or die, whichever came first.

"I should have done this last summer after I killed your first boyfriend."

In her dizzying mind she saw Bobby's face.

She tried to speak but couldn't.

His grip loosened, slightly.

"What's that?" he asked.

"You...you're a monster...deserve to...."

"Go ahead, little sister, say it."

"You deserve...to...die."

He picked her up by the throat and flung her over the railings.

She crashed down to the pavement shoulder first and rolled into a fetal position, gasping for air as her shoulder flared with pain.

She hoped Rocky had gotten his mother and sister free – she wasn't going to last much longer.

"I thought you might feel that way," Gabriel said from the ride's platform. "I figured you'd like to watch me hurt your little lover boy."

November rolled over and sat up. Every muscle was sore and weak.

She heard a sudden cry from above her.

"Come here," she heard Gabriel order. He was talking to someone else.

Clarise Zukas, bloodied and bound, appeared above her as Gabriel brought the woman to the ground next to November.

"You did such a fine job with Uncle Artie, I thought—"

No.

"I thought I'd give you another chance to play the hero and save the day...only, you have to be a *monster* to do it."

Rocky appeared from the other side of one of the vending booths.

"Let them go," he shouted.

"Ahh, and here's our sweet prince now," Gabriel hissed. He dug his claws into Clarise's arm, causing her to cry out behind the rag in her mouth and bend at the waist.

Gabriel forced her to her knees next to November.

"Now, your little lover can see his monstrous girlfriend live and in action."

"You can't make me," November said.

"You haven't a choice, I'm afraid. You see, it's either you bleed this bitch dry or...I do it and then kill every one of you anyway."

She had to do something. She had to.... An idea hit her.

"Okay, okay. I'll do it, but you have to let them go."

"No!" Rocky screamed. He pulled the knife out of his coat and held it out toward Gabriel.

Julie appeared behind him.

"Mom!" she cried.

"Ah, you saved your sister. My, my, what bravery to scale that wheel. I must say you're a better brother than I."

"Haven't you killed enough people? Haven't you hurt your own family enough?" Rocky said, stepping toward them.

Gabriel pressed one of his nails into Clarise's throat and tilted her head so that they could all watch the blood begin to seep down her neck.

"One more step, lover boy, and I'll finish this all right now."

Rocky stopped.

November locked eyes with him and mouthed her message: *Trust me.*

She saw the fear in his eyes even as he gave a slight nod.

"Give her to me," November said.

"Not so fast," Gabriel said. "There is one other stipulation."

"What is it?"

"You drain her here and now while they watch, then we leave."

Julie was crying.

Tears rolled down Rocky's cheeks, too.

November hoped to hell this was going to work.

"Fine, let's get this over with," she said.

Gabriel smiled as he pulled Clarise Zukas to November and wrenched the woman's head back.

"Feed," he said.

November moved to her knees and sank her fangs into the side of Rocky's mom's neck.

She could hear Julie's screams and Gabriel's pseudo-sexual moans of delight.

November drew in Mrs. Zukas's blood, doing her best to hold back and just take enough to follow through with her plan.

She was hit with the surge of fresh blood coursing through her. Her entire body tremored. The pull to suck harder and take every drop crawled over her. Her eyes rolled back in her head.

"November!"

Rocky's cries came in through the fog enveloping her mind.

"You're going to kill her! November!"

She pulled her fangs free, gasping air. She didn't waste another second. November hurled herself at her brother and bit into the front of his throat as he stumbled back startled.

★　★　★

"Get Mom, put pressure on her neck!" Rocky commanded Julie, grabbing her and shoving her toward their mother, who was now lying on her side, her eyes wide, her mouth gasping for air like a fish out of water. "Go, now!"

He ran past them and straight for the vampires.

He was nearly to them when November was sent flying back and into him.

They both crashed like bowling pins to the ground.

Rocky's head bounced off the unforgiving pavement.

November rolled toward him.

"I'm sorry," she whimpered, her mouth covered in blood. He saw a blossoming crimson patch soaking through the stomach of her t-shirt.

"Now," Gabriel said, his voice coming out like a needle scratched across a record. The vampire held a hand to his wounded throat as blood continued to pour between his fingers. "You both get to die together."

Gabriel stumbled to one side, then the other as Rocky gripped the knife hidden at his hip.

Come on, you bastard.

"Any...last...sweet nothings?" Gabriel said.

"Yeah," Rocky said. "Get it over with, you piece of shit."

The creature's face contorted in rage as he drew his free hand back and screeched, launching at him for the final blow. "Die!"

Rocky waited to the last possible second with the monster a foot away and raised the knife, gripping it in both hands and thrusting upward into Gabriel's chest as he crashed down upon him.

The monster moaned out as he landed.

Rocky had his eyes closed, waiting for the thing to finish him off despite the mortal wound he'd inflicted.

He opened his eyes and watched November nudge Gabriel to the ground. The vampire rested on his back, the handle of Uncle Arthur's knife sticking out of his chest, a direct shot to the heart. A tremor rocked Gabriel's body before he fell still. His monstrous features relaxed, leaving behind smooth pale flesh, but Rocky would never forget Gabriel's true face.

They were all too numb, too hurt to react.

Lights broke into the lot, as two vehicles approached, reflecting in the vampiric black pools of November's eyes.

"Go," Rocky said.

She glanced his way, a somber lift to her lips, before she staggered off behind the Tilt-a-Whirl.

"Don't move!" shouted Officer Shannon. "What the hell is going on here?"

"Help! He tried to kill our mom," Julie cried.

"Julie Zukas? Is that you?" Officer Shannon said.

"Yes, please, my mom's....my mom's dying."

Rocky's adrenaline fled him, leaving him weak and woozy. He reached up and touched the back of his skull. He felt the blood and his world began to spin.

★   ★   ★

The rest of the night was a blur he later had trouble recounting. The doctors told him he suffered a severe concussion and had to have twelve stitches. Julie was curled up beneath a blanket in the chair beside his bed.

When he asked the nurse checking his vitals about his mother, she dropped her gaze and said she was in the ICU, fighting to hold on.

He was about to demand the nurse take him to her when whatever medicine she'd given him took effect.

He closed his eyes and prayed....

EPILOGUE

Clarise Zukas is still alive and well. Dr. Naugler said the week following her injuries all those years ago she'd lost more blood and come as close to death as anyone he'd ever seen. My mother has said many times that her love for us and the idea of leaving us without her or our father had given her all the fight she needed. No one tells Clarise Zukas when to say when.

Julie had the roughest time in the years that followed. She dropped out of school senior year and checked in and out of a mental health institute in Portland several times before she could learn to cope with everything that had happened. It was three years later, when she'd finally gotten her GED, that she met a guy named Brett Golden at some church function. They eventually married, had two beautiful girls, and moved up to the Midcoast area to raise them.

I get to see them twice a year, Christmas and Thanksgiving, one at Mom's and one up at their place.

As for me, I ran off with Axel when we decided to start our own rock 'n' roll band after high school. We tried making it in Boston, then New York, before I decided it wasn't happening for us. My Buick Skylark ended up getting stolen in Brooklyn, which was just as well: it held too many memories for me.

When I took the Greyhound home, Axel stayed behind. He'd hooked up with one of the girls from our last gig. He died from a respiratory tract infection two years later. Turned out he'd contracted AIDS somewhere along the way and never told any of us. I never told him what truly happened that summer he was overseas.

No one really knew the truth but me, Julie, Mom, and, well, November.

If they ever discovered anything abnormal about Gabriel Riley, the Beach Night Slayer as he was later christened by the local paper and national media, word never got out. We were his last victims, and the only survivors.

Twenty-three bodies were discovered between the fifteen in the basement of the Segers', the two in the U-Haul trailer later found abandoned in a vacant lot in Scarborough just a few miles up the road from the marsh where they found those four Bath Iron Works workers, and later Officer Pete Nelson. Plus, the body on the Ferris wheel of rookie officer Matt Martin.

I came home from my rock 'n' roll days to join the Fire Department.

No serious relationships. Every woman I've dated seems to be lacking something.

When I find myself stepping from Duke's on my nights off, gazing out at the beauty of the Atlantic, moving, swaying, whispering to me, I think of a girl who was more than anything I could have ever imagined.

I think back to February of that following year after the craziest summer of my life.

★   ★   ★

She was the only thing on my mind for months. Rage, melancholy, shame, disappointment, longing all mixed up and kept me off balance through the fall and winter of 1986. I'd avoided Palace Playland, the pier, and the beach, choosing instead to stay inside and play video games, or watch movies or TV with my mom.

When I finally decided to walk down to the square and out onto the pier, I sensed her before I saw her.

"I had to see you again," November said.

I just focused on the ocean.

"I can't take any of it back and I still think about you every day. Our memories, the two of us here those first weeks...it's the only thing that makes me smile. It's the only thing that keeps me going."

"I think of us, too," I said.

"You do?"

I remember the hope, the joy in her voice.

"Yes."

"I...know you can't forgive me—"

"No," I said.

"Do you think there'll ever be a chance for us?"

"I don't know. I can't imagine that right now. I've tried. I see us and then I see you...and what you've done."

She was silent but near.

"I understand," she said finally. "I have to go away, but I can give you time...if that's what you need."

"I'm sorry, too, you know," I said.

"Why? What do you have to feel sorry about?"

"I love you, but...I can't."

I heard her sniffles.

"I'll wait for you," she said.

I wanted to tell her not to bother. To find someone else. To move on and leave me the hell alone, but even then, I couldn't let her go. Not completely.

"I'm going," she said. "But I'll come back around."

"When?" I asked.

"Maybe when summer comes around."

I remember her hand on my shoulder. I remember wanting to turn around, grab her in my arms and kiss her. But I couldn't.

"Goodbye, Heatstroke."

I closed my eyes and felt the tears there.

"Goodbye," I said.

★　★　★

And she was gone.

She never did come back. If she did, she never made her presence known.

Of all the disasters to hit OOB over the years from the storms of 1898 and 1978 that demolished the original piers to the fire of 1907 that burned nearly every hotel and business to the ground, it was the storm of death in the summer of '86 that sticks with me and plenty of my neighbors here in this great town.

Yet, I still can't let *her* go completely.

Even now, on an early evening like this with the sun going down, the night coming to life, I know part of me is waiting for her to keep that promise.

It's almost ten years to the day she first walked into my life. I wonder sometimes if she met someone else or maybe she succumbed to what she was. But I don't think so.

Somewhere behind me, I hear a familiar song coming from one of the bars.

Sammy Hagar is singing about love walking in.

A cooling breeze drifts in off the sea, an old lost feeling comes over me, and I smile.

"Hello, November."

ACKNOWLEDGMENTS

Thanks first and foremost to my wife and kids for putting up with me on a daily basis, and for letting me do what I do. It takes a lot of patience to deal with me when I'm trying to finish a project like this. So thank you! And I love you.

Thanks to Tim Waggoner for making time for me when I had questions about outlining. Tim, you were a HUGE help. Thank you so very much, sir.

In this story, I took some liberties with details regarding Old Orchard Beach. While some streets and places are there and known by many that frequent my favorite beach town, I was not there in 1986. I've fictionalized my fair share of the town for the sake of this story.

To the wonderful people of OOB, I LOVE your town on and off season. It's my happy place.

I also mention someone reading Stephen King's *IT* in July of '86 even though the book wasn't released until September 15th of that year. I was well aware of the fact, but I couldn't resist putting it in here anyway. I hope my fellow Constant Readers out there will forgive me.

While I love vampire books and movies, I offer my own take on the creatures here. Much love to the classics.

Special thanks to Don D'Auria and Flame Tree Press for taking a chance on me and my little summer love story.